YEST**ER**... **'S SINS**

James Green

Originally published by Lush Press Ltd 2010.
This edition published by Acol Print Press Ltd 2016

Paperback ISBN. 9781909624573
E-book ISBN. 9781909624566

The story contained within this book is a work of fiction. Names and characters are the product of the author's imagination and any resemblance to actual persons, living or dead, is entirely coincidental.

Originally published by Luath Press Ltd 2010
This edition published by Accent Press Ltd 2016

Paperback ISBN: 9781909624573
Ebook ISBN: 9781783750337

This book is dedicated to Tracy and Jackie

Acknowledgements

Gulle Simonson, Hotel Villa Gulle, Nyborg, who made us so welcome.

Dr J. Jacques MBCHB, knowledgeable as always.

Danish Railways; helpful, clean and efficient.

Many thanks to Darton Longman and Todd Ltd, London, for permission to quote from *The Way to Nicea* (1976) by Bernard Lonergan.

Be sure thy sin will find thee out.

Numbers 32:23

ONE

The man was standing still, his hands out of sight in his overcoat pockets, motionless among the steady stream of travellers who filled the station concourse. He was looking towards the table where Jimmy was sitting and Jimmy felt sure the man was watching him. How long had he been there? Jimmy took a slow drink of his Tuborg. If the man was on his own maybe it was nothing, just someone standing, looking, waiting for somebody. *But why me*, thought Jimmy, *why look at me*? Then another man arrived and now they were both looking. Jimmy felt his stomach tighten and he stiffened. Should he get up, leave, head for the nearest exit? Then he relaxed. What was the point? They had him spotted and had shown themselves; any chance of getting out of the station building was already gone.

That was the problem with being on the run: you were never actually going anywhere. You moved around and didn't stop until you thought you were safe. But how could you know you were safe? You couldn't. You couldn't know for sure if they were still looking or if they'd stopped because they'd decided you didn't matter any more. You could never take the risk, all you could do was run. Jimmy took another drink and looked at the two men. Or you could do the other Thing: stop running and wait until they finally came and it was all over.

1

Now they'd come.

The men exchanged words and began to walk towards him. Jimmy watched them coming. Which ones will it be? But it didn't really matter, the end result would be the same whichever they were. Then two women walked past the bar. The men smiled and one of the women waved. They met and moved off together and Jimmy, watching them go, realised his mouth was dry and took another drink of his Tuborg.

The bar was a glass affair inside the main concourse of Copenhagen Central Station. He came here because it was convenient, near the shops and the church. The station was always busy, so he could disappear into the crowd. You could come for a drink most days and, if you changed bars, never become a 'regular'; you could sit and drink and watch the crowds and remain anonymous. He liked the station; a big, florid, Victorian-style building which would have been gloomy except that it had been filled with shops, bars and cafés. They added brightness and colour and stopped it being somewhere just to wait or pass through. They gave it a life of its own. The place seemed to sum up what he had seen of Copenhagen in the months he had been there. Solid and sensible but with plenty of life and style. A happy, well-ordered place for a happy, well-ordered people. A safe place where a tired man could rest.

He took a drink of his beer. The Tuborg had come as a pleasant surprise when he had first tasted it. He knew the name, of course, had seen cans of it in supermarkets at home, but had never been interested in trying it. He felt sure it would be just another gassy lager brewed under license in the UK. When he'd tried it here in Copenhagen he liked it. It was his beer of choice now. He looked at his watch: just gone half past one, time to get back for lunch. He finished the beer, bent down and picked up the carrier bag full of shopping and left the bar.

The main station entrance was a suitably grand affair facing the Tivoli Gardens but Udo's house was five minutes' walk away behind the station in the opposite direction, so Jimmy left by a humble rear entrance. He crossed the road, turned left and headed for what was now home. The street was quiet, almost deserted. This was hotel-land – modern, inexpensive hotel-land, where people on package tours and weekend breaks stayed. During the day they were out seeing the sights. It was at night that it lit up and came to life. Jimmy walked on. Beyond the hotels a few girlie bars began to appear and the buildings became older and a little shabby, a sort of grey area made up of big, dark turn-of-the-century apartment blocks with shops, offices and bars at street level. Not totally respectable nor completely sleazy or run-down. A sort of Danish Soho, but on its best behaviour and wearing a Sunday suit.

Holy Redeemer Church with its attached priest's house was in a side street. It was slotted in between an old office block and a storehouse of some sort. When Jimmy had first seen it, he got the impression that when it was built Catholics in Denmark preferred to keep a low profile. The church matched its two neighbours in style – an ugly, depressing building, certainly not a joyful celebration of the Universal Church.

Jimmy let himself in, went through the house to the kitchen and put away the groceries. Then he went to Udo's study. He couldn't hear him talking to anyone so he went in. Udo was doing paperwork at his desk. He was about Jimmy's age, fifty-something, but where Jimmy was of middle height, thick-set, with a crumpled look, Udo was a big man and looked fit for his age. His short grey hair might have given him a military appearance if he hadn't been wearing a black shirt and a priest's Roman collar. Udo looked up from his papers and smiled at Jimmy. He spoke good English but with a strong German accent.

'Time for lunch already? I lose track of time, though God knows why, I don't enjoy wading through this stuff.'.

'I made ham sandwiches before I went out, they're in the fridge. Do you want me to microwave some soup as well?'

'Yes.'

'Which sort do you fancy?'

Udo shrugged. 'Whatever comes to hand.' Jimmy turned to go then Udo stopped him. 'Not mushroom. I don't like mushroom.'

'I'll see what we've got. I'll call you when it's ready.'

'Thanks.'

Udo went back to his paperwork and Jimmy went back to the kitchen. He looked in the store cupboard and found they had four tins of mushroom soup and no other kind. Then he heard the phone ring in the study. They lunched late. It was a time of day when people phoned so they ate when everyone else had gone back to work. He went back to the study and waited until Udo's voice stopped.

'It has to be mushroom, or I can do beans on toast, if we've got any beans.'

'No, make it the soup, we'll have to eat it sometime.' Udo picked something up from his papers and held it out. 'There's a letter for you.'

Jimmy didn't take it.

'I'll get it after I've sorted lunch.'

'It's postmarked Rome.'

'I see.'

Jimmy took the envelope and went to the living room. He sat down at the table and opened it. There was no address at the head of the unsigned handwritten letter.

I'm afraid I have bad news for you. There have been enquiries made recently concerning your whereabouts. Exactly who was making the enquiries is unclear but from the way they were conducted it seems likely that it was an Intelligence Service. As promised, there is no official record of your time spent in Rome. Everything I have access to was erased. But, as I said to you before, memories cannot be erased so if any of the men you knew when you were here were asked then your presence will have been confirmed. I cannot make enquiries myself as that would certainly arouse suspicion. You should do nothing, you are probably safest where you are. You can put full trust in Fr Mundt. Needless to say if anything further comes to my notice I will endeavour to inform you as soon as possible.

There was no signature but he didn't need one. He took the letter into the kitchen, found a box of matches and burned it, then crumpled the ashes to dust over the waste bin. He washed his hands and went to the fridge, lifted out the sandwiches,

4

collected a couple of spoons and took them through to the living room. Then he went back and got started on the soup.

So, they haven't forgotten me, they're still looking. He wondered which ones it was, but it didn't really matter, one was as bad as the other. Was he safe here? That didn't matter either because he had nowhere else to go; he had run out of places to hide. He left the soup and went back to the study and called to Udo, 'It's ready. Do you want coffee or beer?'

'Whatever you're having.'

Jimmy went back to the kitchen, got two glasses and two bottles of beer and took them to the table.

He thought about the letter – not that there was much to think about. What will happen, will happen, and when it did, it would have to be dealt with as best he could. *Just get through one day at a time*. He ladled the soup into bowls, took them through and sat down, then poured his beer and waited. Udo came in after a couple of minutes, sat down and poured his beer, said a quiet grace and began his soup. He didn't refer to the letter. Letters from Rome were none of his business. They ate their lunch in silence. Jimmy was like Udo, he didn't like mushroom soup either, and the beer was some sort of Pilsner from the supermarket. It wasn't bad, but it wasn't Tuborg. Oh well, sometimes you just had to settle for what you got. Some days it was bad news from Rome, mushroom soup and an indifferent Pilsner. You just had to make the best of it. So Jimmy ate his lunch, drank his beer and made the best of it.

TWO

Six eggs! Surely six was too many? Six eggs, six tablespoons of sugar, one cup of black breadcrumbs, ground cinnamon and butter.

Hmmm. Was it too rich?

More to the point, was it vulgar?

Nothing vulgar could ever be allowed in an Elspeth Allen cookbook. The name was right though. In fact the name was damn good – Black Bread Pudding. It had a ring to it. Something that had grown out of grinding poverty and, over the centuries, matured into a dish fit for the tables of the affluent and discerning.

What about three eggs and three tablespoons of sugar? Charlie looked at his watch. Half past seven. It was Sunday, the day Elspeth gave herself the treat of a long lie-in. She wouldn't be up for another hour. *Time for a cup of tea and then back to it.*

Charlie Bronski put aside being Elspeth Allen, got up from his desk and went to the kitchen. While he waited for the kettle to boil he thought about the recipe. Three eggs, three sugars and what? It needed something. The answer came just as the kettle boiled. Alcohol. But not just any alcohol, Polish vodka. Perfect. Booze was always good, people liked booze, and Polish vodka was bloody brilliant.

He returned to the desk with his tea and resumed work on

the latest Elspeth Allen cookery book, *Poland in an English Kitchen*.

He wrote out a provisional list of ingredients. At least it didn't have cream. It seemed to Charlie that half of the recipes in the old second-hand cookbook he was plundering needed eggs and cream. And this was from the Soviet era when even bread was supposed to be scarce! What a bloody country! Not that excess was bad. Excess was usually good. The success of the books he wrote in his wife's name was based on the simple idea that readers, while reading, liked to feel good. And reading an Elspeth Allen cookbook did more than make you feel good. It made you feel rich. For a while, in your head, you became a part of the glitterati, the fashionable dinner-party set.

Charlie stopped writing for a moment. The sentence that had started it all drifted back into his mind. His wife had come across it in an old Victorian gardening manual she had bought and when she came on it she had to stop and read it out loud to him.

'No matter how small your garden, do try to keep at least one acre for trees.'

From that single sentence Elspeth Allen's 'The World in an English Kitchen' series had been born.

Charlie smiled. Maybe this black bread thing could use a touch of that sentence, a touch of naive extravagance. He reached out to the bookshelf, pulled out a copy of Tanners wine catalogue and turned to the Gin and Vodka section. The entry chose itself immediately, nearly jumped off the page at him – Wiśniówka cherry-flavoured Polish vodka. He looked in the right-hand column. Pricey for vodka but with a perfect name, just what he was looking for. If he couldn't do something creative with that, he'd bloody well eat his own Black Bread Pudding.

He put the catalogue down and got back to work. After a while he heard the bathroom door open and close. Elspeth was up. Soon he would have to stop, but he still had time to get a bit more done. He looked back at the yellowing page of the old book and read aloud.

'Line the buttered pan with breadcrumbs.'

Line it how thick and, if any thickness at all, how do you make the ones not held in place by the butter to stay up? Or does it mean just line the bottom of the pan? He sat back, annoyed. He hated it when the recipe he was stealing made it difficult for him. He tried again but the problem remained. How thick, and how would you make the bloody things stick?

He decided to give up and closed the book. It was almost time to finish anyway, he would sort it out later from another book. He looked at the cheap, plain black cover. It was just bad writing. It failed the first and greatest rule of all 'How To' books – always assume your reader has the intelligence and initiative of a retarded field mouse with emotional problems. Spell it all out, every single step, spell it out so even a moron could follow it.

Oh well, he'd deal with the breadcrumbs when he had a go at the damned thing. He began to close down the computer.

'Morning, darling. Am I making something nice?'

Charlie turned round. Elspeth stood in the doorway in her dressing gown with disordered hair, holding a mug in her hand.

'Not really, this is for your new series, "Recipes to Poison Hated Relatives With".'

Elspeth pulled a face.

'Oh no, I can't have that.'

'And why is that, my love, have you no hated relatives?'

'Plenty, but I can't have an Elspeth Allen book where the title ends with a preposition.' She came to the desk and looked at the screen of Charlie's computer. 'Will I like it?'

Charlie pressed a couple of keys and the words disappeared as the computer shut down.

'Not really, it's got six eggs and you serve it with …' He opened the old book at the bookmark, '"whipped cream or whipped sour cream." I knew it. *Cream.* It always turns up somewhere.'

She took a sip of tea and looked over his shoulder at the recipe.

'Black Bread Pudding. But surely black bread is made with mud or something? Not even six eggs and whipped cream could redeem mud.' Elspeth took her tea to the settee and sat down.

'It doesn't sound much like the upmarket stuff I usually dish out. Still, it's your book and you always seem to know what you're doing. You'd better start getting ready or we'll be late.'

Charlie closed his laptop, tidied his desk and got up. He knew Elspeth liked to be early for Mass. There was only one Sunday Mass, said in the small function room of a local hotel which, many years ago, had been bought by a French couple. Over the years the number of Catholics in and around Nyborg had grown until there were enough of them to justify a priest coming from Copenhagen to say a Sunday Mass for them. The French couple had gladly provided a venue but made sure the Mass finished just nicely for people to stay on at the hotel, have a drink, then have lunch. As the couple refused any payment, many of those who came to the Mass felt it only proper to stay for a drink or a meal. Charlie and Elspeth ate Sunday lunch there about once a month and, as the cooking was excellent, staying was never any kind of penance. By accident or design, the way things had worked out, the couple were well rewarded for their generosity.

'Why can't we have our own priest and use a proper church? Churches get shared these days. If we used one of the local churches maybe we could have Mass at a time that suited us. Not that I mind having to eat there but having to stop …'

'Oh, Charlie, don't moan. I know you only became a Catholic to please me.'

'No I didn't. I became Catholic because you convinced me …'

Elspeth got up and grinned at him. 'That my father wouldn't permit my marrying any non-Catholic.' Charlie followed her into the kitchen. 'And we're lucky to have any kind of priest come to us. Nyborg isn't exactly a Catholic place, is it. If Father Mundt didn't come, it would mean going to Copenhagen or Odense. And here we get the bonus of Mass in English.'

Charlie put his arms round her waist as she washed out her mug and gave her a gentle hug.

'Whatever you say. I'll get the ingredients for that recipe out so I can make a start when we get back, then I'll get the car out.'

He got out six eggs and the sugar. Start with what the recipe says and see how it goes. After he had collected everything he needed and put it on the work surface he left the kitchen and stopped by the door to the bedroom, where Elspeth was doing her hair.

'It's odd though, isn't it?'

'What's odd?'

'A German priest living in Denmark who speaks fluent English. Don't you think that's odd?'

'Not really, Denmark hasn't any native Catholic community to speak of, so the priests have to be foreign. And why *not* German? Germany's just across the border.'

'And I suppose everybody speaks good English these days.'

Elspeth turned from the mirror.

'They do in Denmark. That was one of the reasons we chose it, remember? Now get the car out, or we'll be late.'

Charlie walked to the hall, put on a light overcoat, then went back through the house and out the back door. He stood for a moment looking at the view. At the bottom of their garden, beyond the low fence, was a narrow band of rough grass and beyond that, the beach. It was a calm day with a gentle breeze blowing in from the sea and he could just hear the sound of wavelets gently lapping against the white sand. Beyond the beach lay a blue expanse –the Storebælt, the southern reach of the Kattegat which separated Denmark from Sweden and eventually led into the Baltic.

He loved this view. He loved the whole place. To his left began a wood where the pine trees came down to the beach. To his right was the strand, a favourite summer bathing and picnic resort of locals and visitors alike. Back from the beach was a line of neat bungalows, all looking across the sea to a hazy view of land peeping over the horizon. Beyond the strand, reaching out from the edge of the small town, was the Great Belt Bridge. From where Charlie stood, it looked so thin and fragile; a long ribbon barely above the water, held up by two narrow suspension towers. It grew smaller and smaller as it headed away across the wide channel that separated Nyborg from the neighbouring island of Zealand. The sun shone from a

11

cornflower blue sky. Everything looked perfect on this fine autumn day.

Charlie felt happy. He decided that after Mass they would give lunch at the hotel a miss, come home, walk along the beach or through the woods and have a beer and lunch somewhere. He went round the side of the house to where it faced the road and opened the up-and-over garage door. He got into the car. Elspeth arrived and stood on the drive ready to close the garage door once the car was out. Charlie turned the ignition key. For a split second nothing happened. Then a voice came from the car's sound system.

'Bang, you're dead.'

Elspeth looked round, startled, as the car door banged open and Charlie ran at her shouting.

'Get back, get away from the car.'

But she just looked at him stupidly and didn't move.

Charlie grabbed her and began pulling her away from the garage. 'For God's sake get away from the fucking car.'

Elspeth tried to pull away from him, shocked by his swearing and frightened by his roughness and his words. She began struggling to free herself from his grip when the garage dissolved in an ear-shattering explosion and they were both thrown to the ground.

The last thing Charlie heard before he hit the floor was Elspeth's scream. Then a deep black pool opened at his feet, and he slid in.

THREE

Someone was talking to him.

'Stay with us, Charlie. Come on, stay with us.'

There was someone's voice inside his head. Then the pain came and he opened his eyes. He was lying on his back on the drive. Three faces were looking down at him out of a background of blue sky. The nearest one smiled.

'Thank God.' It turned to the other faces. 'He's conscious.' Then it looked back at him. Suddenly Charlie remembered what had happened.

Elspeth was standing by their neighbour Inga and her husband, Lars, who was kneeling beside him.

'Look at me, Charlie. Do you know who I am?'

There was concern on Lars' face and in his voice. Charlie felt like one big bruise but it was the pain in his head which was worst. He forced his brain to clear; he needed to know if he was really hurt.

'Hello, Lars.'

Lars' face split with a grin of relief.

'Welcome back. You had us worried for a minute.' Charlie tried to move but Lars held him. 'No, stay there until the ambulance gets here. I don't think there's anything serious but don't take any chances.'

Charlie relaxed. When he had tried to move there had been

no serious pain anywhere, he was only knocked about. He didn't have to worry. He could function, he could think, stay in control. He was going to be OK.

'How long was I out?'

'Not more than two or three minutes. We heard the explosion, came out, and there you both were.'

Charlie looked up at his wife. 'Are you OK, Elspeth?'

Then he saw that she was quietly crying and her eyes had a frightened, faraway look. Inga, who had an arm around Elspeth's shoulders, saw the look of concern on Charlie's face.

'Don't worry. We think she may have broken her wrist when she fell. Otherwise she seems OK, except for the shock, of course.'

Charlie tried to get up again but Lars eased him back to the ground.

'No, stay there. You took a bang to the back of your head, you're bleeding and I think you'll need stitches. You fell onto the drive but Elspeth fell onto the grass.' He gave an encouraging smile. 'She got a soft landing. You lie still. The ambulance will be here soon.'

They all fell silent. No one seemed to have anything to say. *What do you say to someone who's just been blown up?* Charlie turned his head and looked at the garage. The whole front of the car was blown open and was burning furiously. But through the smoke billowing out, Charlie could see that the garage looked OK except for the up-and-over door, which was bent and sagging. What the hell had happened? Lars was obviously thinking the same thing.

'Maybe it was petrol? Did you keep any in there? If it vaporised, then maybe a spark as you started the car …'

That will do for the time being, thought Charlie. 'You could be right.'

'You did keep petrol in there? God, that's dangerous. It could …'

Charlie tried to smile. 'I think it already did, Lars, don't you?'

Lars forced a smile but didn't respond. This wasn't the time to tell someone how stupid they had been. Then they heard the siren.

A small crowd had gathered at the bottom of the drive. They talked in subdued voices and had that air of order that was typically Danish. When the ambulance pulled up they parted and let the paramedics through. Nobody pushed or tried to get closer. Quiet and concerned, the Danish way. There had been an explosion in your street, a neighbour's car had blown up, but you didn't make a fuss. Also it was Sunday. Danes still took Sunday seriously, it wasn't a day for too much emotion. The crowd looked on soberly as the paramedics began their work. Now it was clear that no one was dead, the voices seemed to take on a slightly critical air, giving the impression that getting blown up was not something that a good citizen did on a Sunday.

Charlie listened as one of the paramedics spoke to Lars, finding out what had happened. The other knelt beside him. She spoke excellent English, of course, barely a trace of accent.

'Are you in pain at all?'

Charlie slowly shook his head. God, it hurt to do that, but by not speaking and closing his eyes as if he was drifting off she wouldn't ask him questions and he could think. The other paramedic was talking to Elspeth, but Elspeth wasn't answering. He lay and listened as the paramedics spoke to each other. Danish wasn't German but it was close enough to follow some of what was said, close enough to get the gist. They were telling Lars to call the police. Charlie lay still with his eyes closed. He would need to be ready when the questions began. The petrol thing wouldn't hold up. He thought about Elspeth. She was in shock, which meant she might be a problem. He thought about the car and the voice. It had been a neat job, very clean, very efficient.

He felt a support-collar being fitted round his neck, then he was lifted expertly on to a stretcher and carried down the drive. He felt them load him into the ambulance, heard the doors close and then felt the ambulance begin to move. He opened his eyes slightly but the medic wasn't looking at him, she was too busy. Elspeth was sobbing, she looked very close to hysterics. The medic was doing a good job with her, but it wasn't easy.

Elspeth was going to be a problem. She looked like she might be a basket case. Charlie closed his eyes.

Soon, very soon, somebody would be in charge. When they got to hospital, were checked over and sorted out, the questions would begin. Suddenly Charlie felt his age. Physically he was in good shape, very good shape in fact. He could pass for a man in his early to mid-fifties and he was still strong and quick. He kept in shape. But now, in the ambulance, he felt old and tired. He didn't want this, he had finished with this sort of thing long ago. Now he lived with his wife by the beach in a small, pretty town on Denmark's market-garden island and wrote successful cookery books in his wife's maiden name. He lived a comfortable, quiet life. Until today. Today he had been blown up.

He lay with his eyes closed, rocking gently while the ambulance hurried to the hospital with its siren going.

'Bang, you're dead.'

The words in the car had given him enough time to get out and get clear. What did that mean? If you car-bomb somebody you do it so death is certain. That's the whole point. Nobody survives a car bomb if it's done right. And this one was done right. It wasn't any kind of amateur job, not with a relay to the sound system and a delay mechanism. *But why the delay?*

It didn't make sense.

The only sense it could make was that someone was sending him a message. Some message. You blow someone up but make sure they get clear if they're quick and if they recognise what's happening. Was someone going to kill him and wanted him to know he was going to be killed? Someone who knew he would be quick to recognise what was happening and get out. Someone who knew him. He thought about it. Blow up your car but not kill you?

No, a warning didn't make any sense. But what else could it mean?

As the ambulance made its way along the quiet Sunday roads, Charlie drew the only conclusion he could think of. It was all going to have to start again. Charlie Bronski was going to have to go back to work or Charlie Bronski was going to be

16

dead.

The ambulance slowed and pulled to a stop. The doors opened and he heard people moving and quietly talking. He would make sure Elspeth stayed in hospital, maybe for a couple of days. He needed time. Then he felt himself moving. He opened his eyes. Elspeth was gone. They had taken her ahead of him, she was the walking wounded.

'Where is my wife?'

The man pushing the trolley looked at him. 'Sorry, I not got good English.'

Charlie looked at his face. He was almost certainly a Turk, cheap immigrant labour doing the jobs the locals didn't want.

He'd get Elspeth kept in hospital, out of his hair for a couple of days so he could get himself organised. A doctor joined the trolley and smiled down at him as they went along.

'We'll have a good look at you in a minute. Your wife is with a doctor now. It looks like you're both going to be all right.'

Charlie smiled his thanks.

Yes, he was going to be all right. He was going to make damn sure he was going to be all right.

FOUR

An hour later he was sitting by Elspeth's bed in a room off a small ward. Other than a few stitches in the back of his head he was fine, shaken up and bruised but basically OK. Elspeth was in bed with her eyes closed. She had made it easy for him. The hospital medic had lost the battle with Elspeth's hysteria and she had fallen apart. Now she was asleep, sedated.

One arm lay on the bedclothes with the wrist in some sort of strapping. It was broken. Inga had been right. He'd get his two days. He sat back and looked at her sleeping. Soon the questioning would begin and it wouldn't just be the police who did the asking. When Elspeth woke she would also begin asking.

How much to tell them? The problem was the delay. Everything hinged on him getting out of the car. Getting out the way he did and pulling Elspeth away meant that he knew there was a bomb. That wasn't going to be so easy to explain to the police, or to Elspeth.

He looked at her. She was still a good-looking woman. She'd been beautiful when they married ten years ago, the way some women can be more beautiful at forty than they can at twenty. A mature, lasting beauty. How her father, Hugh, had kept her a virgin until they had met, God alone knew. Not that he wasn't grateful. Hugh might be a selfish old bastard, but he'd done Charlie a favour even if he hadn't meant to. The trouble was that as well as looks she had enough brains not to swallow any simple lie. Whatever he told her would have to stand up. It might even have to be the truth, or near enough so only he knew it was a lie. The main thing was that she would continue to trust him, to believe in him. That meant there would have to be window dressing, some nice comforting lies, so she wouldn't be afraid. He didn't want her to know how dangerous this might be or how much worse it could get. The important thing was for her to feel that everything was under control. That way she wouldn't become a liability.

Another possibility occurred to him as his mind got back in gear. If someone was putting the frighteners on him, then getting at him through Elspeth might be an option for whoever was out there. You could never be sure. Only one thing was certain, you never expected the one that got you. *If* they got you.

Charlie's mind was beginning to function again. The soft years were falling away and dormant instincts were reviving. It was all about self-preservation. Somewhere inside his head he was beginning to get that old feeling. Only Charlie mattered. Everyone else, absolutely everyone, was expendable. You used what you had to hand. Keep Elspeth believing in him, trusting him. Keep her predictable.

A voice came from the door of the room. It was a nurse. 'How do you feel, Mr Bronski?'

'OK, thank you.'

'The policeman who's been waiting asked if you could talk to him now? I told him you were with your wife but he still wanted me to ask.'

'Not yet. I don't want my wife to be alone when she wakes. Tell him I'll come when she's awake. I want to be sure she's going to be all right.'

He turned back to the bed. He wasn't ready for the police. He still needed time.

'I understand, Mr Bronski. I'll tell them.' Charlie turned back to the nurse.

'Them? I thought you said it was only one?'

20

'Only one who's been waiting here since you and your wife were admitted. The other one arrived a few minutes ago. I think that's why he wanted me to see if you'd come now.'

Charlie turned back to the bed and the nurse left.

Two of them. And they'd know for definite by now that it was a bomb, a good one. Also that we were far enough away from the car not to be seriously injured when it detonated. They wouldn't be stalled for long. With car bombs in the frame there was very little space for courtesy or consideration, even in Denmark, even on a Sunday. They'd soon have a nurse by Elspeth's bed and it wouldn't be, 'Would you be ready to talk now?' It would be, 'Now we're going to talk.' He had just about run out of time. He moved to the bed and gently but firmly began to shake Elspeth and whisper, close to her ear.

'Wake up, Elspeth. It's me, Charlie. Wake up, darling. Wake up.'

Finally her eyes opened. They were dazed and faraway. She looked at Charlie as if he was a stranger. He hoped she wasn't too drugged to be of any use.

'Stay with me, Elspeth, stay with me.'

Elspeth eyes slowly began to focus, she was surfacing.

Then the recognition came and with it the fear.

'Oh my God, Charlie, what happened? Are you hurt? What happened?'

The fear was taking over. He had to be quick and he had to stop her going hysterical again.

'It's all right, darling. Don't worry. We need to talk. Just lie and try to listen. When we're at home I'll explain everything, but for now you're to say you can't remember anything. Nothing at all. You remember leaving the house and waking up in this bed but between those two things it's a total blank.' He hoped there was enough sedative in her to keep her from falling apart again. He took her good hand, bent down and kissed her.

'It's going to be all right. Nothing more is going to happen. It was an awful accident but we're neither of us badly hurt. I don't want you being questioned until you're safe home with me. Then we can answer things together. After all, there's nothing we can tell anybody. It happened, we don't know why.

21

It was probably something to do with the petrol. I just don't want you bothered while you're in hospital. I want us to be together when anyone talks to you. We don't know anything and I don't want you upset.' He kissed her again. Did she understand? Her eyes were drifting away, she was going under again. 'You remember nothing, OK?' He smiled. 'Nothing until we're together again, safe at home.'

She returned his smile. 'All right, Charlie, you know best.'

Thank God for that. He gently stroked her arm then kissed her again.

'Now go back to sleep and get well. I want you back in your own house, I want us to be together.' He stood up but kept hold of her hand. 'I have to go out for a minute to check something with the doctor. I want you sound asleep when I get back.'

Elspeth smiled in a vague, drugged way and nodded. Then her eyes closed. Charlie waited for a few seconds until her breathing told him she was asleep. Now he could talk to the police. He put her hand down gently, left the room and looked around.

Standing at the end of the short corridor were two men. He walked towards them. As he got nearer and saw them more clearly he became sure that whatever they were it wasn't policemen. He quickly decided which one to talk to first.

They came in all shapes and sizes, men and women. The ones who didn't look the part were usually the best. This one was anonymous except for the small moustache. The moustache was definitely a mistake. Charlie wasn't surprised that he was there, a bomb these days almost certainly meant terrorists, so they'd naturally have at least one of the goon squad on hand. Still, start with the muscle, you're not supposed to know how these things work, so start with the wrong one and see where it goes from there.

He started talking before he reached them. He wanted to be the first to speak, as far as was possible he wanted to control the conversation. When he spoke it was Moustache he looked at.

'I have to get back to my wife. I can't give you much time but I understand that you must ask me some questions. She's sleeping but I'd rather she didn't wake up alone. So, if you

22

could be as brief as possible …'

Moustache looked at him with dead eyes and ignored what he had said. It was the other man who answered and his eyes were anything but dead, they were the eyes of someone who knew exactly what he was doing.

'It was a bomb, Mr Bronski. I understand your concern for your wife but I'm afraid …'

Charlie feigned surprise. 'What? A bomb?'

'A bomb.'

'But I don't understand. Why would anyone put a bomb in my car?'

'Why indeed? The same question has occurred to us. Why would anyone put a bomb in your car?'

Charlie switched to baffled amazement. Baffled amazement wasn't easy but he gave it his best shot.

'I don't understand … are you sure?'

'Very sure.'

'I'm afraid I just don't understand.'

'Of course, Mr Bronski. Please, return to your wife immediately. It was insensitive of us to intrude. One doesn't get blown up every day and I'm sure it can be, well, most upsetting. We understand,' he looked at Moustache, 'don't we, Sergeant?'

The concern in the voice and the understanding smile were so false they were almost as comic as calling Moustache 'Sergeant'. Charlie had to work quite hard to keep the smile off his face and out of his eyes. Moustache just kept on looking at Charlie. He was the straight man, it was the other one who was the comedian. Charlie looked at the Comedian.

'Thank you.'

He was about to turn away.

'My sergeant will come with you and wait outside your wife's room.' Moustache walked towards him. 'In case you need anything.'

'What sort of thing?'

'Oh, one never knows. One wants something and finds it easier for someone else to get it. Doesn't one?'

The urge to say, 'Does one?' was almost overpowering. This guy was going to be a handful. Moustache was pure routine but he hadn't expected anyone like the Comedian. Moustache stood beside him looking at him with the same dead eyes and his hands hanging by his sides. Charlie knew what he was thinking. It was a job, nothing more. If he made a wrong move Moustache would flatten him. But Charlie knew the moves and he would be careful not to make any wrong ones.

They walked together back to Elspeth's room. Charlie went in and closed the door. Moustache waited outside. By the time Charlie reached the bed, the door was slightly open again. It was a small room, Moustache wouldn't need perfect hearing to eavesdrop on any conversation. But he probably had it anyway. From now on privacy was something Charlie would have to work for.

OK, we all know the game, so let's play it and see who gets the last laugh. He tried to smile to himself, but it didn't take. The Comedian was going to be hard to get past and there was still 'Bang, you're dead' out there somewhere. The odds weren't great but he had some things on his side, things he might be able to use. He looked at the bed. He had Elspeth, he had himself and he had his ace in the hole, if he could reach it. Two days at most to work things out and he would be ready. Then, if he needed it, he would go and get his ace in the hole. If there still *was* an ace. *And* if it was still in the hole.

FIVE

The man sitting across the desk from Charlie really *was* a police officer. But the pretty blonde sitting at the end of the table certainly wasn't. She might have been a secretary except she sat there with nothing to do, no notepad, no anything.

There were just the three of them in the interview room and no obvious recording device, but Charlie knew others would be listening. The policeman began.

'Thank you for coming, Mr Bronski.'

'Did I have a choice? I didn't get the feeling I had a choice.'

At the hospital, Elspeth had woken about half an hour after he had returned to her bedside. She seemed better, more in control but still tearful and afraid. Charlie told her she would have to stay in hospital for a couple of days for observation and asked her what he should bring her from home. He helped her to make a short list. Even that small task visibly tired her. He said he would go and get what she needed and be back as soon as he could.

'You'll come straight back, won't you? You won't leave me here on my own.'

The tears were flowing again.

'Of course. Close your eyes, count to ten slowly and when you open them I'll be back here.' She tried to smile but the fear was still too strong and tears continued to run down her cheeks onto her hair. Charlie bent down and kissed her gently. 'Close your eyes, darling. Rest.'

Elspeth closed her eyes. Charlie waited for a minute. She would sleep again. To anybody listening it would have all been very natural. Why not? Elspeth wasn't acting.

When he left the room Moustache silently fell into step alongside. Outside the hospital there was a car waiting. Moustache didn't have to tell him to get in.

Now here he was in an interview room. Simple and effective.

'I was brought by the officer you left at the hospital. I wasn't asked if I wanted to come. I was brought.' A bit of fear, a bit of petulance in his voice and manner. It sounded good. He felt he was doing it quite well and the policeman seemed convinced.

'It should have been explained to you that your visit is entirely voluntary. I apologise. You are here of your own free will to assist us in our enquiries in what is a very serious matter. Once you have answered a few questions you will be free to go.'

Charlie shrugged.

'I don't know anything except what happened, but ask away.'

'Your neighbour, Mr Larsson, says you thought the explosion might have been caused by petrol which you kept in the garage. Is that correct?'

The blonde secretary just sat there in her tight white blouse, open at the neck, and a black skirt. His imagination had to supply the good legs but it wasn't a hard thing to do. It was a nice touch. No threats, no pressure, just something to sit on the edge of your attention, something to distract you. If you were from the outside you weren't being scared unnecessarily and if you were from the inside, well, you would expect pressure. What you didn't expect was a sexy blonde, so your attention wandered, maybe just enough. There was an original thinker behind this. The policeman called Charlie back from his thoughts. Already she was doing her job.

'Petrol in the garage, Mr Bronski?'

'Did I say that? I don't remember.'

'Do you think the explosion might have been caused by petrol in your garage?'

'I don't keep any petrol in the garage.'

'So you no longer think that petrol in the garage was the cause?'

'If you say so.'

'Do *you* say so? That is my question.'

'I no longer think petrol was the cause.'

'Did you ever think that petrol might have been the cause?'

'No, not even at any time.'

'I'm sorry?'

His English was excellent, but only in a formal way. He could be tied in knots.

'Not even for ready money.' Confusion put a crack in the stone front, he was human after all, and now he was getting out of his depth. 'Oscar Wilde, *The Importance of Being Earnest*. "No cucumbers, not even for ready money".'

The stone healed. His English was good enough to recognise piss-taking, but only if you pissed right in his face. 'This is not a matter for laughing. I request you most firmly to answer directly the questions I put.'

His English was falling apart. In effect, the show was over. Charlie wondered what rank he was. Senior certainly. What department? Not that it mattered. He was one of the plodders, a by-the-book man, but that didn't mean anything. The best policemen were the senior plodders, they got the work done.

'So what do you think it was, Mr Bronski?'

'A mistake? A practical joke? Maybe it was the car. Has it happened to any others of that model? Shouldn't they do a recall if the model blows up like that?'

A rebuke froze on the policeman's lips and he stared at Charlie. He was asking the questions, but he wasn't the one in charge. He sat with frustrated anger on his face but he didn't speak, he was trying to get himself back under control before he carried on. Then the door opened and a man came in. It was the Comedian.

'I'm sorry to interrupt, sir, but I'm afraid you're needed. Something rather urgent has come up.'

The 'sir' nearly got a laugh from Charlie and the Comedian noticed it. *Yes, you noticed, and you're probably as clever as you are sharp*, thought Charlie.

The policeman got up. The Comedian came to the desk and sat down.

'I'll finish talking to Mr Bronski, sir, I'm sure he doesn't want to be kept waiting. He wants to get home to collect things for his wife and then get back to the hospital.'

The policeman had his orders, so he left. The Comedian looked at the secretary.

'You can go too, my dear, we won't need you any longer.' The secretary, if she *was* a secretary, stood up. She hadn't been called 'my dear' by a man since she was a little girl and she didn't take it well. She stood up and paused as if she was going to do something about it, thought better of it, and left.

They watched her go.

'Did I upset that young lady? I have the distinct impression she had taken offence. She seemed to leave in a most marked manner.'

Charlie liked this Comedian. He was unorthodox, an original thinker. More importantly, perhaps he was someone who would do a deal if he possibly could.

'Maybe she wanted to stay and listen.'

The Comedian registered surprise. 'Surely not? I hardly think so.'

'Maybe it was me. Maybe I fascinate women.'

'Do you, Mr Bronski? It really is Bronski, is it?'

Charlie nodded. 'Yes it is. Charles Stanislaus Bronski.'

'Stanislaus? Isn't that overdoing it somewhat?'

Charlie shrugged. A Dane who said 'somewhat' wasn't going to have problems with his English.

'It's a Polish thing. My father was Polish.'

'If you say so. Shall we begin?'

'Begin?'

The Comedian was gone, switched off at the plug. Now it was business. The voice was flat and direct.

'I presume you have something to tell me, so why not just tell me? We don't need to wrap it up in games of questions and

28

pretence, do we?'

Charlie thought about it. He had decided not to use the police, to keep them totally out of it. But this man might be useful and whatever he was it certainly wasn't the police. He was different. If he was a sample of Danish Intelligence then they were good, bloody good. He would have to be very careful, but one question wouldn't hurt.

'Who am I talking to?'

The man raised his eyebrows in mock surprise. The Comedian was back.

'Why, the police of course. Who did you think you were talking to?'

'You're a policeman?'

'Very much so. I'm in the Traffic Division of Copenhagen Police Force. Nyborg comes under our jurisdiction – for the purposes of traffic, that is.'

'Traffic! You're Traffic like I'm …'

Charlie stopped in mid-sentence and waited.

'Yes, Mr Bronski. Like you're what?' But Charlie was silent. He wasn't about to get suckered in again, so the Comedian went on. 'Your car blew up, so technically this could be classed as a Traffic matter. A car being driven on the road or sitting in bits in a garage is still a car.'

The Comedian's way worked very well. He had almost been careless and joined in without thinking. Now he would join in, but carefully. This man made the rules so you had to play by them, but you didn't have to play his way.

'And when would you say a car is not a car?'

There was a short pause.

'How about when it's a bomb? Primary purpose would be the determining factor. A table is a table not because of how it looks but because of its tableness, its primary purpose. Not Oscar Wilde but Plato, his Theory of Forms. So, why was your car a bomb, Mr Bronski?'

'But if being a bomb was its primary purpose doesn't that rather take it out of Traffic's hands, out of your hands, or have I misunderstood Plato's Theory?'

The voice was flat and direct again.

'Your story, Mr Bronski. You have a story ready and I haven't got all day and I'm sure you want to get back to the hospital.'

He had finished trying to get some advantage, now he just wanted to get on. That was fine by Charlie.

'I have no idea what this is all about. I don't see how I can help you.'

'Why weren't you in the car?'

'How do you mean?'

'You and your wife were far enough away to avoid serious injury but you had been in the car. The ignition was switched on, the door was open. Why did you get out of the car? Did you know there was a bomb?'

Charlie remained silent. He knew this question would come and now here it was. Now he had to decide whether to bring this man in or shut him out. He was good and he wasn't the police, also he was coming across as someone who would deal, if he could. And he was direct, he didn't mess around too much, he had made his view of things clear almost from the word go. He already had a foot in the door. But he was still too much of an unknown factor. Never bet a doubt against a certainty. Charlie decided to shut him out and took on a slightly bewildered look. He did it very well. Most people would have believed him.

'I didn't know, not actually know. More like, I sort of felt it.'

'Sort of felt it? Could you explain that?'

'Before I retired I was in the US Air Force, working in base security. I only ever found three devices in all the security work I did, but three is plenty, believe me. In that line of work you're always looking, you're always careful and you're always suspicious. It becomes a habit, you develop a sixth sense. Sometimes you notice things before you realise you've noticed them, if you see what I mean. One package too many, a parcel with no reason to be there, a wire too many or the wrong colour or where a wire shouldn't be. Nothing really, but your mind notices it before you do because you have trained your mind to look in a special way.'

30

'And you think your mind noticed something?'

'It's all I can come up with and I really have thought about it. But if it was a bomb then it comes back to, why me? Why would anyone put a bomb in my car? And for that question I have no answer. I don't even have a guess.'

The man sat and looked at him. Charlie let him look. The story would hold up no matter how deep they dug. There was nothing this man could get hold of, however clever or original he was.

'Mr Bronski, if you were to be quite frank with me perhaps I could help. It's not nice having people putting bombs in your car and trying to blow you up. I really do think I could help, if you were quite frank with me.'

There it was, the offer. The man wanted to deal. He was asking the price to get inside this. But the answer still had to be no. Charlie shook his head.

'I'm trying to help, believe me, but I can't because I don't know anything. I'm not important or high-profile but maybe it was a lone terrorist thing, someone who sees any American as a target and decided to take out his hate on me, or maybe someone who got the know-how off the internet and wanted to plant a bomb for the hell of it. Who knows?'

'Who indeed? You're sure you don't want to change your story and take up my offer before we have to talk again?'

'I'm sure.'

'Then I must tell you, Mr Bronski, that the "I don't know anything" story is not one that I can subscribe to.'

The man waited. He was making sure Charlie understood there were going to be no neutrals in this. Charlie stayed silent and his silence made him a new enemy. Then the man stood up.

'Perhaps you're right, perhaps it was a lunatic, perhaps a crazed cookery writer who can't get published and is jealous of your success.'

'You know I write?'

'Mr Bronski, in Denmark when someone gets car-bombed we know all there is to know about them very quickly.'

'You knew about me being in the Air Force, in base security?' The man nodded. 'Then why the hell did you let me go through it if you already knew?'

'To see if you knew the story as well as I did.'

Charlie had had enough. He decided he didn't like this man any more.

'Can I go now? I want to get back to my wife.'

'As you were told before, you are free to go at any time.' Charlie got up. 'Oh, if our friend the crazed cookery writer has another go, you will let me know, won't you?' Charlie didn't answer, he just went to the door. The man followed him out. Moustache joined them as they walked along the corridor. 'Of course if there is a next time it may not be a bomb. I read only the other day that someone has put the details of how to develop anthrax in your own kitchen onto the internet. An American like yourself, I believe.'

'I'm British. I became a British citizen just before I married my wife.'

The man ignored Charlie's remark.

'Although with some of the kitchens I've seen anthrax would find itself hard pressed to deal with the local competition. Not your kitchen of course, Mr Bronski, I'm sure a professional like you has a spotless kitchen. Not a hint of anthrax anywhere.' The trio came to the exit. 'This officer will take you home and then if you wish he will take you back to the hospital. I regret he speaks only Danish.'

Charlie looked at Moustache. 'When he speaks at all.'

'Ah, a little joke. That's good, Mr Bronski, it shows you're bearing up. Well goodbye, for the time being. As I said, I'm afraid we will have to speak again. But, for now, go and look after your wife.'

He said something in Danish to Moustache then turned and walked away. Charlie watched him for a second then went out.

When the car reached the bungalow he got out and leaned down.

'I don't need a lift. You can go back to your boss.'

As soon as the its door was shut, the car pulled away. For someone who didn't speak English, Moustache understood it well enough. Charlie waited until the car was out of sight then

32

let himself into the house. He took off his coat, hung it up and went into the kitchen. The garage was attached to the bungalow, on the other side of the far kitchen wall. The door through to it which the explosion had blown open was hanging drunkenly on the upper hinge. Charlie went into the garage. It was empty. Beyond the twisted, scorched, up-and-over door he could see the police tape across the bottom of the drive. A bit of tape wouldn't keep anybody out and the garage door wouldn't close so he would have to fix the door into the kitchen. Even in Denmark there were people who couldn't resist an open door. Back in the kitchen a few things had been knocked off shelves. Some plates had fallen and the fragments were scattered over the tiled floor. Also splashed on the floor were the remains of his ingredients for Black Bread Pudding.

As he surveyed the mess there was a ring at the front door. Lars was standing there looking concerned.

'Inga saw you come home; she sent me round to ask if you needed anything. Something to eat, maybe? Someone to talk to?'

'Thank you, that's thoughtful and kind but I'm only here to pick up a few things for Elspeth. I must get back.'

'They're keeping her in?'

'Yes, for observation. You were right about her wrist and of course she's badly shaken up. She's sedated, sleeping a lot. I want to be there when she wakes up.'

'Of course, we understand. Go, and give her our love when you see her.' Lars turned away then stopped and looked back. 'Can I give you a lift to the hospital? The police took your car.'

'I don't think it would have been much use even if they'd left it.' Charlie smiled and Lars looked a little embarrassed at his silly remark. 'And thanks, but no. I'll call a taxi. I know this may sound rude but I don't want company at the moment. I just want to take a breather and then get back to be with Elspeth.'

'Yes, I quite understand.'

'There is something you can do, though.'

'Anything, just ask.'

'The door from the garage to the kitchen got blown in. After I've gone, could you make it secure? Anyone could walk in.'

'Sure, glad to.'

'Go in through the garage and then let yourself out. Thanks, Lars, thanks for understanding.'

'It's nothing. I'll see to it as soon as you go. Ring our bell when you leave and it will be done before you're back.' And he walked away.

Charlie went back to the kitchen and the remains of his Black Bread Pudding among the broken plate shards. He looked at the mess. Six eggs. It *was* too many, he'd known it all along.

After he had cleaned up he went to the living room, made himself a stiff drink and sat down. He made a decision. He wasn't going to run, whatever happened he wouldn't run. He wasn't going to start all over again, whoever it was that was after him.

If he stayed, he would have to fight. And if he had to fight, he needed to know what sort of enemy he was taking on. Who wanted him to suffer before he died? Not any of the people he was hiding from. They wanted him dead and they didn't play games. If they had found him and planted a bomb in his car, he would be splattered all over the inside of the garage. This was someone who wanted to make it personal. Not that it helped. If all the people who had a reason to kill him got together, they could start a small soccer league. But it had to be a professional, the bomb wasn't the work of some clever amateur who got his information from the internet. The way that bomb was wired wasn't something you picked up off the web, like how to make your own anthrax, and the components for it weren't on eBay.

Charlie sat and sipped his drink. He liked the view from this room at the back of the house, over the garden to the sea. He was looking east and the colour of the water was darkening as the daylight began to fade. His watch told him he had been gone from the hospital for nearly two hours. If Elspeth had woken up she would be frightened and wondering where he was. Well, that couldn't be helped – he needed to begin working this out.

It had to be someone based locally who could watch their movements and knew their Sunday routine, especially that Elspeth didn't get into the car until it was out of the garage. He smiled to himself. Someone who wanted him dead but was careful not to put Elspeth in harm's way. A professional with compassion, now *there* was a novelty. And it had to be someone new, someone who had arrived not very long ago and recognised him, or someone who had found where he was and had come to kill him. He was looking for a new face, somebody who could watch him without being noticed. Someone new who had a good reason for being there, who fitted in. It wouldn't be someone acting as a visitor or tourist. Nyborg was a small place and the tourist season was over, so a new face should help him, if the face was in Nyborg. But whoever it was could just as well be based in Copenhagen or Odense. Odense would be his bet, one stop up the line from Nyborg, only fifteen minutes on the train and big enough to hide in if anyone came looking.

Whoever was after him had slipped into the local woodwork and would take some dislodging. Charlie took a drink. Remember the rules, be careful and thorough and don't make any mistakes. You know what has to be done, so do it. *OK, whoever you are, you can watch me, maybe even try to frighten me once more if you're quick. But then I'll kill you.* He stood up and finished his drink. Now, what was it Elspeth had asked for?

SIX

'I brought your things.'

Elspeth was sitting up in bed nursing her strapped wrist with her good hand. Charlie put the bag he had brought on the foot of the bed and sat down beside her. She didn't ask him why had he been so long or tell him she'd been frightened when he didn't come straight back. She didn't need to, it was in her eyes and he'd seen it as soon as he walked into the room.

'I'm sorry I've been so long but the police insisted on taking me to the police station and asking me a lot of pointless questions, and when I got home I had to do some cleaning in the kitchen and sort out the door through to the garage. It was blown open, it was just hanging there. Anyone could have walked in. I asked Lars to see to it so that I could get here to you. I'm sorry, I came as soon as I could.'

Elspeth's eyes immediately forgave him. She should have known he wouldn't leave her alone if he could help it.

'What cleaning was there?'

'The Black Bread Pudding finished up all over the floor with some plates that had fallen, it was a mess, I couldn't just leave it.'

There was a silence. Charlie was waiting for the question and Elspeth was getting ready to ask it.

'Charlie, now can you tell me what this is all about?'

37

'Yes, I can tell you, but it's hard to know how to begin.'

'It's something from your past, isn't it?'

Charlie nodded but remained silent. *Don't speak, let her take her time to get where she wants to go.*

'I was thinking about things when you weren't here. About what I really know about you, from before we met, and I realised I know nothing about you except what you've told me. You were in the Air Force but you never told me anything much about that, just that you did a tour of service in England. I've never met any family or friends. I've never even met anyone who ever knew you.'

Charlie waited. She was about ready to ask her question.

'Charlie, is anything I know about you true?'

Fear of the answer was clear in her voice. Charlie put on his puzzled look. He wanted to do this well, for her sake as well as his own.

'Of course, dear, everything you know is true. What do you mean?'

'It was a bomb, wasn't it?' Charlie nodded. 'And it's something to do with your past, something I know nothing about, something you've hidden from me?' Charlie nodded again. She was doing very well. Elspeth made the final effort. 'Is your name really Charlie Bronski?'

'It is, except that there used to be a Stanislaus in front of the Charles and Bronski's my mother's maiden name. But it's been the name on my passport from before we ever met.'

'So am I really Mrs Bronski?'

'Yes, you really are.'

'And were you ever in the American Air Force?'

'Yes. I was in base security. But security is a young man's game and eventually I lost my confidence and that made me dangerous, so they retrained me. I became an accountant.'

'An accountant? Do they have accountants?'

'Sure they have accountants, lots of them. I became a very good accountant and by the time I retired I headed up a whole department of them. When I left the Air Force, being an accountant made it easy to get a job. I got a very good one with a small investment bank. Its main office was in Italy, in Milan, but it had two branches in the US. I worked at the branch in Miami, the other one was in New York. They didn't have a whole lot of clients but those they did certainly had the stuff. The bank moved it around so the money made money. I kept track of some accounts. Unfortunately it turned out my clients weren't simply hard-working businessmen or pension funds.'

'They were gangsters?'

'Not all of them. The bank was very good at what it did so it picked up some genuine clients – not a lot, but enough. They provided window dressing and gave the bank an air of respectability.'

'And you found out?'

'Me? No. I didn't suspect anything. It was all too well done, it all looked perfectly straight to me.'

'So what happened?'

'Have you ever heard of the Witness Protection Programme?'

'Yes, it hides gangsters who give evidence against other gangsters, doesn't it? It gives them new lives.'

'That's right.'

Elspeth paused. She didn't like to say it but ...

'Were you some sort of gangster, Charlie?'

Charlie grinned. 'No, dear, I was an accountant like I told you. It was the FBI who told me what was going on.'

'The FBI?'

'Sure. They knew it was a front for Mob money. They wanted me to help prove it and get the guys who were running the thing. Actually I found they didn't give a shit ...' Elspeth winced. 'Sorry, dear, that's how I used to talk. This is all bringing old times back. Times I want to forget.'

Elspeth smiled and put her good hand on his arm. 'That's all right, I understand.'

'Later I found what they really wanted was for the government to get the money. If they got the bad guys, fine. But what they really wanted was the money.'

'So you agreed to help?'

'Like hell I did. The Mob kill people, especially people who take their money off them.'

'So where does the Witness thing come in?'

'Once the FBI told me what was going on, I knew, and if the Mob found out I knew then I was dead. If I suddenly left the bank without any good reason it would look suspicious and I might as well save everybody time and effort, go somewhere quiet and blow my own brains out.'

'But couldn't you have gone on for say six months and then leave, making it look natural?'

'I didn't have six months. If I said no, the Feds made it clear someone would tip off the bank that I knew what was going on and that I had been approached by the FBI.'

'But they can't do that. That's blackmail. It's worse than blackmail, it's …'

But she couldn't think what it was.

'Look, dear, the Feds are the Mob with badges, they do whatever it takes. To them it's a war and wars have casualties and sometimes the casualties are innocent bystanders. In the military we called it collateral damage. It was either help, or become a piece of collateral damage. Anyway, the FBI had me where they wanted me and I knew they were the only people who could get me a new life where the Mob wouldn't find me, so I did what they wanted and then went into the Programme. Everything you know about me is true. You just didn't know the bit between leaving the Air Force and coming to England as Charlie Bronski.'

Elspeth thought about it. Then she gave a slight shudder. 'Is it the Mob, Charlie, did they try to blow you up? Is the Mafia after us?'

'Absolutely not. If they had found me, you would have had to collect me from all over the garden.'

'Oh don't, Charlie. It's too horrible to think about.' She paused. 'But if it's not them, then who?'

'My guess is somebody has recognised me and thinks they see a way of making money.'

'By selling their information to the Mafia?'

'No. I think this will turn out to be nothing more than old-fashioned blackmail. Pay me or I'll tell the Mob where you are.'

Elspeth let it all sink in.

'But we don't have a lot of money, do we?'

'You have what your Aunt Anne left you but that's all tied up. You get the income during your life but the capital goes back to your family when you die. I have my Air Force pension and we've got some savings. There's the house and there's the money from the books. We have all we need but we're not rich. We certainly couldn't afford any blackmail. Once it starts it doesn't stop.'

'Do we go to the police then?'

Charlie put plenty of urgency into his voice. He needed Elspeth to trust him totally.

'No police. Definitely no police.'

'But why, couldn't they ...'

'What the cops know today the Mob would know tomorrow and the day after that I'd be dead. Somebody would sell me out.'

He watched her. She didn't like it but she believed it.

'So who else is there? Is there anybody who can help us?' Charlie nodded.

'Yes there is. The people who got me into this. The FBI. I'll get in touch through the Protection Programme.'

'Will they help?'

'They'll have to. What good is a Witness Protection Programme if it can't keep its witnesses alive after they've testified? I'll make sure they understand that if I die, everyone is going to know why and what it was all about.'

'Isn't that a bit like blackmail? Like the way they treated you?'

'It's exactly what they did to me. That's why I'm sure it will work.'

There was a soft knock at the door. It opened. A big man with short grey hair, a black jacket and shirt topped off by a priest's collar, half came in.

'May we come in?' The accent was German. Elspeth looked at him past Charlie.

'Good evening, Father Mundt. Please come in. Charlie, get Father a chair from somewhere.'

The priest came into the room, followed by another man.

'You know Mr Costello, Jimmy. He is on a placement with me, getting parish experience.'

Charlie went and shook hands with Fr Mundt.

'Sure, Father.' Then he turned to Jimmy, 'We've seen you serving at Mass on Sundays.' Then back to Fr Mundt, 'I'll go and get a couple of chairs.'

'No, don't bother. We won't stay. I just wanted to be sure you were both all right. The doctor I spoke to says no real harm done but I thought I'd pop in and see for myself.'

Charlie stood aside as Fr Mundt headed for the bed. 'We came as soon as we heard, Elspeth.'

Charlie studied Fr Mundt's back while he talked to Elspeth. He looked just like a Catholic priest should look. He was a priest, and that was all he was.

'A terrible thing. Thank God neither of you is badly hurt.'

'No, Father, we're fine, but it was good of you both to come.'

Don't bother the priest, don't make a fuss. Somebody blows you up and you're in hospital but don't bother the priest. She was a little girl again. In the close presence of any priest she couldn't find a way to be more than ten years old. She smiled. You always had to smile. Unless, of course, you were crying. Crying was all right too. Priests could deal with crying, they got a lot of it.

'It must have been a terrifying experience for you both.'

Charlie turned his attention away from the bed to the other man, the placement. This was no fresh-faced young seminarian. In his late fifties, thick-set and badly dressed, he had a crumpled look, a lived-in face, short grizzled hair. But it wasn't his appearance that concerned Charlie. It was the way he had looked at him when they shook hands. His eyes seemed to say, you mean no more to me than the furniture.

It wasn't the sort of look you expected to see in the eyes of someone thinking about becoming a priest, it belonged to people like Moustache, and it registered with Charlie.

As Elspeth talked to the priest, Charlie's mind kept running. Up close, the man now standing quietly by the door looked very much like another Moustache and that had set an alarm bell off

42

in his head.

Here was a new face, a face that fitted in and got no questions asked. Charlie hadn't thought of him because he had the perfect cover story, a placement with the priest who just happened to say Mass for the Catholics in and around Nyborg. Charlie wondered how hard it would be to set up a phoney placement. Maybe not so hard – I'm thinking about becoming a priest, could I have a placement to help me decide? But why Copenhagen? He hadn't given it any thought before. Now he did. This guy was English, why come to Denmark? He walked over to him.

'How is the placement going, Mr Costello?'

Jimmy didn't try to smile, he knew he was no good at smiling.

'Fine.'

Not a chatty type, thought Charlie. Neither was Moustache.

'How long is it for?'

'Sort of open-ended.'

'Isn't Denmark an unusual choice for an Englishman?'

The man shrugged. 'Fr Mundt agreed to take me so I came.'

'Must be a big decision, thinking of becoming a priest. I mean, at your age.' The man didn't answer so Charlie pressed on. 'What did you do before?'

The man looked at Charlie and when he finally answered he obviously chose his words with care.

'I was in the Civil Service.'

Charlie made up his mind. This placement man was wrong. This was no apprentice priest. If this man wasn't another Moustache then Charlie was the Pope.

'Goodbye, Elspeth.' The priest turned to Charlie. 'We'll be on our way now we know you're both all right. I can see Elspeth needs to rest. Please let me know if there is anything I can do.'

'What time will Mass be in Copenhagen tomorrow, Father?'

'Ten thirty.'

Charlie nodded his thanks. The priest shook his hand and smiled. The man called Costello came to Charlie. They looked into each other's eyes as they shook hands and Charlie suddenly felt that this could be the one who had come to kill him. He had seen killers before. He was sure he was seeing one now. It was in the eyes, the way he looked at him. That meant that if he was right, there would be no more frightening, next time it would be for real.

After they left, Charlie went and sat by Elspeth, thinking. If Costello was the one then the clock would be running. Charlie would have to move very quickly.

'Will you have to go to America?'

Charlie pulled himself out of his thoughts. 'America?'

'To get help from the FBI.'

'No, I don't think so. I should be able to make contact through the embassy. I'll go tomorrow after Mass.'

'Going to Mass is nice. I'm glad you're going, I wish I could come with you.'

'No, don't even think about it. You rest and get well.'

Elspeth smiled at him.

'You know, somehow I feel better, as if everything was getting back under control. I don't know why but that's how I feel.'

'Good.'

Charlie was pleased, that was exactly how he wanted her to feel. He had worked very hard to get her to feel like that. Charlie was in control, she could rely on Charlie and trust him because she believed in him. Just one last thing and he could go.

'The papers and television will be covering this, it'll be quite a story. If they get wind of who you are, the Elspeth Allen of the books, they may bother you. If they do, remember what I told you, you have nothing to say. If you know nothing and say it often enough they'll go away. They can't make a story if there's nothing to say. You know nothing.'

'All right, if you say so.'

'I do say so. I'll have a word with the nurse or doctor to make sure you're not bothered while you're in hospital. Now, get under the clothes and get some sleep. I'll come in tomorrow as soon as I can.' He kissed her then went to the door, switched out the light and left.

SEVEN

'I know very little about them. He's American, she's English. He writes cookery books in her name. They were already living in Nyborg when I came to Copenhagen. They seem a nice couple.'

'I don't like him.'

'What do you mean, not like him? You don't know him.'

'Do you?'

'No, I told you what I know, which is very little.'

'Do you think he could be wrong?'

'Wrong? About what?'

'No, him. Could he be, well, wrong?'

'In what way "wrong"?'

Jimmy poured the last of the Tuborg into his glass, as Father Udo Mundt waited for an answer.

'It's difficult to explain.'

'Take your time. I'll get us both another beer.'

Udo got up and went to the kitchen, collected two more plastic bottles and returned to the living room. Jimmy watched him as he sat down. He liked this man, he was calm, patient and kind and he never intruded. He was a man you could talk to.

'I used to be a copper, a policeman ...'

Udo smiled.

'I know what a copper is, Jimmy, I think everyone knows

45

what a copper is.'

Jimmy pulled the top off his bottle and poured some beer.

'I was a detective sergeant in North London.' He took a drink. 'And I was bent.'

Udo pulled the top off his Tuborg and poured some beer. He didn't look up as he asked his question.

'Bent as in corrupt?'

'As in corrupt.' The conversation stalled for a minute. Udo let it. He took a drink. You didn't hurry someone when they were telling you things like this and you didn't show any curiosity. You waited and you listened.

'I took money and I did things. Bad things.'

Jimmy waited for some sort of response. He wanted the priest to make it easier for him. Priests were supposed to help. Udo understood so he helped.

'Bad things?'

'How bad can you imagine, Udo?'

'Oh, very bad I should think, just about as bad as it gets.'

'Then you've got it.'

Udo made sure his face registered nothing. Jimmy tried to struggle on but somehow he couldn't find the right way. *Once it would have been easy*, he thought. *I was a bent copper. I took money. I hurt people. My wife died. I smashed up a couple of blokes and was given early retirement to cover it all up. I went away, thought about things and decided to become a priest. That's me, take it or leave it, I don't give a shit one way or the other.*

But now he was going to try and tell it properly and he found he really did give a shit after all.

'I had a wife and two kids. I told myself I was doing it for them. I'd got mixed up with a bad crowd as a young man. I found I liked it, I could have been good at it. I knew how to hurt people so I fitted in. A mechanic, they called me. But Bernie, she was my girlfriend then, well it wasn't a life for her. So I decided that if I knew about the bad guys and how they did things the best thing to do was to stay in the business but move to the other side of the street. So I became a copper.'

Udo sat very still. Jimmy wasn't really talking to him, he

was trying to talk out his past, trying to face the man he had once been. If he did, it would be hard and painful. So Udo waited. 'Anyway, when I became a detective I got in with another bad crowd, bent coppers this time. Like I say, I took money and did other things, but I told myself I was doing it for my family, it was all for Bernie and the kids. I told myself that, at home, I was a good dad and off duty, I was a good Catholic.'

Jimmy sat forward, hunched up, looking at the carpet. He felt sick. Then he looked up at Udo. 'My daughter got married and went to Australia. My son became a missionary priest. They both left home and got far away from me, as far away as they could. They didn't want me in their lives.' He could taste a bitterness in his mouth, like after you'd vomited. Maybe he was going to throw up. God knows, he was sick of it all. 'I deserved it, I know now I deserved it, but Bernie didn't, she didn't deserve to lose her kids. And she didn't deserve never to see her grandchildren in Australia. But she stuck by me. I was doing it all for her, so that one day I could say, look at all this money, Bernie. It's for you. Now you can have a nice house. You can visit Eileen and the kids. You can give Michael money for projects. You can do whatever you like, it's all yours.'

Udo watched. Tears were running down Jimmy's face. This was a man suffering, saying out loud to another person the sort of man he had been and, maybe for the first time, truly regretting what he had done to his family, to others and to himself. It wasn't a confession, it was a confrontation, perhaps even an execution. This man was bringing out his old self and confronting not only what he had been but what he had done to those he held most dear. This was a man trying to lay to rest a ghost that had haunted him for a long time.

'But she died. Just like that, she died. There was nothing I could do. So I was left with all that money and ...'

Fuck all else, were the words that almost came out, but he held them back. It was a small thing, but now life was no more than a series of small things and he tried to get them right. The big things he left alone. He had tried changing the big things and he knew he couldn't, so he stuck to the things he could change. He tried not to swear now, at least not out loud. Bernie

47

had never liked bad language.

'Money and nothing else. After the funeral I had a bit of a breakdown, I suppose. I was angry, I lashed out. I hurt a couple of blokes – I sort of took it all out on them. One was a heavy villain and, when he got out of hospital, I was going to be found in little bits distributed across London so I was given early retirement to cover everything up and I hopped it.'

Jimmy looked up at Udo who sat very still watching him. He wiped the tears from his cheeks with the back of his hands and sat back. He took a drink then poured himself some more beer, it was something to do.

'Udo, I've looked into the faces of thugs, pimps, liars, cheats and not a few killers in my time and that guy's face has most of those in it. Whatever he is, he's not just a nice bloke who writes cookery books. And I'll tell you something else, he doesn't like me. When we shook hands at the hospital you could see it in his eyes, the way he looked at me. There's something wrong about that guy.' Jimmy waited. He'd said what he wanted to say – now it was up to Udo.

'You said that when you retired you decided to become a priest. How long ago was that?'

Jimmy didn't want to think about those years, they weren't great memories.

'It took time, it needed thinking about.'

'I can see how it would. So, how long?'

'A long time. Can we leave it at that?'

'OK. So, if you wanted to be a priest, why wait what you call "a long time" and then settle for a placement like this? Why not just apply to Rome or wherever and begin training?'

'I did, I applied and started training. I was a Duns College student.'

'Duns College?'

'It's a funny set-up, a sort of one-at-a-time college for mature men of independent means who can pay for their own training and never need to get paid by the diocese where they work as a priest. They don't turn up often so, as I say, Duns College is a funny set-up. It comes and goes. It's really just an office in the Vatican, some headed notepaper and an honorary rector when needed. It gets wheeled out when a suitable candidate comes along. All the training is done by other places in Rome.'

'So why are you here on a placement starting all over again? Why aren't you still in Rome?'

Jimmy paused. This was going to be tricky.

'I'd been a detective so I was asked to do a job for the rector, me and another bloke, a sort of research job, finding things out about somebody. When it was over the rector thought I should go away and think about things. She wrote to me after I'd gone and told me if I still wanted to consider training for the priesthood she would get me a placement to see what a parish priest's life was like. I thought about it, then said, OK, and here I am.'

It sounded thin to Jimmy; he hoped it didn't sound quite so thin to Udo.

'Tell me, the name of this honorary rector you did the research for. It wouldn't have been someone called McBride would it, Professor Pauline McBride? An American, black?'

'Yes, how did you know that?'

Udo smiled at him. The smile turned into a grin. 'That explains a great deal, Jimmy.'

'It does?'

'Oh yes. You see, I was asked to take you on this placement by Professor McBride. Oh, she didn't ask personally, you understand. If you know her at all you'll know that isn't her way. The actual request came through a Monsignor, but it was made clear that the request originated with her. And if you know the professor at all well, you will know she is not the kind of person you say "no" to. So here you are. But when I was told to take you on, I asked myself, why would an Englishman with no foreign languages be put on placement in Copenhagen? You will agree it's an odd thing to do?'

Jimmy nodded. He could see how anyone would think so.

'This job you did for her, this research job – you said there was another man?' Jimmy nodded again. 'And what became of him when the job was done?'

'He died. It turned out he was a very sick man.'

'I see.'

Jimmy hoped he didn't, for his own sake. For a short while they both sat in silence. Then Udo began again.

'So you think Charlie Bronski might be a bad lot?'

'It's possible, if not now, then before.'

'Perhaps a retired crook, you think? Living off his ill-gotten gains? Come on, Jimmy. He writes cookery books. How many retired crooks write cookery books?'

He was right of course, Jimmy knew that. What sort of villain wrote cookery books and retired to a small seaside town in Denmark? It was none of his business but Jimmy's mind couldn't leave it alone. He didn't like Charlie Bronski. He was too smooth and he asked the wrong questions. He had been nearly blown up in the morning and by the evening he was as calm as you please, making polite enquiries about Jimmy's placement while his wife was across the room in a hospital bed. He was in control of himself, very tight control. That was the problem, Jimmy decided, that was why he was wrong. He was too much in control. Bronski was used to that kind of pressure and he could deal with it. What sort of person could do that? Not a cookery book writer.

'Look, Udo, I shouldn't have said anything, it's none of my business. Even if I'm right about Bronski I don't want to get involved. I should have left it alone. I don't want any trouble, not for me, or you, or him, not for anybody. Whatever he was doesn't concern me. If, now, he's a nice married guy who writes books, let him get on with it.'

'Somebody doesn't agree with you. Somebody blew up his car.'

'You think somebody tried to kill him?'

'Don't you?'

'I suppose so. How else does a car blow up?'

'What about some sort of accident. A gas leak, something like that?'

'That doesn't work, Udo. If it was something in the garage and starting the car set it off, how come he and his wife were watching when it happened?' Jimmy might not want to get involved, Jimmy might want to be a priest, but Jimmy's mind was still a copper's mind and the questions kept coming whether he wanted them or not. 'Why wasn't he in the car? Why plant a bomb and then give your target time to get clear?'

'Good question, Jimmy, but there's another one. If it *was* a bomb, how did he know to get clear? It doesn't seem to make much sense whichever way you look at it.'

And Jimmy suddenly understood why his mind wouldn't leave it alone. *Because* it made no sense. It made no sense if Bronski was a nice bloke, happily married, who wrote books. It might begin to make sense if Bronski was not only wrong, but *very* wrong.

'I don't know what this is all about but I was in London during IRA bombing campaigns and I know enough to know that if someone puts a bomb in a car they don't delay it so the target can get out and get clear. It goes bang and you're dead.'

'Which means what?'

'I don't know, but I bet Bronski does.'

'How can you be sure?'

'I can't, I don't even want to be. But I don't like the way he looked at me and the way he asked his innocent questions. I've interrogated plenty of people and I've been interrogated, by experts. He was sniffing for something. God knows what, but he was sniffing.'

'"Sniffing"?'

'If he is a wrong 'un, he'll be an extra-careful man just at the moment, he'll be looking out for something.'

'What sort of thing?'

'How should I know? But he'll be looking. When he looked at me you could see the wheels turning, what's an Englishman doing on a placement in Denmark? Maybe he had me pigeonholed as someone using this placement as cover to look into him. He said it was a funny place for an Englishman to do a parish placement.'

'He's right, it *is* very unusual.' Udo paused. 'I have never asked because I don't want to intrude but as you've brought it up. Why Denmark? Why Copenhagen?'

Jimmy didn't answer.

'May I make a guess?'

51

Jimmy nodded. *Why not?*

'Denmark is not a Catholic country. Our community here is mostly foreigners. If you wanted to be somewhere ... how shall I put it ... somewhere out of the way, unnoticed, this placement would suit you very well.' Jimmy remained silent. 'Is anybody looking for you, Jimmy?'

'You could say something like that.'

'I think I did just say something like that.'

'Yes, they're looking.'

'And it is to do with the job you did for Professor McBride, your research job?'

'Yes.'

'And if you were found would you be arrested?'

'Oh no. Whatever else might happen, I wouldn't be arrested.'

'I see, except of course I don't. But it's none of my business, so I think I'll leave it there. As far as I am concerned you are here exploring whether you have a vocation, that is enough.'

'I can see why Bronski gave me the once-over. Apart from being English I'm not exactly your usual vocational candidate, am I? I don't look like a bright young graduate who got hooked by the university chaplain.'

'I don't know, are mature students so uncommon? So, what do you think? He's a gangster of some sort whose past may have caught up with him and he suspects you're part of that past, come looking for him?'

'He's something and he took a serious interest in me and, like I said, it wasn't because he thought we might be friends. Maybe he thinks I'm police. I was, remember, and maybe it still shows if you know what to look for.'

Udo didn't like it. If Jimmy was right about any of this it could get very messy.

'Do you think he might do anything? About you, I mean?'

'If he does, his first move would be to try and check me out. If he's got contacts in London he could get questions asked. But that won't matter.'

'No?'

'My story will stand up. I was a copper, my wife died and I

52

took early retirement. It's all in my record. I'm an ex-copper. End of story. But if he's here lying low, I doubt he'd want to break cover, so I don't think he'll contact anyone.'

'And Rome?'

'If anyone asks in Rome I was never there, not as a Duns student, not as anything. And again he would have to break cover to get anyone to check.'

'And this placement? What is that?'

'Is it as much a lie as my London record or the one that doesn't exist in Rome? No. Being here isn't me lying low while people look for me - not exactly. It really is me finding out about life as a parish priest. Look, Udo, I told you everything because I thought you deserved to know it all. As for Bronski, if he wants to check me out, the simplest way would be for him to come here and ask questions, that would be a safe first step. If the questions were careful enough he could find out what he wanted but still keep his cover intact.'

'So if he comes asking questions, that would mean …'

'It would mean he came and asked questions. I don't have to be right. I'm just thinking out loud. I'm probably a mile wide of what this is about, if it's about anything at all.' He hoped he was convincing Udo, because he was bloody well sure he wasn't convincing himself. 'And even if he is hiding out, it's nothing to do with us. I don't want to know anything or do anything about this bloke, whoever he is or whatever he did. I don't deal with villains any more, not for justice, not for profit. And I don't hurt people now, not if I can help it. I don't help punish people for their crimes and I don't bring retribution to the wicked. I just do what I can so Bernie won't be ashamed of me.'

'Ashamed of you?'

Jimmy nodded.

'She must have been ashamed of what I was for most of our married life. She never said anything but she must have known, yet she stuck by me. God alone knows how many times she must have thought about walking out on me and going down to Australia and having a proper life with Eileen and the kids, but she stuck by me.' Udo could see that the tears were back in his

53

eyes. 'I thought I was doing it all for her, that I was looking after her, when all the time she was doing it all for me, looking after me. So now I do what I can. I tried being someone she would be proud of but that didn't work. It was the same me, being the good guy and making it so Bernie would have been proud of me and not caring a damn who got hurt in the process. It was – "Look at me, Bernie, be proud of me, Bernie, I'm doing it all for your sake. I know I'm not doing the right thing but I'm too busy making you proud of me to think about what the right thing is.".' He looked up and wiped the tears out of his eyes. The self-pity had gone. 'So now I do what I can, I try not to make her ashamed of me. It's not much but it's all I can manage.'

Jimmy finished his beer. Udo reached across and picked up Jimmy's empty bottle.

'Another?'

'No thanks. I think I'll turn in.' Jimmy got up and went to the door. 'Thanks for listening.'

'It's OK, I get to do a lot of listening.'

'I know you do.'

And Jimmy left Udo to his beer and his thoughts.

EIGHT

Charlie Bronski arrived at Nyborg Station, bought a return ticket to Copenhagen and boarded the seven fifteen train. The train was already well filled with passengers and by the time it reached Copenhagen Central it was packed. It was just before quarter to nine when Charlie joined the crowds of commuters on the platform and they climbed, shoulder to shoulder, up the stairs into the main concourse. There he left the hurrying crowds heading for the exits and went into the ticket office. It wasn't busy and he was out in a few minutes with a return ticket to Østerport, a local station on the main lines to the north. He looked at the departures board. Almost all of the trains heading north stopped there and he had a choice of two leaving within five minutes. He walked down the stairs onto the platform where the Helsingør train was waiting. The platform was empty and when he got on the train there were only a few passengers scattered about the compartment. He sat down.

Half an hour later they arrived at Østerport station. Three other passengers got off and began to walk along the platform towards the exit sign. Charlie waited for a moment looking at a poster, then he turned and headed for the exit. He didn't want anyone from the train behind him. A small and probably unnecessary precaution.

Once out of the station he walked past a few parked cars

onto a footpath with a high wall on his left and a park on his right. The autumn sun was shining, giving the trees in the park long shadows across the well-tended grass and gravel footpaths. After a couple of minutes the footpath came out onto a wide street, Kastelvej.

From Kastelvej he could see the main buildings of the British Embassy in their own grounds behind the footpath wall. He passed the tall, elaborate iron gates which only opened for special visitors, past the security building at the side of the gates where routine traffic came and went, and turned into an imposing white building that fronted onto Kastelvej. It was squarely handsome in that formally attractive way that many official buildings had in Copenhagen. This was the front office of the Embassy complex where the small business was done. Here came the tourists who'd lost their passports, here all the other little jobs concerning the British traveller in trouble got sorted. This was where the press would get briefed if, as very rarely happened, a British subject in Denmark became newsworthy.

The lobby had a high ceiling and dark marble floor and a clean, austere Scandinavian style, but two substantial aspidistra plants, a large portrait of the Queen and a middle-aged, uniformed man who looked like a West End commissionaire claimed it for Britain. Apart from two leather chairs facing each other on either side of the lobby the only other furniture was a substantial desk.

Charlie walked up to the desk. A young woman smiled at him. Charlie smiled back.

'I would like a message to be given to Henry Clarke-Phillips.'

The young woman checked her lists and informed him that no one of that name was on the Embassy staff.

No, he knew Henry Clarke-Phillips was not a member of the Embassy staff, Henry Clarke-Phillips was based in London. Could the Head of Embassy Security be given the name and arrange for the message to be sent to London? It was urgent and it was important.

No one was smiling any more.

The young woman looked across at the commissionaire, then the smile returned and she asked Charlie to wait. He smiled back at her then went to a chair and sat down while she made a phone call. The commissionaire never took his eyes off him.

After about five minutes a man who seemed too young to be out of sixth form came through a door and walked across to the desk. He bent down and spoke to the young woman, she answered, then they both looked across at Charlie. The young man walked across to him.

'I understand you wish the Embassy to send a message to someone?'

Charlie stood up.

'To Henry Clarke-Phillips.'

'There is no one of —'

'That name at this Embassy. I know. Henry Clarke-Phillips works out of London.'

'In what capacity?'

Charlie looked at him. Was he being careful or snotty? He decided he didn't care.

'Are you the Head of Security? I asked for the Head of Security to be given the name.'

'I'm afraid I can't discuss —'

'Tell the Head of Security someone wants a message sent to Henry Clarke-Phillips in London, that it's urgent and important. Tell whoever it is to look up the name. It will be in the Dormant Contacts Register. I'm not in too much of a hurry …' he looked at his watch, 'but I do have to be somewhere shortly after ten o'clock, so if you could get on with it.'

The sixth former paused. He wasn't sure. But a Dormant Contacts Register sounded as if it might be something that actually did exist. He was a very junior diplomat, so he made the decision all very junior diplomats make. He would pass the thing on to someone else higher up.

'Wait here please.'

Charlie sat down again. He wasn't in a hurry but he didn't want to be too late. After another five minutes someone else came into the lobby. Mature, smartly severe, she didn't waste any time.

57

'Good morning, I understand you wish us to send a message?'

'Yes.'

'And you are?'

'It doesn't matter who I am. I want a message sent to Henry Clarke-Phillips in London.'

She didn't even pause. 'The message is?'

'Hamburg, Louis C Jacob, tonight, nine thirty.'

'Is there anything to go with it to say who it's from?'

'No. Thank you. Henry will know who it's from.'

Charlie left with the Head of Security watching him. Outside he turned off Kastelvej back onto the footpath. He hoped they were at least halfway efficient, he didn't want to make the trip to Hamburg for nothing. Well, it was done now and when he got to Hamburg he would find out if he still had an ace in the hole. He walked back along the footpath to the station, crossed over the bridge and stood on the platform.

This was a very exclusive suburb. The men and women who stood and waited with him on the platform were the ones who travelled to central Copenhagen after the nuisance of the rush hour had subsided. These were the ones whose offices were at the top of those formally attractive buildings. They arrived late, lunched well and left early. Why not? If success doesn't mean rewards then what's the point? He looked at his watch, the trains were frequent and the journey was short. He should be just about right for the ten thirty Mass.

There were about twenty people in the congregation scattered around the church. Jimmy was serving as he did on Sundays at Nyborg. He noticed Bronski slip in and kneel at the back just as Udo was about to give out communion. He wasn't happy about the arrival; he hadn't wanted to be right about Bronski but there he was. A few minutes later, at the end of Mass, Udo gave the final blessing, bent down and touched his lips to the altar, and Jimmy led him off the sanctuary back to the sacristy.

Charlie waited a few minutes until almost all the congregation had left the church. Then he went to the door of the sacristy, knocked and went in.

Fr Mundt turned to him. 'Hello, Charlie, how's Elspeth?'

'She'll be fine, Father, she just needs rest. Listen, I want to say thanks to you for coming yesterday, and I want to ask a favour. I'd also like a bit of advice.'

'Certainly. Let me finish here then we can go and talk over coffee.'

'Fine.'

Jimmy was unsuccessfully trying to be invisible, busying himself tidying away the chalice and other items used for Mass into the sacristy safe. He didn't want to be around this man but he knew Charlie was watching him. He closed the safe door and turned the key. He handed the key to Udo.

'I'll go and do some shopping, Father.'

But Charlie wanted him where he could see him and talk to him. He was, after all, the reason for the visit.

'No, Mr Costello, please don't go yet. You may be able to help with the advice. Two heads are better than one. I'm sure the shopping can wait.'

Charlie and Jimmy looked at each other. *So*, thought Jimmy, *the game's on*.

'I'll go through and get the coffee ready, Father.'

'Thanks.'

Jimmy went through the door that led from the sacristy into the house and went to the kitchen. After a couple of minutes Udo led Charlie into the living room where Jimmy was putting milk and sugar on the table. Udo and Charlie sat down. Jimmy looked down at Charlie.

'There's only instant, Mr Bronski. I hope that's OK?'

'Instant's fine.'

Jimmy left for the kitchen and heard Udo get down to the supposed business.

'So, Charlie, what's the favour?'

'I didn't tell Elspeth but I've got to go away for a day or two. I didn't tell her because I thought we'd be going together, I was going to turn it into a surprise break. It's to do with my writing, nothing very important in itself but there's a deadline. There's a publisher who thinks he can bring out a German edition of the series, God knows how … oh … sorry, Father.'

'It's all right, I've heard the expression before.'

'Anyway, how "The World in an English Kitchen" series could sell in Germany is his business, but he needs to see me today to make a decision. It was all arranged weeks ago. Would you go to the hospital and tell Elspeth what's happened and tell her I'll be back without fail tomorrow? If I go to the hospital myself I'm not sure I'd get away. If she got upset, which she probably would, I'd have to cancel. I know it sounds like I'm being a wimp but I need to go and if Elspeth …'

Jimmy came in with three mugs on a tray. He put it on the table.

'Help yourself to milk and sugar.'

Jimmy took his mug and went to sit by the dining table. Udo picked up his mug. He didn't take sugar or milk. Charlie took both.

'It would be a real help.'

'Certainly I'll do it. I'll fit it in as soon as I can after lunch. The world has to go on. You go and see your publisher and get back to Elspeth as soon as you can. Now, what's the advice?'

Charlie hesitated, took a drink of his coffee then sat back, ready to talk.

'It's about the police.'

'The police?'

'They interviewed me yesterday and made it clear they think I'm holding something back about what happened to the car.'

'And *are* you holding anything back?'

'No, nothing. But if someone puts a bomb in your car the police seem to think you must know who and why. I'm not sure what to do. I have no experience of the police, at least none of being questioned by them in a situation like this. I don't know how I should handle it. I don't know who to talk to about it. I wondered if you knew anybody who could advise me. I don't want to go to a lawyer, I think that makes it look as if I'm guilty of something. I need someone who has experience of the way these things are done. I wondered if you knew anyone, Father?'

There it was, out in the open, the careful question Jimmy had been waiting for. This bloke was good, he really sounded genuine, slightly confused and slightly afraid. He even got it into his eyes. This bloke was very good indeed. *Well*, thought Jimmy, *if he's guessed it he's guessed it, he just wants it confirmed, so why not*?

'I don't know if I can be of any help, Mr Bronski, but I have some knowledge of police procedures.'

'But I thought you said you were in the Civil Service?'

'In the UK the Civil Service covers a lot of ground. What is it you want to know? If I can help, I will.'

'Well, thank you, I appreciate it. And please, call me Charlie. Everyone calls me Charlie.'

Jimmy looked at him. *Amazement and relief.* Yes, he was very good. *Maybe I should clap.* Someone ought to clap.

'What should I do, Mr Costello?'

'Have you cooperated?'

'In so far as I can.'

'Then I would say keep on cooperating.'

'So just answer their questions as best I can and if I know nothing, say so.'

'If you know nothing where is there for them to go? If you have nothing to hide there's nothing to find. Do you have anything to hide, Mr Bronski?'

'No, nothing.'

'Then I'd say that for a beginner you're doing OK. I'd say up to now you're doing fine.'

Charlie stood up smiling. Jimmy watched him. Now it was relief and thankfulness. *I wonder if he can dance as well and maybe sing a bit or play an instrument*?

'That's two things off my mind. You really don't think I should put off this trip, Father?'

'No, Charlie, if it's there and back by tomorrow then you go. I'll let Elspeth know you've gone to your meeting. Something very terrible nearly happened but life has to go on. The sooner you both get things back to normal, the better you'll feel.'

Udo stood up. Jimmy sat and watched. They shook hands then Charlie came and shook Jimmy's hand. Jimmy didn't get up.

'Thank you, Mr Costello, you've really been a help. I think I know where I stand now.'

Jimmy knew it was meant to mean something, he didn't know what, but Bronski was definitely telling him something and it was nothing to do with where he stood with the police.

Udo led his visitor from the room, leaving Jimmy to sit and think about the visit.

The curtain had come down and the show was over. He felt sure he would find out sometime soon what the price of admission would turn out to be. For such a good show it could be quite a high price.

When Udo came back, Jimmy was sitting drinking his coffee. Udo sat down.

'Well, he came, like you said he would. Do you still think it means something?'

'I said he *might* come. I hoped he wouldn't but he did, and he didn't waste any time. And, yes, I think it means something. He made one mistake though.'

'A mistake?'

'He didn't thank us for the coffee. He did just about everything else, but he didn't say thank you for the coffee. Maybe he didn't like it.'

Udo looked at Jimmy.

'What are you talking about?'

'He's good, Udo, too good to just be a straight ex-villain. He's trained, some kind of professional.'

'You think so? Ex-police maybe?'

'No, not police – not even the Special Branch sort – but I know the type he would fit. He's like the ones who sometimes turned up to keep Special Branch company, the sort who never got introduced. There was always at least one around when there was IRA involvement or even the chance of their involvement.'

'And that cryptic remark means what exactly?'

'He's some sort of Intelligence, or was. He's not some ex-Mob guy that's retired or is being looked after by some Witness Protection Programme.'

'How do you know? How can you be sure?'

'I can't be sure, just like I couldn't be sure he had me clocked as a policeman and would come to suss me out. But it turns out I was right then and I think I'm right now. What sort of successful villain retires to Denmark, for God's sake?'

'And writes cookery books? Yes, I see what you mean. But it's like you said, a good place to disappear into. If you wanted to live a nice comfortable life well away from anyone who was looking for you, the sort who would want you dead if they found you, I'd say it's a very good place.'

'Until someone finds you and puts a bomb in your car.'

Then Jimmy noticed that Udo was looking at him in an odd way.

'I'm sorry I have to ask but things seem to have changed. Is that what you're really doing here, Jimmy, are you hiding from someone who wants you dead? If it is, I think I have to know.'

Jimmy didn't want to tell him but he couldn't just shut him out. Udo was a good bloke, he shouldn't have to get involved but it was beginning to look as if there was no choice. Telling him could hurt him, not telling him could hurt him worse. There was only one other way.

'I'll leave. It's the best thing to do. I'll just leave.'

'And where will you go?'

'I don't know. I'll find somewhere. I don't want you mixed up in this any more than you already are.'

'Getting mixed up in the messy things of life is one of the things being a priest is all about. You don't just say Mass and then close the door on all the problems. I'm supposed to bring the Good News to people. If that means anything, it means I bring help to those in need. Are you in need, Jimmy?'

Jimmy didn't have to think about it to answer that one. 'That job I did in Rome for Professor McBride.'

'Yes?'

'It made some powerful people prefer me dead, so I got out, probably just ahead of them. That's why she got me this placement. It was because of her they were looking for me so she got a letter through to me after I'd done a runner and offered to find me somewhere ... well, where I could have a low profile. I suppose I'm hiding out, but I *do* want to know what life as a priest is like. In the unlikely event of things turning out in my favour I still might go back to Rome. But in the meantime, like I said, Denmark is a good place to hide.'

'Can you tell me who these powerful people are?'

'No.'

'I see. Is Charlie Bronski a threat to you?'

'I don't know. I don't see why he should be, but I get the very strong feeling he has me marked down as trouble. If I'm right about him he could have contacts in the Intelligence world. He might be able to get someone to take a look at my file for him.'

'And?'

'My story will stand up to ordinary scrutiny but not to anyone who knows what to look for.'

'And then what will happen?'

'I don't know but my guess is the people who want to find me will get told.'

'Is there no one at all you can go to? There must be somebody.'

Jimmy shook his head.

'Udo, try to understand. I don't mind if they find me, I don't mind if they kill me. Dying isn't something I have a problem with. Living is what I have a problem with.'

Udo sat for a moment.

'Well, it's different, Jimmy, I'll give you that. Normally I have to be the one who helps people overcome a fear of dying. I'm not sure what to say to someone who doesn't care if they die but has a problem with staying alive.'

'It's like I said, I don't want Bernie ashamed of me. I won't fight them but I won't give in. Giving in would be like committing suicide. Bernie stuck it out with me until it killed her. I'll stick it out until it kills me. It's not much but it's all I can do.'

Suddenly Udo stood up.

'Come on, Jimmy, you've told me what you wanted me to know and I've asked what I needed to ask, but the world doesn't stop just because your bit looks like it's coming to an end. We've work to do. You do the shopping and I'll start my visits. I'll be back at one to do some paperwork then we'll have lunch. After that we'll go and see Elspeth Bronski.'

And that was that. Jimmy's problems were put away for the time being because, whatever was happening to him, life went on.

For Udo, and maybe one day for him, if he ever made it back to Rome, you didn't stop, no matter what. You said Mass for them, you baptised them, married them and buried them, but most of all you kept going, because it never stopped. Life went on with or without you. That's how it was and how it always would be, for ever and ever. Amen.

NINE

On the platform a group of last-minute passengers hurried past the window looking in for seats where they might sit together. They were young people with rucksacks, probably students, noisily laughing and shouting at each other. Charlie looked at his watch, eleven forty, the train should leave in two minutes. He hadn't been on the train more than a few minutes himself but they were cutting it fine, even for students. He leaned forward and looked up and down the platform. The students were out of sight, he could only see an elderly couple who were smiling and giving small waves to what he guessed was a young child further down the carriage. *Grandparents saying goodbye*.

The group of students came past, still laughing, still looking for somewhere they could all be together. He watched them make their way to the end of the carriage and begin to unload the rucksacks. People already in seats smiled and got up, offering to move around so the young people could sit together. Everything was very casual and friendly, typically Danish.

The train suddenly began to move. The students stacked their rucksacks and settled down as it slid out from the semi-gloom of the station buildings into the sunshine. Charlie watched the students settle. Why would students catch this one? It was the fast train, direct, you had to pay a supplement. Then he relaxed and sat back. No, no one would be following him.

Not yet. Up to now they didn't have any reason to put those kind of resources onto him. That was why now was the right time to make a move, to collect his ace in the hole, if it was still there.

The Hamburg intercity express left the platforms of the main station behind and began to pick up speed. Charlie felt pleased with himself. If they had been watching him in Nyborg, which was unlikely but just about possible, then before anybody realised for sure he had gone he would be well on his way, maybe he'd even be on his way back. *Keep it simple, get it right. Thank God for the European Union*. Even if they realised he'd skipped and got an alert out quickly, no one would know where he was or where he was going. They could cover airports but on the ground the borders were all open doors. It wasn't like the old days, now all the exit routes were soft exit routes.

The train was moving faster now, through Copenhagen's urban landscape. It could be any European city. Offices, factories, depots. The elegant architecture of the city centre was behind them. Not that Charlie cared what the view looked like. A journey was a journey, you went from one place to another. He watched the city passing and decided that when Hamburg was finished he'd fly back to Copenhagen. Once his business was done it didn't matter if they knew where he had been and he preferred flying. It might be pricey but it was better than a train journey, even this fast one. A little bit of expense was OK, especially if things went well. He watched the city passing. Once the train was well on its way he'd go along to the Bordbistro and get something to eat, a light lunch, nothing too heavy to spoil his dinner. He was looking forward to dinner. Another little treat, if things went well.

Charlie settled down and began to work on the story he'd tell when he came back. He didn't need to work too hard, getting it ready was really just something to pass the time until he went to the Bordbistro. It didn't have to be a good story; after all, no one was going to believe it except Elspeth, and Elspeth wasn't going to be a problem. She trusted him, she believed in him. He sat back and let the train begin to eat up the miles.

Just over four and a half hours later the train slid into

Hamburg Station dead on time. It was just gone quarter past four. Charlie got up with the other passengers. The students were in no hurry, taking their time sorting out their rucksacks. He joined the crowd on the platform heading for the exit. Everything was going well, just as he had planned.

He walked across the main concourse making for the ticket windows. The station was busy, the end-of-day rush was getting under way. He stood in line and eventually bought a single on the S-Bahn for Klein Flottbek and then headed for the right platform. He knew the way. Hamburg had been familiar to him once and he'd made this same journey more than a few times. The trains he wanted ran every five minutes from platforms one and two, there would be no delays. The place he was going was a classy suburb, quiet but easily accessible by road or rail, twenty minutes away from the bustle of central Hamburg.

There was a train waiting at the platform. It was already about half-full of people commuting home after work. The crowds in the station and a compartment of anonymous faces were perfect cover for any watcher. But Charlie didn't care; he wasn't looking for any kind of tail. He was close to his ace now the only thing that concerned him was whether it would be there. He sat down opposite a pretty girl who looked at him from over her glossy magazine. He unbuttoned his overcoat and smiled at her. She retreated behind her magazine. He looked at his watch. He was going to be early, too damned early. Maybe he should … But the maybe was too late. The carriage doors shut and the train began to move.

He looked out of the window at the city – big, prosperous, full of history but still full of life. You could get anything you wanted in this town and, if you weren't careful, a few things you didn't want.

The train rolled on until it cleared central Hamburg and moved into the outer districts. Charlie took out his phone and made a call. When he spoke it was in German.

'Louis C Jacob? I'd like to book a table for dinner tonight and I might need a room, a single. You can? Good. I won't be eating until about half past nine. Fine. One last thing, I'm on the train coming from Hamburg and I'll be into Klein Flottbek in about fifteen minutes. Can you get a taxi to meet me? Bronski, Herr Bronski. Thank you.'

The girl sitting opposite him lowered the magazine and smiled as he put away his phone. He smiled back. Was it an invitation? If he was staying, maybe he should say something to check? But he only smiled back at her and looked out of the window. The magazine went back up.

Keep it simple. First, get the job done, after that he could relax.

Klein Flottbek station was a two-platform affair, busy at the rush hours but otherwise quiet. Outside the station a taxi was waiting. He walked over to it.

'Bronski?'

The driver nodded.

Charlie got in and the taxi pulled away.

The Louis C Jacob was a find Charlie had made many years ago. A five-star hotel high up above the Elbe on the Elbchaussee, the road going west out of Hamburg that ran along the north bank of the river. The hotel had begun life as the palatial home of a local merchant when the Hanseatic League dominated international trade in Northern Germany. Now it was a place where visitors, and Hamburg locals who could afford it, soaked up past glories and modern conveniences. The taxi pulled up in front of the big white building and the door of the taxi was opened by a smiling man whose uniform made him look vaguely like a Lufthansa pilot but without the peaked cap. Charlie got out and paid off the driver. The taxi pulled away.

'But your luggage, sir?'

'Nothing.'

The smile didn't disappear, he was too well-trained for that, but the eyebrows went up slightly.

'Sorry, sir, I took your call myself, I understood you were staying.'

'I might be, my plans are fluid.'

Charlie headed for the door but Lufthansa got there before him and opened it. Charlie slipped a note into the hand that was almost not there and got the smile again. Without apparently looking, Lufthansa noted the denomination. It was enough, more than enough. No luggage maybe, but with tips like that Lufthansa had passed Charlie as OK.

Charlie walked into the lobby. Heavy chandeliers hung from the ceiling which was all ornate plaster mouldings. The carpet, furniture and decor were all solid luxury, forcing itself on your attention. Charlie liked it. Excess was comforting, you knew where you were with excess. He walked over to reception. This time he spoke English.

'I'm meeting someone for dinner tonight. I've booked a table, Bronski.'

The smart young man, another pilot, checked a list.

'I have your booking, sir.' He looked again. 'But it says nine thirty?'

'Yes, sod's law I'm afraid.' The young man looked puzzled, excellent English but no colloquial experience. Charlie explained. 'It was a last minute thing; I had to leave in a hurry. You know how it is. If you're in a hurry, everything goes wrong and you're late, so I allowed for delays.' He shrugged. 'But there were no delays, so here I am,' he looked at his watch, 'about four hours early. Sod's law, see?'

The young man didn't see, but he understood an English joke had been made so he gave a polite smile and carried on.

'Do you want to change the time of your booking? It would not be a problem.'

'No, leave it. If I change it, my friend will be delayed.' He laughed. 'Sod's law?' The young man smiled again but obviously didn't understand. 'Never mind. I'll go out to the terrace and watch the world go by. Send some coffee, would you.'

'Certainly, sir.'

Charlie walked away from reception through the bar and out onto a wide terrace that was fringed by trees and looked down over the Elbe. It would have been a magnificent view if there had been anything worth looking at on the other side of the river. As it was, the far bank was low and flat, with modern industrial buildings and farm land stretching beyond. He walked to the balustrade and looked down. Below, a fully laden container ship was heading downriver towards the North Sea.

The containers were stacked as high as the bridge and filled the entire deck. Charlie counted. Six-high above the deck! It looked top-heavy. How come the bloody thing didn't capsize? It didn't look safe, even in the dead calm river. How did it stay upright out at sea?

He turned back and sat down at one of the tables. He had the terrace to himself. The sun was low in the sky and evening clouds were beginning to drift in. When the sun disappeared behind one, Charlie noticed how cold the breeze along the river was. With the sun setting, the light was going and the terrace was getting cold. He would probably have the terrace to himself for as long as he had to wait.

A waiter came out with a tray and laid out his coffee on the table.

'I'm eating here tonight and probably staying over. Put it on my bill will you? Mr Bronski.'

He was still speaking English.

'Certainly, sir. Is there anything else I can get you?'

'Not at the moment. I'm early for my appointment; I'll wait out here until my visitor arrives. Bring me another coffee in an hour and when anyone asks for me tell them I'm out here.'

'It will be cold, sir. Wouldn't you prefer to wait inside, in the bar perhaps or ...'

'No, here's fine. I like my own company.'

'Just as you wish, sir.'

The waiter left. Charlie poured his coffee and settled down. He knew how to wait, he'd had practice. You set yourself, turned off your mind and let the time pass. There was no watching or thinking to be done, just letting the time pass. He sipped his coffee and began.

The second cup of coffee had come and gone and Charlie had buttoned up his coat and turned up the collar. The waiter had been right, the breeze from the river had strengthened as the dark descended and for the past two hours it had been bloody cold. No one had come out onto the terrace except the waiter. He looked at his watch. Nearly there but still half an hour to go. He let his mind think about the Louis C Jacob to distract himself from the cold. He liked this hotel; it had history, elegance and luxury. It even had its own art collection. Charlie knew nothing about art and didn't want to know, but, in a vague way, the art collection pleased him - art went well with serious money. In the Louis C Jacob you could feel wealthy - art-collector wealthy. It was like reading an Elspeth Allen cookbook but with more noughts on the end. In the old days he had always used it when he came to Hamburg and it hadn't changed. That set his mind on another line of thought. Something else in Hamburg that wouldn't have changed. When his train had got in he knew he had plenty of time, time to kill. He should have picked up a call girl and treated himself to a quick session of Hamburg sex. Why hadn't he? It wasn't really a mistake but it niggled him. He should have thought about it instead of rushing straight to the hotel.

He felt annoyed with himself. He needed to do better, he needed to get back up to speed. He stood up and began to walk about, occasionally stamping his feet and rubbing his hands together against the cold. He went over to the terrace edge and looked down at the river. The view was better at night. Down below it was black except for the line of lights on the far bank. Their reflection in the water gave a strange and attractive effect to the darkness of the river.

God, he was hungry. What if Henry Clarke-Phillips didn't come? Maybe he should eat.

No, if his London contact didn't come, he'd get going again. He wasn't on expenses any more and with the prices as they were in this place he'd wait for Henry Clarke-Phillips to show up. If not, then …

A voice came from behind him.

'Not drinking anything, Charlie?'

Charlie turned. Henry Clarke-Phillips was standing by his table. *Thank God.* Now she was actually standing there he could let himself think about how worried he had been ever since his visit to the Embassy. But now the worry was over. London had sent someone. He walked over to the table.

'Not until you came. I thought you could buy them. I'm paying my own way these days so I'm careful about money.'

'I see, that explains why you chose to meet in this place.'

Charlie smiled. 'Surely you don't mind? I'm not on expenses but you are. And I even waited to get your OK before I booked in and ordered dinner.'

'Oh, so London's picking up the bills on this, are we?'

'Just get the drinks. I haven't had one yet, remember? It took me seven and a half hours by train to get here from Copenhagen then I had to get across Hamburg. I'm knackered and all I've had is a couple of cups of coffee, so get the drinks, then we'll talk. After that we can get inside out of the cold and have something to eat.'

Henry Clarke-Phillips put her handbag on the table. 'What do you want?'

'Highland Park, a large one, and don't let them put any ice in it.'

Charlie watched her as she walked away. He had sounded full of confidence but that was just show, he hadn't been at all sure how this would go. He still wasn't sure. They had sent someone, which was good, but was it good enough? They were supposed to look after him, but no commitment is ever open-ended. A line gets drawn under everything after a time. London might have decided to draw a line under him. He had gambled, in the Embassy that morning, that they would still be interested enough to answer a crash call. Not because of who he was but because it was a crash call. Now it looked as if the gamble had paid off. She had come right on time.

Now everything depended on the reaction when he told her he needed her to kill someone for him.

It didn't seem to him like a big thing to ask but British Intelligence could get annoyingly picky about some things and there was always the cash angle. Extra work meant extra calls on their budget and they hated anything that took money out of their precious budget. Sometimes he thought he should have gone to the French, but that would have meant learning their bloody language and that was one yard too many. He sat down at the table and waited.

Henry Clarke-Phillips came back with his whisky. She had a coffee. She put the drinks on the table and sat down. She wasn't wearing an overcoat. *God*, thought Charlie, *she must be freezing*. He took a grateful sip and then raised his glass in salute.

'What do I call you?'

'I don't know, what do you want to call me? Call me whatever you like.'

The whisky was good. You had to be somewhere in the Louis C. class to be sure they would have it.

'I'll call you Henry, it's easy to remember.'

She sipped her coffee. 'Get on with it. Why the crash call? And it better be good because I had to fly budget to get here. I even had to fly out of bloody Luton, for God's sake, and when budget say Hamburg they mean Lübeck so I'm not in the best of moods.'

'Money still tight in London these days?'

'Yes, money's always tight. But this wasn't money, it was schedules. I wasn't exactly sitting on my arse twiddling my fingers when I was given your call. By the time I could leave, it was the only flight that would get me here on time. Everything out of Heathrow or City seemed to want to go via Zurich or Geneva and take four hours. So, what's this about? And it better be good, the journey was hell and I'm not wearing my thermal underwear.'

Here goes, thought Charlie, and he tried to ooze confidence. It oozed, but only on the outside. Inside he was very nearly running on empty, but the whisky helped.

'I know it's a nuisance but someone is going to kill me and I think I might need your help.'

'I'll kill you if you don't get to the point. Anyone else will have to get in line.'

'Somebody put a bomb in my car but fixed it so I could get clear. It had to be a message, something to scare me. "I can reach you, I can kill you, I'll kill you when I'm ready.".'

'You're talking rubbish, you know that? Who puts a bomb ...'

Charlie held up his hand.

'Stay with me. I've thought about it, believe me, and I know it sounds nuts. But what else is there? Who puts a bomb in your car and lets you get out?'

'How was that done?'

'"Bang, you're dead" through the sound system. I got out and off it went.'

'No, I don't buy it. You have to be wrong.' He was losing her.

'No I'm not. It has to be someone from the old days, from inside the system. There's this guy called James Costello ...'

The coffee cup went on to the table. 'Again.'

Suddenly he had all her attention.

'A guy called James Costello turned up in Copenhagen about a month ago and yesterday morning ...'

She stood up.

'Wait here. I'm going to make a call.'

She went to the far end of the terrace, took out her mobile and made a call. It didn't take long and when she came back and sat down he could see he didn't have to ooze confidence or anything else. Now she really wanted to hear what he was going to say, so he told her about the bomb, the Comedian and James Costello. He told her everything. When he had finished he watched her. Costello had hit a chord all right. He was pleased with himself, he could still make the right call about people.

'I knew I was right about Costello. If you know him then he's from inside the system somewhere and that makes it certain. He's the one who has me as a target. Somebody must have told him where I was.'

'Why? You've never seen him before, you don't know him.'

'I made plenty of enemies I don't know and plenty I've never seen. Sometime or other I must have done something and he's taken it personally. Now he thinks it's payback time. It doesn't matter what it's about, I don't care what it's about. I just want him out of the way. I want him dead.'

But she seemed to have switched off her interest. He didn't like how this was going. One minute she was all over him and couldn't listen carefully enough; now he'd told her what had happened and why, she'd completely lost interest.

She stood up.

'Book in and then we'll get something to eat. It's cold out here and I'm hungry. I'll be in the restaurant. What shall I order for you?'

'Steak will be fine. Rare.'

'Hurry it up, I have to get back to London.' And she walked away.

Charlie went to reception and booked in then he joined her in the restaurant. It wasn't busy so she'd been able to get a table where they could talk. But when he sat down she didn't seem to want to talk. She just sat there with her mobile on the table and, as he had nothing more to say to her, he sat there as well until the food came. They were well into the silent ritual of their meal when her mobile rang. She didn't bother to leave the table to answer it. She just listened. Then put it away in her handbag. Now she was ready to talk.

'Well, well, aren't you the lucky lad? It looks like you're going to get your wish.'

'Was that London?' She nodded and resumed her meal. 'And they agreed?'

She nodded again. It was too simple. He had asked her to kill someone, to kill Costello, and he was going to get what he had asked for, just like that. It was too simple. There had to be a catch. He went back to his steak, it was good. He decided to forget the catch and enjoy it. She would tell him what the catch was when she was ready. He summoned the waiter.

'Sir?'

'We've changed our minds. We will have wine after all.'

'Certainly, sir. I will bring you a wine list.'

'No, don't bother. Just bring us a bottle of your best red that's under a hundred euros. You have a red at that price?'

'I'm sure we can find you something, sir.'

The waiter left. She was looking at him. What the hell, it wasn't her money and now he had something to celebrate.

'See how economical I'm being with your money. Less than a hundred euros won't get you much of a wine in a place like this but, for your sake, I'll drink it. I know you wouldn't begrudge me a little celebration drink after getting my good news.'

The waiter returned and placed glasses on the table then left. She went back to her meal. The waiter returned with the bottle and was about to pour some wine into Charlie's glass.

'Don't bother, we'll pour it ourselves.'

The waiter put the bottle on the table and left. Charlie poured himself a glass and held the bottle out.

'Not for me. It's your celebration. You drink it.'

Charlie took a sip of the wine. 'Do you know, it's not at all bad. Are you sure you won't have a glass?'

'I'm sure.'

Charlie took another drink, refilled his glass and got back to his steak. He was happy, things were going well, better than he could have hoped for. It would have to be one hell of a catch to spoil things.

When they had finished the meal the waiter cleared away the plates and Charlie sat back with his glass in his hand. He had nearly finished the bottle. It really wasn't bad for the price. But you got that in a good hotel, nothing was cheap but nothing was crap either.

'How do I pay for tonight?'

She took a credit card out of her bag and handed it to him.

'The pin number is one two three four.' Charlie took the card. 'Then you cut it up and throw it away. And don't try to be clever. It's a once-only card. We'll know if you try to use it a second time and we won't be happy if you do that. No withdrawals, nothing. Only the hotel.'

'How do I contact you?'

'You don't, I'll contact you.' She took out a business card and threw it across to him. 'Put your mobile number on the back of that.'

Charlie took out a pen and picked up the card. Caroline Lewis-Hughes. Lewis-Hughes Design Ltd. The phone number prefix wasn't London and there was no address. Charlie turned the card over and wrote his mobile number.

'Do you want the landline?'

'No. I won't be phoning your home. Make sure you'll be on your own between five and six tomorrow afternoon. Is there anybody else, are you married or anything?'

'Married.'

'Then get rid of your wife, send her away somewhere.'

Suddenly a worried look came into her eyes. 'For God's sake, tell me there's no children.'

'Six, alternate girls and boys.' He grinned. 'And no pets either.'

'Just be sure you're on your own. If we need you to do anything in this we don't want any innocent bystanders getting in the way.'

Charlie flipped the business card back. 'How long do you want her gone?'

'Make it at least a couple of weeks, and make it well away, not some hotel in Copenhagen. Make it out of Denmark.'

She stood up, picked up the card and put it in her handbag and walked away. No goodbyes, nothing. Not that he gave a damn. He poured the last of the bottle into his glass. He still didn't know what the catch was but he was happy, things were going to be OK. They would get rid of Costello. Not that he thought for a moment they were doing it for him. Costello was a target for some other reason. But that was also OK because it meant he was right. Costello was an Intelligence insider, otherwise how would London know about him? Yes, everything was going to be all right. He finished his wine and got up. It had been a hard two days he would sleep well tonight because he still had his ace in the hole. London would look after him. They would kill Costello and then things could get back to normal. Charlie left the restaurant and went up to his room satisfied with a job well done. The waiter came to clear up the table. There was no tip. Charlie had been sorry about that but he would have had to use his own money and it was London who were paying. It was a pity because the meal and the service had been excellent. *But that's life*, thought Charlie, *not everybody gets what's coming to them. And hey, what can you do? You can't hand out happy endings to everyone, can you?*

TEN

'How did it go?'

'Fine.'

'Did you tell him anything?'

'Only that we would get Costello off his back.'

'He didn't ask any questions?'

'Why would he? He knew I wouldn't answer any.'

'What was your take on the car bomb thing?'

'It didn't make sense. Why rig the car then let him get clear?'

'What about his idea of a message, someone trying to frighten him?'

'It's possible I suppose, just about. A bit left-field though.'

'Danish Intelligence are playing the whole thing very cagey. They got the police to put out that it was a leaking gas cylinder. That keeps the media out of things while they look into it. Why does he think it's Costello who's out to get him? Where did he get that crazy notion?'

'I told you, he thinks it was all done to scare him, that someone from his past wants it to be payback time. Someone who wants it up close and personal.' He gave her a look. 'Don't look at me. I'm only telling you what he said. He thinks someone from inside the system is out to get him.'

'For what?'

'God knows, it's all a bit crazy …'

'A bit! It's bloody *Alice in Wonderland* stuff.'

'Agreed, but the bomb did actually happen and it's being taken seriously by the Danes. The way they're handling it rules out anything terrorist. However mad it seems, it had to be a professional to wire the bomb and fix the sound system.'

'But that brings us back to why he thinks it's Costello? Costello's not connected with any service and never has been. How did Bronski make any connection?'

'I suppose he assumed it had to be a new face and Costello was a new face. When Costello and the priest came to the hospital he got a close look at him and was convinced that Costello wasn't what he was pretending to be, that he didn't fit the apprentice priest thing. He reckoned Costello was some sort of plant.'

'And he was right in a way, but I still don't see the connection.'

'He went to the priest's house, played the bewildered innocent and, bingo, Costello says, "I was in the business."'

'But as a copper, not Intelligence.'

'Costello didn't make himself clear, just said Civil Service. Bronski took the wrong angle, the angle he was looking for.'

'So there's a bomb in his car and a newcomer Bronski thinks is not what he's pretending to be. That's enough to make a crash call?'

'I suppose the way he looked at it, even if it wasn't Costello there was someone out there. So he went to Copenhagen and made the call. I got sent. The rest you know. You're damn lucky it was me; no one else would have dropped Costello straight in your lap. So make sure I get something when the medals start getting handed out. An extra two weeks' holiday, maybe.'

But he wasn't listening, he was thinking it through.

'So when he saw Costello's name rang a bell with you, he thought it gave him the Intelligence connection, and that made him certain it was Costello? It sort of brought all the nonsense together?'

She nodded. He'd got there at last. Sometimes it was like

trying to hammer a nail into concrete.

'Now I've found him for you, what are you going to do?'

'What do we know about Bronski?'

'I pulled his record and read the summary before I went. He wasn't a real high-up but he knew the ones who were, the ones who moved over from KGB into Russian Intelligence and which desks they were at. And he knew which German and Baltic operations the Russians had kept going. He knew a lot of background. He was worth bringing over and he wasn't exactly expensive. He started life as a Moscow-trained thug but when the Soviet Union folded he could see the career prospects of the goon squad had pretty much folded with it. Muscle wasn't going to be in so much demand any more. He was ambitious and clever so he worked himself a desk job in the new outfit and began to collect enough info to make him worth buying. When he was ready, we bought him.' She waited so it had time to sink in. 'If you're thinking of using him, he's had plenty of field experience.'

'Yes, he might be useful.'

She watched him. His eyes had a faraway look. He was plotting, thinking about how he might use this to his own advantage. She had guessed he would, that was why she had given it to him. The devious bugger couldn't very well give her nothing if it helped him up the ladder.

'I thought you might want to use him so I told him to make himself a free agent for a while just in case, to lose his wife for a couple of weeks, somewhere well out of Denmark.'

His eyes changed, he was back, he'd got his plan. He could be damned good. Clever, quick and ingenious where his own career was concerned. It was a pity his judgement wasn't so sharp when it came to actual Intelligence matters. The only quick thing he did then was delegate blame, but he was clever and ingenious at that as well.

'That was good thinking. We'll need someone sitting on Costello until I get things sorted. What about this bomb? Do you think it's a real threat?'

'How should I know? All I know is his car was blown up and he wasn't in it. Like you said, *Alice in Wonderland* stuff.

How could anyone know for sure what it's all about?'

'Do you know who's on it in Denmark?'

'No, like I said, they're playing it very close to their chests. It's not terrorist, so they don't have to share it. We know there's an Intelligence involvement but we can't be sure who's running it. Whoever it is knows what he's doing. The smokescreen went up very quickly. The bomb story got spiked at birth and the leaking gas cylinder story was out before anyone could get a sniff of anything else – silly man stores faulty bottled gas in his garage and nearly blows himself up. No real story.'

'Hmm. All very neat and efficient.' *At least he can recognise efficiency when he sees it*, she thought. 'But it's still a mess, a total mess. It's the blind leading the partially sighted for God's sake.' He sat back, he was ready. 'OK, if we're going to do it let's get on with it. Bronski's going to take your call tomorrow at five like I said?' She nodded. 'Then get to Copenhagen on the next available flight and get to – where is it?'

'Nyborg.'

'Get there and locate him. When he's on his own, waiting for the call, you tell him we're going to use him.'

'Beater or gun?'

'Beater. I want you as the gun.'

'That's how it's going to be is it?'

'How else *could* it be?'

It was too sudden, she didn't like it. *An operational decision that quickly*?

'This isn't you on your own, is it? It's fully cleared?' He raised his eyebrows. 'Pardon my caution but I'm not killing anybody just on your say-so.'

The eyebrows came down again.

'It comes from all the way up. I went upstairs as soon as I knew.'

She relaxed. It was official.

'This Costello must be quite something. As soon as Bronski used his name I knew you'd want to hear about it, but I'm surprised you got clearance for a termination so quickly. He's flagged, I know, that's why I called you, but all I've seen is "locate and inform", nothing close to "terminate on sight".'

'Yes, it rather threw me as well. I took his name upstairs and the next thing I know I'm told to arrange things and do it now. To happen that quickly means it must have had confirmation from the very top. I wish our illustrious leader could be as bold and incisive when it comes to domestic politics. Then maybe the country wouldn't be in the mess it's in and we'd get the cash we need to do the job properly. Anyway, there it was, "do it and do it now".'

'Where do you want it done?'

'Anywhere that would be good for us. Anywhere that could make it look like it's something left over from the old days. That way it muddies the waters. The Balkans would be ideal but I don't see a way of getting him there so do it as soon as he's on suitable turf. I want something that won't interest anyone. I want to read in the papers that a shady ex-copper called Costello was killed by a dodgy ex-KGB agent who had become hooked up to any number of illegal goings-on. I want it all very hard to pin on anybody. An ex-Intelligence freelancer hired by nobody knows who. I want it so no one will take it to heart, do anything, or ask any really awkward questions.'

'And when it's done?'

'No loose ends; when Costello is sorted, Bronski will have to go. We can't leave him lying about, can we, actually or metaphorically?'

'And what do we get out of this? We must get something good.'

'The Americans and the Israelis were the ones interested in Costello, they got him flagged. What he was up to was never anything to do with us, but *that* unholy alliance wanted him and wanted him badly. On the surface it was supposed to be connected to a foiled terrorist bomb attack in Rome. That was the story that got put about, that and Costello being connected to the Vatican in some way.'

'The Vatican!'

'Yes, I know, but it was Rome and the world was hooked on Dan Brown at the time so everybody threw in the Vatican when they could. As far as we could ever find out, there never had been a James Costello in Rome, at least not one who had anything to do with the Vatican. Whoever he was working for, it wasn't them.'

'We looked into it?'

'We had a semi-official glance to satisfy ourselves. We used an old Vietnamese priest connection, a China-watcher we sometimes use. He put us on to a Professor, an American woman. She worked for some sort of college and had access to the records and according to the records he was never there. We ran the terrorist story by the police and it turned out to be exactly what we were told, a busted terrorist-bomb thing. We weren't really interested. It was nothing to do with us, we just checked out the story. But whatever Costello did in Rome and whoever he did it for, he really pissed off the Yanks and the Israelis. They've been looking for him ever since but, up till now, no one's had a sniff. Now, out of nowhere, he's fallen into our lap, so we do the job for them.'

'Why not hand him over, if they want him that badly wouldn't they pay for him? There must be some juicy Intelligence tit-bit we could get for him.'

'No, my orders were black and white. He's got to go.'

'Why?'

'Because we don't know what Costello did and the Americans and Israelis do. It's important to them but they won't share it with us. When those two get together and shut everyone else out it's bad news all round, almost certainly something HMG wouldn't like. So, if they won't share and they want to talk to Costello, we shut down Costello. We don't help them when they're keeping us out of it. We eliminate him.'

'Well I hope it's all worth it. I had a night of unbridled passion with Sam planned before that bloody crash call came.'

He opened a drawer, took out a folder, put it on the desk and looked pleased with himself.

'By the way, I'm using a yellow folder for this and it's getting a three-star rating. One copy kept in my office safe. To be read only in my office by the people on a very short list. And I report straight to the Director who reports directly to the PM.'

Look at him, she thought, *like a kid in a candy store. Now he has his very own little yellow three-star folder*. Costello would be killed, but for him this wasn't going to be about shutting anything down or screwing the Americans or Israelis. This was going to be about a bit of empire-building, about treading on the faces of rival department chiefs. Not that she cared. Past a certain level of superiority it was always about office politics, whether it was Intelligence, banking or selling bananas.

'Do I get to have a shower before I go?'

'Get one at your hotel in Copenhagen and get some sleep on the plane, the next available flight. I want you in Nyborg in plenty of time to set things up properly. This is a yellow file job now. Everyone gives it one hundred and ten per cent.' He looked up from the folder. 'But make sure you keep the expenses down. Being top priority doesn't have to make it cost more than it needs to. And make sure that all the chits come directly to me. I don't want accounts handling anything, anything at all.'

She couldn't say anything but that didn't stop her thinking. *"Everyone gives it one hundred and ten bloody per cent"? Who's "everyone"? There's only two of us in this and I'm the only bugger going to be in the field doing anything that isn't shuffling papers or signing chits.*

'And I want a full verbal report every twenty-four hours. Use my direct line. You only speak to me.'

His head went down and his eyes went back to the sheets in his beloved folder. She was dismissed. The meeting was obviously over so she left the office.

There was no one else in the lift so she spoke out loud. It made her feel better saying what she had to say so it could be heard, even if she was the only one listening.

'It's straight off to bloody Copenhagen, is it? Well, fuck the next available flight nonsense. I'm damn well not going budget this time and I'm *certainly* not flying out of Luton. It's going to be business class on a scheduled flight and the VIP lounge at Heathrow, and in Copenhagen a suite at the Hotel D'Angleterre.' She felt better. He could have all the fits he wanted when he got her expenses chits. When the job was done and he was using her success to brown-nose with the Director he would *have* to OK them, even if she gave them to him by stuffing them up his arse.

On the ground floor she called in to the duty officer and collected the suitcase she'd left there when she arrived. She had come straight back to report when she got in from Hamburg so the same case would have to do for the Copenhagen trip. She told the duty officer to order a taxi and book her business class on the next flight to Copenhagen out of Heathrow or City, then book her a suite at the Hotel D'Angleterre.

In the taxi she turned her mind to the job in hand. It wasn't killing Costello she needed to think about, it was killing Bronski. Getting a Soviet-trained thug to walk on to a bullet wasn't going to be so easy. The trick would be making sure he didn't see it coming, which was going to take a bit of working out. The taxi moved quickly through the pale dawn of the early-morning streets. Her mind slipped back to the present.

And the most expensive meal I can find in Departures. With champagne. She'd make the sod wish he'd given her time for a quick bang with Sam and a shower before he shoved her off to Denmark. That shag and shower were going to cost him so much it would give him apoplexy and she hoped to God it bloody well killed him.

ELEVEN

When Charlie got home from the airport Elspeth was sitting in the living room on the settee quietly crying. She had a damp handkerchief in her hands. She didn't look up at him when he came in. He sat beside her and put his arm round her shoulders. She still didn't look at him - she wiped her eyes with her damp handkerchief and he knew she was still crying. Shit. He tried to make his mind form the words he needed, but his mind wouldn't, or couldn't, help him. He did the best he could.

'I'm sorry.'

It wasn't much but it got her head up. She didn't look at him but at least she spoke.

'I was worried, Charlie. In the afternoon Fr Mundt came to see me with some silly story about you going to Hamburg to see a German publisher. It didn't make any sense.'

'Was he alone?'

'No, Mr Costello was with him.'

'Did you say anything to either of them?'

Now she looked at him. It wasn't the look of a woman who trusted him.

'No. What could I say? There's no German publisher.'

'No, there's no German publisher. It was just something to tell Fr Mundt, it was the only way I could think of to try and let you know I had gone to Hamburg. It was the best I could do at

89

short notice but he accepted it. He came and told you where I was.'

Elspeth looked at the handkerchief in her hands. She was trying to believe, God how she was trying.

'I wanted to talk to you, to find out what was going on. I tried to phone you as soon as they had gone but your mobile was switched off. You *never* switch your mobile off.'

Charlie knew where he was now. She had been left on her own too long and that had started her thinking. The fear was taking over again and that wasn't what he wanted. He didn't mind her scared but he didn't want her terrified. Scared made her rely on him and stopped any risk of independent thought. But too much fear would make her irrational, she might do or say anything. He had switched off his mobile for the very simple reason that he didn't want Elspeth talking to him, going on about 'where was he' and 'what was going on?'. But he could hardly tell her that now.

'I'm sorry, Elspeth. What time did you phone?'

'I don't know, about three, maybe earlier.'

'I would have been on the plane to Hamburg. That's why my mobile was switched off. Look, darling, I'm sorry about what happened but in the morning I went to the American Embassy and I eventually managed to get through to someone connected with the Witness Programme. They told me there was an agent passing through Hamburg who could help but he would only be around for twenty-four hours. I had to take the opportunity while it was there. It was nothing short of a miracle that someone was so near just when I needed them. If I didn't go to Hamburg it meant waiting, maybe for a couple of weeks, or having to go over to the States. What could I do? It was too good a chance to pass up.'

He waited. She was trying to believe him. 'I wanted to do what was best for you, best for us. I don't want you worried more than you have to be about this thing. Trust me, darling, just trust me and soon it will all be over and we can go back to being a boring old couple who write cookery books, live by the seaside, love each other very much and just want to live long quiet lives minding their own business.'

Elspeth turned to him and gave a weak smile. She was trying, but he could see it wasn't easy, though the charm was helping. She dabbed her eyes with the handkerchief.

'I tried to phone you again when they told me I could leave.'

'What time was that?'

'They told me I could go home after the doctor had seen me. It was about ten thirty when I was actually told I could leave.'

'And was that when you tried my mobile?' She nodded. 'It was just bad timing, darling, that's all.'

'Bad timing?'

'I was on the plane again, coming home.' This time it was true. He smiled his encouraging smile. 'Never mind, we're together and home now, and we're not on our own any more. Now we have help.'

He saw her whole face brighten up.

'The person you saw said they could help?'

'Yes, they can help. He said they would get a couple of FBI agents here in about a week. They'll find out who's behind this and then it will all be over.'

'Oh, Charlie, I hope so, I don't think I can stand much more.' Charlie tightened his arm round her shoulders into a hug. She smiled again. 'What will they do when they find whoever it is?'

'I don't know and I don't care. I'm happy to let them handle it. They're the trained guys, they'll do whatever they think is necessary.'

She was coming round. It had been a lousy story but it had worked. She wanted to believe him and she wanted to trust him and that was more than half the battle.

'So what do we do until they come?'

'You go and stay with Hugh.'

'With Father?'

'Yes, he'd love to see you and you'd love to see him. You've not seen him since we left the UK.'

'But ...'

'But what?'

'Well, Daddy is funny in some ways, you know he is, and ...'

'Your father is a bigoted, narrow-minded old bastard and when he dies I'll be happy to dance a polka on his grave. But until then he's still Daddy and you're not the one he can't stand. That's always been me, remember?' She smiled again and Charlie could see that now it was genuine. He kept going on the same track. 'You're the one he loves and lights candles for because you married a newly converted American with no family worth spit and he's a high-class Catholic snob whose family goes back to God knows when.'

'William the Conqueror, he says.' He had almost got a laugh. That was good. But the laugh didn't last. 'What will you do? I don't think I could go to Daddy while you stayed here. What if something happened before the FBI men got here?'

Charlie knew he had a window of opportunity so he went for it.

'Listen, Elspeth. The man I met in Hamburg told me to get away and lie low until the agents get here and do what they have to do. He told me I was to go alone, that if we go together we'd be too easy to follow. We have to split up, dear. The agent said that it's the only safe way. I'm the one whoever it is out there will try to follow, so I have to move quickly and I have to move by myself, and I want to be absolutely sure that when I do you're somewhere safe. And you couldn't be safer than spending a couple of weeks with Hugh.'

He waited. It had been a good pitch made at the right time and she was thinking about it. God knows why she wanted to see Hugh. The old bastard had kept her under his mad Catholic thumb until Charlie had woken her with a kiss and a few other things. But Charlie knew that seeing Hugh wasn't what would make her drop. She might want to see her father, but getting this thing finished was what she wanted most. She wanted things back to normal, she wanted to do whatever would end the nightmare. If he offered her that, then she was almost there. Charlie waited. Sometimes silence was the best persuader.

'When would I go?'

Charlie gave a mental sigh of relief. *Done*.

'Phone Hugh today and go tomorrow, early. I can't leave until you're gone and I need to be on the move.'

'Where will you go?'

'I have an old Air Force buddy who was stationed in Germany for a long time. He married a local girl and retired there. I'll arrange to go to him. It'll be perfectly safe and it's not far to travel. I'll go to morning Mass then go to the station and get a direct train to Hamburg. I'll just slip away. I'll buy the ticket online and get on the train at the last minute. Even if I'm being watched I should be away before anyone can get after me.'

'Did the agent you saw in Hamburg tell you what to do?'

'No, I thought it up on the flight back. Going to Hamburg gave me the idea.'

He could see Elspeth had bought into it. Now she would be all right and, most importantly, out of his way, and he could forget about her. She got up.

'I'll phone Daddy right away.' She stopped at the door. 'Will you see to the ticket? After I've phoned I'll pack and get everything ready.' She paused. 'Can we go out to dinner tonight? It would be nice to do something normal and we'll be apart for however long it takes. We haven't been apart from each other for any real time since we were married.'

Charlie smiled. She was always shy about asking for sex, she always wrapped it up. It was never – do you fancy sex? It always had to look like something else. A night out and the sex tagged on when they got home as if it was an afterthought. He was different. When he wanted it he asked for it and, to be fair, he always got it. She wasn't a passionate or experienced woman, she had never been good in bed, but she was always willing.

'Of course, dinner somewhere quiet and romantic. We'll be on honeymoon again. We'll turn the clock back and forget everything else.'

He saw the look of happiness that came into her face. She loved it when he played the game and wrapped up his answer as she had wrapped up her question.

'Thank you, darling. I'll go and phone Daddy straight away.'

Charlie sat back. That was Elspeth sorted. Now he had to give some thought to what was coming. *What a mess - and if the British weren't careful, it could get messier*. True, he was getting what he wanted, Costello killed. But he had no idea why, and that unsettled him. Certainly it wasn't because they were worried about what might happen to him. So who was this Costello guy and how good was he? If it was something personal then he had probably faked himself into the placement, which meant he was on his own. That meant he made the bomb and planted it himself and that meant field operative experience. Whoever he was, he was good enough to be dangerous. The Brits would have surprise on their side, which was good, but they would have to get him first time. If they missed they'd lose him and he could come back any time. And if he came back it wouldn't be to play games. It really would be – 'bang, you're dead'.

'I wonder what I did to him to make him so mad at me?'

'Who, dear?'

He looked up. Elspeth was in the doorway. He hadn't realised that he had spoken out loud.

'Oh, somebody yesterday on the plane. He kept on giving me dirty looks. I've no idea why. Maybe he thought I pushed in front when we boarded, or maybe he just hates Americans. How did the call go? It didn't take long.'

'Daddy's delighted. He wanted to talk but I told him I had to pack, we can talk all we want when I get to St Anthony's.'

Crazy bloody family, thought Charlie. Fancy naming your house after some saint, it made the place sound like a monastery. Although maybe it was, in some ways. With the exception of Elspeth, they were all religious nuts. They'd all got the Catholic thing bred into their gene pool.

'I'm pleased Hugh's pleased. It's been too long since the old bastard saw you. You should have gone back before this.'

'Well I'm going now, so let's forget it. I'll start packing. Can you arrange the flight?'

'Sure.' He went and put his arms round her waist and pulled her close to him. 'And I really *am* glad the old bugger's delighted. I know it's not really his fault. If your family's been Catholic in England for over five hundred years you're entitled to have an oddball or two in it.' He kissed her and then put his hands on her shoulders as if he were telling her off. 'Now listen. This is an order. You two have a good visit together and forget all this for a couple of weeks, and when you come back it will all be over.'

'Are you sure, Charlie?'

He let his arms fall and tried to look as relaxed as possible.

'Sure I'm sure. When the FBI get here, it will all be over bar the shouting.'

She stood in the doorway smiling at him. He could see she had convinced herself. She wanted to believe him, so she believed him. Tomorrow she would be gone, he'd have got rid of her like Clarke-Phillips said, and at five he'd be told what the Brits were going to do. Then he could just sit back and enjoy the show.

'Charlie, I'm so glad. It's all been like an awful dream, a nightmare. But after it's over we can forget all about it, can't we? Like when you wake up and forget your bad dreams.'

She was trying very hard, so Charlie helped. He put his arm round her again and kissed her gently.

'Of course we can. We can forget about it and get on with our lives like it never happened.'

It wasn't really a lie, it was the truth, but in someone else's suit. When she got back it would indeed be over. Costello would be dead and things *could* get back to normal. He would get back to being just another agent from the East who had defected, who had been bought and paid for by a Western government for betraying his country and was now hidden away in their affluent woodwork. A normal guy just like all the other normal guys. All that it needed was Costello to be dead. And that was all arranged.

The doorbell rang.

'I'll get it. Whoever it is I'll get rid of them. It's probably Lars seeing if we need anything.'

Charlie went to the door. It was the Comedian.

'Yes?'

'I need to have a word, Mr Bronski. Can we go inside?'

'No.'

The Comedian switched on his false smile.

95

'Thank you.' He walked past Charlie and made his way into the living room. 'Hello, Mrs Bronski, I've come to have a few words with your husband.'

Charlie had followed him into the room. He could see there was no point in trying to get rid of him. Best to let him ask his questions and then he would go.

'I'll deal with it, Elspeth, you go and pack.' She started to move.

'No, I would rather you stayed, Mrs Bronski, it would save me having to see you later. Shall we all sit down?' He sat down and Charlie took Elspeth's hand and they sat opposite him on the settee. He smiled at them. 'Does anyone want anything to drink, tea, coffee, something stronger?' Elspeth shook her head and Charlie ignored the question. 'No, then we might as well begin. Yesterday you left Denmark rather suddenly, Mr Bronski. You went to Hamburg. Why was that?'

Charlie had to make up his mind very quickly. Opposing him would mean trouble. He didn't mind trouble but it wouldn't be good for Elspeth to see it, not now, not after all his hard work. He could feel by the pressure of her hand that she was already slipping. Cooperating meant telling him enough so he would accept it. On balance it probably wouldn't do any harm, there was no way he could find anything out.

'I went to see an old friend who was passing through Hamburg. We had dinner together at the Louis C Jacob hotel then she left to catch a flight to London. I stayed for the night and flew back today. My wife was here already. She left hospital this morning.'

The false smile became a false beam. Charlie thought he was overdoing it.

'Wonderful. So complete and yet so concise. You can confirm Mr Bronski's arrival here today, Mrs Bronski?' Elspeth nodded. 'Wonderful.' He got up. 'Then I'll go. There, that wasn't too bad was it? Don't bother to come to the door, I'll see myself out.' But he stopped at the doorway and turned back. 'Have you seen the papers or TV since the explosion, Mrs Bronski?' Elspeth shook her head. 'And your husband hasn't told you?'

'Told me what?'

'We thought it best to put the explosion down to a leak from a bottled gas cylinder. We don't want people thinking car bombs have arrived in Denmark, do we? No need to upset people. I do hope you'll both cooperate if you're asked any questions by the media or anyone else.' But he didn't wait for any response. 'But of course you will. You're both cooperating so beautifully, the question doesn't need asking. Goodbye, and thank you once again.'

And this time he left.

Charlie and Elspeth sat on the settee for a moment. 'What was that all about, Charlie? Who was that?'

'He's a policeman, he was the one who interviewed me.'

'He didn't behave like a policeman.'

'No, he doesn't. He has his own way of doing things.'

'He behaved as if it was his house and we were visiting him. And his manner was, well, odd. I didn't like it. He seemed to think it's all a joke or something. As if it isn't real. But it is real, Charlie, isn't it?'

Charlie could see she was worried again. The Comedian had upset her. He had been right not to make waves.

'It's nothing, dear, he just wanted to check where I'd been, that's understandable. The hotel will back up what I said. I met someone, we had dinner, I went to bed. Next morning I left. There's no way he can find anything out. He seemed satisfied and now he's gone. It's over.'

Elspeth didn't say anything. Charlie could see she was thinking. The Comedian had really upset her with his bloody act. *Damn the bastard and his clever ways*. He knew how to do the most damage in the shortest time.

'Charlie, I think I've changed my mind about dinner. Do you mind if we stay in?'

'No, we'll do whatever you want.'

'I'll go and get on with the packing. Book a flight, will you, I'd like to know when I'll be going.'

She slipped her hand out of his, stood up and left.

Shit, thought Charlie, *that bastard has just put me back to when I came home.*

He went to his desk and switched on his computer. He'd get her on the first available flight, even if it meant flying out tonight. The way things had gone, the sooner she was on her way the better. *Damn that fucking Comedian. But I'll beat the bastard, and Costello, and I'll come out of this smelling of roses. Yes I will.*

After a short while he had the flight booked. He went into the bedroom.

'It's at one a.m. I'm afraid, but I can cancel if you don't want to use it. I took it because it's a scheduled flight and it gets into Heathrow. After that one there were budget flights but nothing scheduled to Heathrow until much later. I don't want you hassled around on some cut-price ticket. I want you to have an easy journey and be looked after. I booked business class. But just say if it's too early.'

It was all a lie, but a safe one, she wouldn't check.

'No, Charlie, if I'm going I want be on my way. Will you come to the airport with me?'

'Of course.'

'Suddenly I'm very tired. I think I'll go to bed when I'm finished packing. Can you call me when it's time to go?'

'That's exactly what I was going to suggest.'

He went across and gave her a kiss on the forehead.

'A visit to Hugh for a couple of weeks, some rest in that big old house and plenty of country walks will sort you out. Then when you get back here everything will be just as it used to be.'

'Everything just like it used to be?'

'I promise. Now finish packing and get some sleep.'

He left the room. Elspeth watched him go. She thought about the funny policeman as she packed the last few things. He didn't seem like a policeman but Charlie said he was. She was frightened. Charlie had said everything would be like it was, he had promised, so she had to try and believe him. But the funny policeman had made it harder somehow, much harder. But she would try, she really would try. What else could she do?

TWELVE

When the doorbell rang Udo remained in his chair and Jimmy went to see who it was. It was a new rule. When Jimmy was in, he always answered the door.

'You never know who it will be,' Udo had told him, 'some down-and-out who wants a cup of coffee and a sandwich, someone suicidal, someone asking the times of Mass, a baptism, a funeral or the postman. You just never know. Always be ready for anything.'

The 'anything' Jimmy found at the door was a man who said he was a police officer although he wore no uniform and showed no police identification.

'Is Fr Mundt in?' Jimmy was about to answer but he never got the chance. 'Good. Is this the way?' The man was past him before the question was finished. Jimmy suppressed his natural instinct to grab him and throw him out. He followed him to the living room. If he'd made a mistake, Udo could tell him afterwards. Besides, the man had all the earmarks of officialdom. If he was a loony, he was a very official-looking one. Udo looked up at the visitor from his chair. 'Good morning, Fr Mundt.' The loony didn't wait to be asked, he sat down then made a slight gesture towards a chair. 'Please sit down, Mr Costello.' Jimmy looked at Udo, who said nothing, so he sat down. 'I won't have anything to drink, thank you,

Father.' Udo hadn't asked him, but that didn't seem to matter, he was making himself right at home. 'If one drank something on every visit one makes, well, you understand, Father, I'm sure. One doesn't want to drown in a sea of coffee and good manners, does one?'

Jimmy and Udo exchanged glances. Who the hell was this and what was he up to? It was Udo who asked the question.

'Who are you and what do you want?'

'I am a police officer and I want information.'

'May I see some identification?'

'But of course.'

The man produced a warrant card and passed it to Udo who looked at it and passed it back.'

'You both visited Mrs Bronski in hospital two days ago?'

Udo nodded. 'Yes.'

'I understand it was your second visit?'

'That is correct. We visited her on the day she was admitted.'

'What was the reason for your second visit?'

'I was asked to take her a message from her husband. He had had to go away unexpectedly and asked me to let his wife know.'

'I see. Why do you think he didn't he tell her himself?'

'It was a trip to Germany, a business trip, but he'd wanted to surprise her and make a break of it for them both. She was in hospital so that was not possible. He wanted me to tell her that he had gone and would be back the following day. He felt that if he went himself he might not get away, she might not want him to go. He told me to tell her not to worry.'

'And *was* she worried when you told her?'

Udo thought about it. 'Yes, now you mention it, I think she was. At the time I put it down to something left over from the accident but, now I think about it, it could have been telling her that her husband had gone away suddenly that worried her.'

'Was that your impression as well, Mr Costello?'

Jimmy had been studying the floor, trying to be invisible.

He surfaced.

'Yes. She took it badly but tried to hide it. Considering what she'd been through she didn't do too badly. But it definitely shook her.'

Udo turned to him. 'You didn't say anything at the time.'

'What was there to say? Her husband had suddenly gone to Germany without telling her. He sent a message, didn't come himself even though she was in hospital and it was the day after their car got blown up. It's not exactly normal behaviour, is it?'

'But he explained that.'

'He told you an obvious lie. He wanted his wife to know he had gone to Germany but he wouldn't go and tell her himself.' Jimmy turned his attention back to their visitor. 'When he left us it was just after eleven, about quarter past or half past, but wherever he was going he said he would be back the next day so he wasn't going far.'

The policeman smiled and nodded as if congratulating Jimmy on his contribution.

'Good. Tell me, when he visited did he have any luggage, a bag of any sort?'

Udo answered. 'No, no bag.'

'The Bronskis live in Nyborg, so if he had gone home to get things he wouldn't have been able to set out for wherever he was going for over three hours, if he was leaving from Copenhagen that is. I wonder why he didn't take anything with him.' He paused but neither Udo nor Jimmy offered any suggestion, so he went on, 'And if he was going to Germany, as he said he was, then I think he must have left from Copenhagen, the station or the airport, don't you?'

Udo was studying the floor now so Jimmy responded. 'If you say so.'

'And did neither of you think it odd, travelling with no luggage?'

Udo looked up and shrugged. 'I just didn't notice.'

'And you, Mr Costello. Did you not notice?'

'It was none of my business one way or the other.'

'But if it *had* been your business, Mr Costello, what then?' Jimmy didn't want to get into it, whatever it was. But this man was trouble. No ordinary copper would behave as he had done. He was making some sort of point by his behaviour and his questions. What point? Jimmy decided he would need to go very carefully. The visitor gave him a big smile as if to encourage him. 'In your own time, Mr Costello, I'm not in any hurry and I *do* want to hear what you make of it all.'

Why not, thought Jimmy. *Bronski's up to something so why not give the police any bit of help he could.* If this guy *was* the police.

'My guess is that he wanted to get going as soon as he'd left us. He asked the day before about Mass times, that meant he planned to come to Copenhagen at a time when he knew he could talk to Fr Mundt and me. I think he set up some other contact or meeting before Mass which he knew would result in him having to travel to Germany at short notice. I think he intended to leave for wherever he was headed as soon as he'd finished here and got Fr Mundt to deliver his message to his wife.'

'And why do you think all that, Mr Costello?'

'Because he came into the church late. He knew the time of Mass but he got there only a few minutes before it was all over. If you've planned to come to Mass, why be so late unless you'd had other things to see to first?'

'Yes, I see. Did he make a point of asking to see you both?'

Udo nodded.

'And why did he say he wanted to see you both?'

Udo didn't answer so Jimmy filled in. 'He told us he needed advice about how he should deal with the police.'

'A very silly story.'

'A weak lie just like his other story – could Fr Mundt tell his wife he'd gone to Germany to see a publisher because he had to meet a deadline? Who leaves a wife in hospital after they both nearly get killed to see a publisher, deadline or no deadline?'

'Who indeed?'

'He probably went to the station as soon as he left here.'

The policeman sat back, smiled and raised his hands. Jimmy thought for a second he was going to clap.

'Very good, very good indeed.' The hands went back down and he put a serious look on his face. 'But tell me, you seem very sure of what you are saying. Would that be because you have more information about Mr Bronski or his visit?'

'I have no information about him or his visit. I have my own opinion on what happened. If I seem sure, it's because I used to be a police detective in London and I got to hear lots of stories that were lies, although you wouldn't have to be a detective to see through the ones Bronski told.'

'Fr Mundt believed it.'

'If you say so.'

'But do *you* say so, Mr Costello? That's the point.'

Jimmy looked at Udo who said nothing. It wasn't his conversation.

'Fr Mundt gets told lots of stories. He doesn't have to believe them. Bronski asked him to tell his wife something, so he went and told her. Why not? He's a priest, he tries to help people and it wasn't much to ask, even if part of it was a lie.'

The visitor switched from Jimmy to Udo. '*Did* you believe the story, Fr Mundt?'

'I suppose not, but, whatever I believed, he was going away and his wife needed telling. She had been in a bad way when I saw her the previous evening. Her husband suddenly going away wasn't going help her condition. I thought it best that I was the one who told her, not the hospital, so I went.'

'Do you agree with Mr Costello that he probably caught the train after his visit here?'

'I've no idea. I didn't give it any thought.'

The visitor switched back to Jimmy. 'But you, Mr Costello, you think he went to the station?'

Jimmy nodded. 'If he had a meeting in Germany he would have needed to get going whether he went by train or air.'

'Let us say, for the sake of argument, he did indeed go to the station as you think. Where would you say Mr Bronski might have been headed?'

'If he went by train I'd say Hamburg. There's a direct connection that leaves around the right time. If he went to the airport he could have been going to quite a few places that are close enough to get to, have a meeting and get back, Berlin for instance. But I think it was the train.'

'Ah, now why do you think that?'

'He's near the station, a short walk, he had probably checked the train times. If he'd already got his ticket, waited until the last minute and hopped on the train it would be difficult to see how anyone would be able to follow him.'

'Why do you think he was being followed?'

'I didn't say I thought he was followed. I said it would be difficult for anyone …'

'Can we stop there?' They both stopped and looked at Udo. 'As you see, we are both quite happy to answer your questions, but I think that before we go any further you should give us some idea of why you are asking them. Is Mr Bronski suspected of anything?'

'Mr Bronski is involved in a very serious crime. Attempted murder at the very least.'

'His car?' The visitor nodded. 'Not a gas cylinder like the papers said?' The visitor shook his head. 'A bomb?'

'Oh, yes, Father, it was a bomb and you'll forgive me, I'm sure, if I say that I cannot believe that either you or Mr Costello put any credence in the gas cylinder story.'

'So you think he is involved in whatever caused his car to be blown up? Is that it?'

'We are following every possible line of investigation.'

'I see.'

'I'm sure you do, so please tell me in your own words, Father, about his visit here.'

'Well, he came to Mass at ten and when it was over he asked to talk to us …'

'Both of you?'

'Yes, he particularly asked Mr Costello to be there while we talked. He said he wanted a favour and some advice. The favour was to visit his wife and tell her he was going to see a publisher and would be away overnight.'

'And the advice?'

'How should he deal with the police.'

'Deal with the police, in what way?'

'He said he felt the police suspected him of something but that he knew nothing. He wanted to know what he should do. He said he wanted to talk to someone who could advise him.'

The policeman registered surprise and turned to Jimmy. 'So he came here because he knew you had been a policeman, Mr Costello?'

'No, I told him that when he asked us how he should deal with the police.'

'Are you saying he came here to ask for help with the police without knowing you had been a detective?'

'He was lucky, I guess.'

The policeman nodded slowly, as if considering it.

'Yes, I'm sure you're right. Mr Bronski strikes me as a man who would be lucky. What happened then?'

'I told him to cooperate.'

'That's all, nothing else?'

'Yes. Wasn't that the right thing to say?'

'Yes, Mr Costello, that was the right thing to say. A good citizen always cooperates with the police and Mr Bronski strikes me as a good citizen.' He got up and beamed a false smile. 'Thank you both for your cooperation. I can see that you are also good citizens.' Jimmy stood up but the visitor held up a hand. 'Please don't bother. I'll see myself out. Good day, Fr Mundt.'

No one shook hands when he left. Jimmy waited until he heard the front door close then sat down again. It needed talking about.

THIRTEEN

'What the hell was that all about?'

Udo shook his head. 'No idea. What do you think?'

'I think our visitor has an odd sense of humour.'

'It was a very odd visit, I agree. You told him you were English?'

'No, he spoke English as soon as I opened the door. I didn't have to tell him, he already knew.'

'He was a strange sort of policeman. I got the feeling he didn't much care about our answers to his questions, that he was looking for something else, but I have no idea what.'

'Whatever he came for, I don't think we scored any credit points with him.'

'No, I don't think we did either, but we told him what we know, didn't we?'

'That's right, we told him what we know. But we didn't tell him what we think.'

'He didn't ask us.'

'Would you have told him if he had asked?'

'No.'

'Neither would I.'

'So, Jimmy, you were the detective. What do *you* think?'

'I think that ever since his car went up, Bronski's been very careful to be in control of himself, too much in control for anyone who isn't trained to handle situations like that.'

'Yes, I noticed that in the hospital. For a man who had seen his car go up in a ball of fire that morning he seemed, well, abnormally normal.'

'That's right, too normal and very much on the alert. I think when we visited the hospital and he got a close look at me he decided that maybe I wasn't what I seemed, that I might be some kind of a plant and possibly connected to the car bomb.'

'Why? Why should he think that?'

'Because he might have asked himself, why is an Englishman with no foreign languages doing a placement with a German priest in Denmark?'

'Yes, when you put it like that you *are* a bit of a plant, aren't you? He wasn't exactly right but unfortunately he was close.'

'Whatever that car bomb was about, he was on the lookout, he would pick up on any face that didn't quite fit, especially a new face. Once he put his mind to it then you can see how I'd fit the bill for him. Someone must have watched his Sunday routine and knew when to plant the bomb. When we turned up at the hospital he focused on me, saw that I fitted what he was looking for, so next day he arranged to come here to check me out. When I told him I had experience with police methods he must have felt sure I was something more than I was telling him. I think that's why he was late coming to Mass. He was arranging to get in touch with someone who could help him, maybe someone who could check up on me.'

'I wonder why a car bomb? It's not run-of-the-mill violence, is it? It's usually a terrorist thing. Could this be terrorist-related?'

'How should I know? I was only ever a bent detective sergeant, I never blew anybody up. If he has me down as the one who planted the bomb, then God knows why.'

'How about if he was an ex-terrorist, someone who'd sold out some sort of terrorist group and was now living undercover.'

'That would make sense except for one thing. They wouldn't frighten him, they'd kill him.' But Udo's idea had set Jimmy thinking. 'Whatever he is, he's a trained bugger, he got straight into action after he'd put his wife safely in hospital.'

'Trained as what?'

'God knows. But if he's on the move, it probably means he's been in touch with an emergency contact, one he'd been given if he thought his past had caught up with him. If he is an ex-terrorist or ex-something else then he'd be in some sort of programme, he'd be protected by an agency. If they'd given him a new life, he'd want to live somewhere quiet, like Nyborg.'

Jimmy waited. He wanted Udo to act as a sounding board on his thoughts. He didn't want to do it all in his head. He needed to do it out loud to somebody.

'No, you're going too far on this. Isn't it all a bit far-fetched?'

'Maybe, but isn't it always, when something like this turns up on your doorstep? What you read in the papers or see on TV always happens to someone else. When it happens to you, it always seems far-fetched.'

'I suppose so. Car bombs aren't exactly routine in Denmark.'

'And like I said, if it's a new face he wants, a new face with a shaky story, I fit the bill.'

Udo hesitated for a second.

'You're *not* involved, are you? You're not making some kind of case against yourself to tell me something, to warn me? After all, what do I know about you except what you've told me?'

'No, I'm not involved, Udo, you can pick up the phone any time and check with the Monsignor or even Professor McBride. If I'm right, then I'm just an innocent bystander who's in the wrong place at the wrong time.'

'And we both know what happens to innocent bystanders.' Jimmy nodded, he knew. 'So what do you propose? Tell the police what you think is happening? We could try to get in touch with the one we've just had here.'

'Why, what can they do? I've no proof of anything and if Bronski's what I think then he'll have been given a watertight story. If I tell the police what I've told you, all that will happen is that a whole crowd of people will get to know I'm here and it won't be too long before my visitors turn up.'

'And that would be bad?'

Jimmy decided it was time to let Udo know what he was getting into just by having him there.

'When they come it will be either the CIA or Mossad. Would you say that was bad?'

Udo didn't say, he didn't need to, he waited. It was Jimmy's problem so it was Jimmy's choice. But Jimmy was certainly right about one thing. He was very much in the wrong place at the wrong time, a bystander. But not so innocent if it was the CIA and Mossad after him.

Jimmy didn't think for too long. He knew he really didn't have a choice. It was stay and die, or do the other thing. So it had to be the other thing.

'I'm going to run, Udo, it's best for both of us. I don't like the way things are going. It was bad enough when I was hiding out from Mossad and the CIA but now it's Bronski, and he's right here beside me, and soon I think he'll have help. There's no way I can hide or defend myself. So I'll run.'

Udo didn't argue. He had nothing to offer, so he accepted Jimmy's choice.

'Where to?'

'I don't know and even if I did I wouldn't tell you. Once I'm gone I want you to go straight to the police and say I've disappeared. I don't want you to have to lie for me, I don't want to put you in any danger. Tell them what you know, all of it. That way, if anyone else turns up you're in the clear. You don't know where I am.'

'What do you think your chances will be if you run?'

'Not great. If anybody at all in the Intelligence community gets to know about this then I'm located and that's pretty much that. But it doesn't matter. I told you, dying isn't something that I worry about, but I can't just sit here and let someone come and finish me off. I've got to make the effort. I'll run, but I doubt I'll get all that far.'

'How long will it take you to get ready?'

'A couple of days. I need to fix the money end of things.'

'Will money be a problem?'

'No. There's plenty. I suppose you'd call me well-off.'

'Ill-gotten gains?'

'Mostly, and well invested. I fixed a drugs charge against a young bloke because his father was an investment banker.' Jimmy gave a small laugh. 'Can you believe it? By that time, I'd got to the stage where I needed an investment banker. Fixing the evidence was my price to get him to look after my money and make it work. He was good at it and either he's still grateful or he's still afraid of what I'd do if he didn't do well by me. One way and another I never got round to telling him I was a reformed character and didn't hurt people or fix evidence any more. I have all I'll ever need and when they catch up with me it's all set up so it will go to my daughter and her kids. It will be a nice surprise and when I'm dead it won't matter where it came from.'

'So, you reformed but you never got round to giving any of the money back?' Udo was smiling. 'Very sensible. It makes everything easier. Listen, if you run you'd better try to do it properly.'

'Properly?'

Udo sat back and didn't say anything for a moment. Then he began.

'You've told me your story, Jimmy, now let me tell you a little bit of mine. Before I became a priest I was a minor official in an East German government department. When unification happened nobody needed or wanted our department. We just duplicated people who were doing the same thing in Bonn so we got closed down. It happened to a lot of government people. I worked out of an office in a little town called Dassow, about twenty kilometres east of Lübeck. Being a government official I could cross the border whenever I liked so I visited Lübeck pretty often. It was always a nice town but quiet in those days, too near the border for foreign visitors. Our border fence didn't have any of the attraction of the Berlin Wall and there was no Checkpoint Charlie to take photos from. Since reunification, Lübeck's back on the tourist trail and these days I suppose it's very nice, now there's money about. I'll give you an address

111

there, an old colleague of mine. Go to him. I'll get in touch and ask him to look after you, find you somewhere discreet to stay. An ex-copper wandering through Europe who only speaks English with a London accent isn't going to blend in. You need a few friendly faces round you. I'll try to see that you get them. It isn't much, but it may help.'

Jimmy wanted to refuse. Deep down inside he wanted the whole stupid mess of his life over and done with. But Bernie had stuck it out, so he had to stick it out. He had to take any help he was offered, otherwise he might as well sit in Copenhagen and wait for whoever came. He made one last effort.

'Thanks, Udo, but I can't let you do it. I don't want to get you into trouble and I don't want you to put your friends in danger.'

'I'm used to trouble and my friends won't mind a little danger, especially if they're well paid. It won't be a free ride, it will cost you. I'm glad you told me money wasn't a problem; you'll need it, plenty of it.'

That was his last chance, and now it was gone. Udo was going to help him stay alive.

'OK, Udo, and thanks. I'll be ready the day after tomorrow. I'll go out the same way as Bronski.'

'No, nobody was watching when he left. They will be now. They'll almost certainly be monitoring the trains and airport. If anyone connected to that car bomb buys a ticket out of the country the police will be informed. And I think our visit from the policeman with the odd sense of humour means we're very much connected. They won't want anyone else involved slipping away like Bronski. Anyone else might not be coming back. If you go to Hamburg you'd be stuck on the train for over four hours. They'd have no trouble getting you. It's too risky.'

'So a plane?'

'No, same problem. You buy a ticket and then you sit in Departures until they come and pick you up. Even if you get on the plane they get you at the other end.'

'So how do I get out?'

'Go to the station and buy a ticket for the direct train to

Hamburg, make sure it's the right one, the one you pay a supplement for and has a Bordbistro on it. Find a train, a fast train going west that leaves at about the same time or as close as you can get. Take that train just before it leaves. On it buy a ticket for Aarhus. That will make it look as if you're headed for the airport either there or at Billund. Get off the train at Fredericia. From there you can get a train into Germany. Buy a ticket for Hamburg. By the time the police are told you bought a Hamburg ticket at Copenhagen and start looking you'll be well on your way. If they find you didn't take the Hamburg train but headed west, the first thing they'll probably do is cover the airports, especially Billund.'

'Why Billund?'

'It's the airport for Legoland. It would make sense for you to head there; it's a tourist airport with plenty of budget flights to the UK. An Englishman wouldn't be noticed. By the time they find you've not gone to Billund or Aarhus and backtrack to the Fredericia train you should be into Germany.'

'But once they find I've bought a dud Hamburg ticket in Copenhagen and scarpered in the opposite direction, any doubt they might have about me and the bomb is gone. They'll have the German police waiting for me at Hamburg with an arrest warrant.'

'They may have the German police watching for you, but that will be in Hamburg, so get off at Padborg just before the line crosses the border and get a ticket to Bad Oldesloe. At Bad Oldesloe you get a ticket to Lübeck.'

'Why can't I just get a ticket straight through to Lübeck?'

'Because there are two routes from Padborg to Lübeck. On one you change twice, at Neumünster and Bad Oldesloe. On the other there's only one change.'

'So why not get that one? Fewer changes means less chance of me getting myself screwed up.'

'Because the change is Hamburg.'

'Oh, I see.'

'Also the Bad Oldesloe train is faster even with the changes, three hours as opposed to nearly four if you go through Hamburg.'

'OK, I suppose you know best.'

Udo could see Jimmy was getting nervous about the journey.

'Don't worry, after Padborg you'll be in friendly territory, northern Germany. They're nice people - slow and without any sense of humour, but friendly. Just show your ticket to any railway official when you have to change and they'll get you on the right train. If you can't find an official just show it to anybody who's there. Like I say, they're friendly. If you travel on an intercity express there'll be a Bordbistro, if not you'll have to do the best you can for food and drink at the stations. The whole journey will take ...' Udo did quick calculation, 'about five and a half to six hours.'

'That's not bad. I expected longer.'

'It *will* be longer. That's travelling time - it doesn't include waits between trains. You could add up to three hours, depending on connections.'

'Shit, that's long time to be on the move. Still, if you think it's the best way.'

'I do, I think it's the only way if you want to get where you're going. At Lübeck you get a taxi from the station to an address I'll give you. After that you're out of my hands but you'll be with old colleagues of mine. They will tell you the price and if you pay it you'll be safe. Then you can decide where you want to go and how you'll get there.'

Now he had his exit all laid out for him, Jimmy still didn't look happy.

'Don't look so worried, Jimmy, it'll go fine, I promise. Trust me, I know about these things.'

Jimmy didn't look encouraged. 'You *used* to know. Like you said, there was a bloody great wall and a whole country that have both disappeared since you used to arrange things like this.'

Udo laughed.

'You English, how did you ever get an empire being so pessimistic, so defeatist?'

'By being realistic.'

'Look, I'll write it all down for you. If you like I'll even teach you how to ask for a ticket in German and make small talk with the ticket inspectors.'

They grinned at each other. It was a little joke between them. In the time he'd been in Copenhagen he'd picked up almost no Danish. He could barely say hello and goodbye.

'What about documents when I get to Lübeck, if I get there? Can your friends help?'

'Fresh documents can be provided, if you can pay.' Jimmy didn't say anything so Udo leaned forward. 'This way you'll have a chance - how good a chance, you'll know better than me. But you won't be sitting here waiting for anyone to come and get you. They'll get a run for their money and, who knows, you may even get clear.'

Jimmy thought about Udo's plan - he was impressed. 'What was your department in East Germany, tourism and immigration? You seem to have all the moves at your fingertips.'

'In the East under communism, everyone who could was in the black market, buying, selling, importing. A few of us had a little smuggling scam going. Cigarettes, booze, nice things from the West you couldn't get in the Democratic Republic but which higher officials were happy to pay for and not ask where they came from.' Udo smiled. 'You weren't the only bent official. In the East, for some of us, it was a way of life. We did OK. When the Wall came down and there was no more border fence it wasn't unrestrained joy all round, you know. Some of us lost a living. In the case of me and my friends it was two livings, my government job and the black market racket.'

'Bloody hell, Udo, has everybody connected with this thing got a past? Me, you, Bronski.'

'I hope Bronski's past isn't all you think it is. The police will be bad enough but if there's any government involvement, you're not going to be so safe, even if you make it to my friends. And Bronski may decide to come looking for you himself; he won't want you turning up sometime in the future with another bomb, or something else.'

'But it isn't me. When whoever's out there makes their next move, he'll know I'm not involved.'

'But what if he doesn't wait? We can't exactly go to him and explain, can we?'

'You're right. I know you're right.' Jimmy got up. 'Well, if I'm going to set things in motion I'd better get going. Thanks, Udo, I hope this works out and you don't get into too much trouble.'

Udo got up.

'I've had my share of dealing with trouble. I'm not too worried about it. Listen, I know I don't need to tell you things are pretty much stacked against you but I will anyway. If you really mean what you say and dying isn't a problem for you, well, I think you're likely to get what you want. I have to say that; I can't let you go thinking it's all going to work out.'

'I'll take whatever comes, but I'll be trying. I won't make it any easier for them.'

'Then God go with you, Jimmy. Not that he ever makes any difference in situations like this, at least not that I've ever noticed.'

'No, me neither.'

Jimmy left the room and went to start setting things in motion. Udo stood for a moment after he'd gone.

'I'll pray for you, and light a few candles, but I've never noticed them make any difference either, especially when the ones after you will be putting their faith into something like a soft-nosed bullet, up close and very personal.'

And Fr Mundt started to get ready for a meeting he had to attend with some local Protestant ministers and a couple of imams. They were going to talk about interfaith dialogue. Not that the meetings ever made any difference, at least not any difference he could ever notice.

FOURTEEN

'Hello, Candice? Yes, it's been too long, ever since that conference in Washington. The man closed the yellow file and slipped it into a drawer. Look, I think we should meet, where are you at the moment? ... Still in Berlin. That's good, there's something we should discuss ... no, I don't want to talk about it over the phone and I don't think you do either ... yes, it's exactly like that ... well, let's just say it's about a bit of flag waving ... of course I'm being cryptic, we're in the Secret Service, we're supposed to be cryptic ... all right, I'll make it as plain as this, look at the flags you've got out ... yes, it's about that sort of thing. The problem is either we meet within the next twenty-four hours or there's no point in meeting at all ... I know it's short notice but I think, when you hear what I've got for you, you'll find it was worth it ... look, never mind the blah, meet me and if I'm wrong and you're not interested I'll give you dinner at a restaurant of your choice and throw in all the Royal Navy battle dispositions tied up in pink ribbon ... OK, saffron then, any colour you like. Good ... oh, no, I don't think Berlin's a good idea at all. This is for your ears only and strictly off-the-record ... no, Candice, listen. I mean *off-the-record* off-the-record. Not off-the-record and you pass it on upstairs if it turns out to be really important.

'This is between you and me, you'll see why when you hear

117

it … all right, that's better. I'm going to the Louis C Jacob hotel in Hamburg. Officially I will be checking out the story of a dormant agent who sent in a crash call and held a meeting there with one of my staff. The story will hold up because he really *was* dormant, did make a crash call and met one of my staff there … yes I can tell you. The call came from Copenhagen … of course it's true, I told you because you could check the hotel and find out for yourself. But don't check, Candice, not you and not someone in Hamburg. If you do then any deal is off. So don't do anything except get to the Louis C Jacob by …' He looked at his watch. It was just gone five a.m. 'Say three this afternoon. Good. Oh, and really be alone, Candice. If you bring back-up, you'll regret it. Hear what it is before you do anything silly like let someone else know we're meeting. You won't regret it, I promise. And for your own sake, use a cover for the visit that will stand up to some scrutiny from your own people. If this runs, we'll want to keep it very much to ourselves … right, see you in Hamburg at three.'

He rang off and made another call.

'Get me on a flight to Hamburg. I want to be there at two. Book me in at the Louis C Jacob for one night and arrange a return flight for about ten the next day. Lay on transport from my home for the flight out.'

Something down inside his Ted Baker boxer shorts stirred. Being at the beginning of something really big always made him horny. It must be the adrenalin, or hormones, or something. He would go back to his apartment, wake up David, have a quick frolic then a shower. He'd be missing his lunch so he'd have to have something to eat at Heathrow, which would carry him through the day until an early dinner. He looked at his watch again. It was now a few minutes more past five. He did a time check of progress so far.

He had sent Clarke-Phillips off to Copenhagen at about two in the morning so she would be well on her way. Soon she should be sitting on Bronski, then she would get Bronski to sit on Costello until he gave her the go-ahead. After three this afternoon he would be sitting on all of them, but from a safe distance. He smiled. The Director would retire in six to eight months. He had been running down his workload for some time and his deputy was already expected to field too much for him. The Minister must have been looking round for a replacement ever since the Director said he wanted to go, but there was no clear front runner and time was running out. The Minister needed somebody, somebody who showed talent, initiative and above all a safe pair of hands.

He ran over what had happened when he had taken Costello's name upstairs. His surfacing had gone straight through to the Director, not stopped on the deputy's desk. That made it very important.

Well, he thought, *if this is as big as it looks and I can bring it off they can stop looking for a front runner. Bless you, James Cornelius Costello, God bless and preserve you. Until I arrange otherwise, of course.*

The scheduled BA flight from Heathrow to Copenhagen touched down just before eight, local time. Henry Clarke-Phillips went to the baggage hall and collected her suitcase which was one of the first to arrive on the carousel. She'd arranged with baggage handling at Heathrow for it to be stored so it was among the first of the bags to be unloaded. Strictly speaking they weren't allowed to do that, it compromised security because it told the baggage handlers there was a government bod with special pull on board. But what the hell, if you couldn't get the VIP lounge and a few favours then you were just another traveller, one more business suit. As she told herself, if you weren't in it for the money, but to serve Queen and country, then you were entitled to the few little perks that were available.

She walked out of Arrivals and through a shopping mall which was lined with the inevitable glass-fronted shops selling glitzy tat. Outside them all, she bought a ticket to Copenhagen and went down the stairs to the platform. The trains from Kastrup Lufthavn station were fast, frequent and comfortable, and in twenty minutes she was in a taxi leaving Copenhagen Central station headed for the Hotel D'Angleterre. She registered, went up to her suite and told the porter to leave the suitcase on the bed. Once he was gone, she took off her clothes and went to take a shower.

Relief swept over her as she stood under the hot water. For a while she just stood there, becoming human again. After the shower she put on the soft towelling robe that was hanging on the bathroom door, went back into the main room of the suite, called room service and ordered fresh orange juice, coffee, a plate of cooked meats and a Danish pastry. *A light breakfast*. Later, after she had located Bronski, she'd find somewhere to pick up a light lunch to get her through to five and the meeting. Once Bronski was set up she could come back to the hotel and make up for things at dinner. *Something special with a really good wine*.

After breakfast she went into the bedroom, pulled her suitcase to one side of the queen-sized bed, dropped the robe onto the floor and slipped between the sheets. She didn't need to set an alarm; years of practice had enabled her to wake up when she wanted to. An hour's rest to recharge the system, then she would head off to Nyborg. In a couple of minutes Henry Clarke-Phillips was asleep.

Nyborg was a small town on the eastern edge of Denmark's small middle island, Fyn. A modern road bridge carried vehicles over the narrow strip of sea separating Fyn from its larger neighbour but the train went into a tunnel when it left Zealand and came out almost on the outskirts of the town. Henry Clarke-Phillips left the neat, modern station and walked across the road to the taxi rank beside the station car park. There were two taxis. She got into the first. The driver turned and said something in Danish.

'Do you speak English?'

'Of course.'

'Where's a good place for lunch?'

'What sort of price?'

'Price doesn't matter.'

'OK.'

The driver liked the sound of that, maybe there would be a good tip if she felt she'd had the right kind of service. The taxi took a road which took them round the edge of the town beside what looked like a pretty canal, except it didn't seem to go anywhere. They drove for a couple of minutes until they came to what had obviously been a small commercial harbour. The driver turned into the car park by a brightly painted two-storey building which stood on its own between the road and the harbour edge. The name painted high up on the road-facing wall said "Café Rembrandt". It looked a nice place. There was covered outdoor seating on the harbour side of the building. The driver turned round and indicated another building across the road they had just left. It was the back of a hotel which stood at the end of a terrace of big, three-storey houses on the other side of the little canal which came to an end in front of the hotel garden.

'If you don't like this place there's the Villa Gulle across the road. The food is simple but good and it's usually quiet at lunchtime. If you prefer to look around for yourself, the town centre is two minutes up that street over there. If you want something more expensive, just say so. There's a hotel out of town …'

She nodded to the Café Rembrandt. 'This place looks fine.'

She got out and looked round. The harbour obviously hadn't handled commercial shipping for many years but it was still active. There were a few yachts moored and an elegant tall ship tied up on the far wall. On both sides of the harbour were modern apartment developments, some new-build, some warehouse conversions. It all looked very classy. The restaurant should be OK.

'What do I owe you?' The driver looked at the meter and told her.

'Does that include the tip?'

'No, the tip is for you to decide.'

'Double the fare and give me a receipt.'

The driver's face split in a grin. He had been right, this one tipped well for good service. She held out some Danish notes, which he took, then wrote a receipt on the back of a business card and handed it over.

'If you need a taxi, just call.'

'I don't suppose you know where a Mr and Mrs Bronski

121

live?'

He shook his head.

'No, but I can look them up if they're in the phone book.'

'They had an explosion in their garage recently.'

'Ah, that place. Yes, I know where it is. It's out beyond the station, by the beach. Do you want to go there?'

'Yes, I'm a reporter from the UK. I want to go and look it over and do an interview. I'll call you when I've had lunch. No, on second thoughts wait here for me. Let the meter run.'

'Sure.'

Better and better, he thought, *it's my lucky day*.

She went into the restaurant and took a seat by a window. In the middle of the room was a long buffet of cold food with the fixed price on a sign above it. Something from that would be perfect. The waiter came up.

'I'll use the buffet.'

It wasn't really expensive enough but unfortunately it was what she wanted.

'Anything to drink, madame?'

'A glass of red wine.'

The waiter left and she got up, collected a plate of cold lunch and sat down again. The waiter arrived and put the wine down beside her. As she ate she looked out of the window at the new harbour side apartment blocks. They were very Scandinavian, all glass and clean lines. Beyond them there must be another harbour, she could see the masts of what looked like a crowded marina. Nyborg looked like a nice place to retire to.

She turned her mind back to the job in hand.

Tomorrow she would have to go to the Embassy in Copenhagen to get a gun. She wondered what sort she'd get. She hoped it wouldn't be a Glock - a good gun but too heavy for a pocket or handbag, and a shoulder holster played havoc with the hang of your suit jacket. A hip holster did the same for your waistline. She had a good figure and she didn't like it messed about. No, she hoped it wouldn't be a Glock. She would try and get something that would fit into her handbag.

After all, this shouldn't turn into a shooting war. If things worked out right, it would be a two-bullet affair, up close. She wouldn't need a cannon; something quite small-calibre would be enough to get the job done. Something neat to go in her handbag. She'd stick out for a Beretta or something like that.

When she'd finished her meal she paid and left. Time to check out Charlie. Time to get the show on the road.

FIFTEEN

'It may be very Little Englander of me but I don't take afternoon tea on the continent, not even in a good hotel like this. They just don't know how to do it and it always disappoints if you try.'

'So you stick to London dry gin?'

'Only one, Candice, and it does less damage in the long run than all that coffee you Americans swill.'

The truth was, he felt like a grubby field agent anywhere outside central London. He was only truly happy at his desk with his ever-faithful secretary Gloria on guard as his gatekeeper.

Candice hadn't come from Berlin to the Louis C Jacob for chit-chat so she got down to business.

'Look, I came and I didn't tell anybody …'

'Nobody at all?'

'Nobody. So can we cut the crap about tea and coffee and discuss what this is all about.'

'What did you tell them you were coming here for?'

'I told them the truth.'

'The truth!'

'That an old friend from British Intelligence was unexpectedly passing through Hamburg. He knew I was in Berlin and asked if we could meet for old times' sake to chew the fat. I asked my boss if it would be OK to take the rest of the day off. I wasn't handling anything urgent so he said "get going but be back at your desk tomorrow morning". I guess I may have given the impression we'd been in the sack together at some time and that I fancied one more roll. He's something of a romantic, so here I am. But don't get any ideas. It was just a story and it's going to stay that way.'

The man smiled. It wasn't exactly a compliment, but it pleased him. A James Bond stud type, he could play that part if he'd wanted to, play it well. Unfortunately the opportunity would never arise because, outside of James Bond films, the part didn't exist.

'Strictly business is fine by me.'

'Then let's get to it.'

'I'm going to give you a name and you're going to think about it. If the name is important to you, very important, then we'll talk further. If the name is no big deal we'll finish our drinks and both go home. Agreed?'

She nodded. Brits did things in funny ways, roundabout and crab-wise, but she would hear the name.

'James Costello.'

They both sat in silence looking at each other. He had gambled that Costello was important. That was why he had started this. If he was right then he could use what he knew to become a player, maybe even a big player. But the question was, was he right? Was Costello important?

She sat there looking at him, thinking. That was good. If she needed time to think that meant he must be right. Costello was important. But was he important enough to be his ticket to the top table?

Finally she spoke. 'I'm listening. Talk some more.'

There it was. He had something they wanted, and wanted it badly enough to deal. So now he had to get ready to pitch. 'Why do you and the Israelis want Costello?'

The smile wasn't because he had said anything funny, although, to Candice, what he had said could be classed as a joke.

'Sure, I'll tell you. Why not? Costello owes my boss and a

guy from Mossad twenty bucks each from an old poker game. We both flagged him because we began to suspect he was trying to welch.'

He ignored the irony. The question had only been a way of letting her know he hadn't a clue why Costello was wanted. Next step.

'Would you deal to get him?'

She had to think about that one. 'We might, but it wouldn't be my decision. It would go way above my head.'

Whoops! *Free information*. The name must have really shaken her. She didn't let it show in her face or voice, but that was a definite slip letting him know it would be a high-level decision. It was going better than he could have hoped for.

'How would your people react to an auction?'

'An auction?'

'Well, Mossad want him and you want him …'

'And you've got him?'

He wasn't shaken. There would be no free information from his side. 'I didn't say we had him.'

Anger came into her eyes but not her voice. 'Then what the hell is this all about?'

'But I know where I can lay my hands on him at very short notice.' The anger got switched off. Now it was out in the open. Now she knew what it was all about she was back in control. That was good. You couldn't deal with anyone who wasn't in control. 'My problem is that I don't know the price I should ask. You see, it's very hard to know what to do in a case like this when you don't know the true value of the article you're handling. Wouldn't you agree?'

'You're right. I wouldn't agree. So can we cut the British whimsy and you say what you came to say?'

Now she was working. Now they could get down to it.

'I have a suggestion, one I think you will like. One I think both of us will like. One in which all parties come out as winners. Except Costello, of course. Costello is going down. The only question is, how much is he going down for? And that's what I got us here to decide.'

The taxi made a slow pass. The house was the last in a series of bungalows between the road and the beach. There was still police tape across the entrance to the drive and the garage door still hung down on one side. This was the place. To the side of the bungalow, the woods that stood between the beach and the road began.

'OK, take me up the road a bit then stop.'

The taxi went on about a hundred yards and stopped.

'If I go through those woods and get to the beach is there a path back along to the houses?'

'Yes.'

'Where does it go when it reaches them?'

'Along beside the beach down to the Hotel Hesselet and the Nyborg Strand hotel.'

'And can I get back to the road easily?'

'Sure, there are lots of places to come between the houses back out on to the road.'

'OK, I'll walk along the beach path. You wait about five minutes then come down the road and pick me up.'

She got out of the car and found a path. She walked through the pines and came out onto the grass between the trees and a long strip of white, sandy beach. She stood and looked out at the sea - it was very picture postcard. *I might come back here in the summer*, she thought, *it's a really nice spot. I can see why Bronski doesn't want things upset*.

She set off along the well-worn path in the grass towards the houses. She passed Bronski's bungalow and walked on. She didn't see anybody inside, but that meant nothing. She walked on past the backs of the other bungalows.

Going out from the beach at intervals were raised wooden piers with handrails. At the end of each pier were steps down into the water. The piers made bathing areas and when the tide was in the water would be deep enough to dive. She thought they looked cute.

After a few hundred yards she chose a path between two houses and went back out to the road and slowly began to walk away from Bronski's bungalow.

The taxi pulled up alongside her and she got in. The driver

turned.

'What now?'

She looked at her watch, it was five past two. She didn't want to sit around somewhere killing time for three hours. On the other hand, it was never a good idea to change things at the last moment. She decided it would have to be sitting it out until five.

'My appointment's for five. Take me somewhere I can sit comfortably and wait, then pick me up and bring me here at five.'

'There's a nice hotel where you can have coffee.'

'Fine.'

The taxi pulled away and headed for the hotel where she could kill time and maybe work on how she would kill Bronski, when that time came.

'Do we have a deal?'

'No.'

'No!'

'What you have is me thinking about maybe having a deal.'

'Look, Candice, we don't have time to piss about on this. I can't just sit on Costello while you keep me hanging about. Either you commit today or the deal's off.' It was a bold throw, it might do the trick or it might blow the whole thing out of the water. But boldness was what you needed to get to the top, boldness and balls. And he had both. 'You don't need to go and get any OKs on this from your boss or anybody else. It's between you and me, and *just* you and me. I'll sort Costello out for you but I want to get something for my trouble. If we're going to set it up like it was your work, not mine, I need a pay-off that helps me with my firm. That's only fair if you're going to be the one who's taking all the credit at your end; the one who found Costello and got the job done.'

She was thinking about it. He was asking a lot, but then he was offering a lot. But what he was suggesting was a high-risk strategy. The problem was, she could see no way of accepting the deal and then selling him out. If she went in on this, she would have to do it his way. He had all the cards. So, the question was, could he deliver in such a way that she would take the credit?

'OK, just go through it one more time.'

'Christ, woman, have you started to suffer from short-term memory loss or something? Don't go stupid on me or I may have to decide I'm better off with Mossad.'

'Listen, buster, I'm the one in deep shit if this goes wrong. If I want to hear it all again, I get it again.'

He sighed. This was hard work.

'You were the one who got the call, it was you who came to Hamburg. If they've swallowed the story you gave them about our meeting, that could be now, this meeting. Bronski told you his story, the bomb story. He asked for your help, and here's where we get creative: he wanted it kept unofficial, no Agency involvement, none at all. He wouldn't budge on that. Given the position he was in, it's quite believable. He'd come to us and asked for our help but we wouldn't play ball because Costello meant nothing to us. So he looked elsewhere, got in touch with old contacts and came up with a sniff that the CIA were interested in Costello's whereabouts. Through the same old contacts he came to you.'

'That's the part I worry about.'

'Why?'

'It seems thin to me and it'll seem thinner when I tell it.'

'No it won't, because by the time you tell it. Bronski won't be alive to screw it up. They'll have to take your version because there won't be any other.' That seemed to reassure her so he carried on. 'Bronski made the call but he was very cagey. He wasn't going to risk being ratted out by your firm as part of some deal after the Costello job was over. You owed him nothing so it had to be a straight swap. He gave you Costello's whereabouts on condition you took Costello off his back. He said if you turned him down he'd run and Costello would disappear. You'd lose him. And he wanted a quick answer, it had to be a hurry-up job. It was like it is with us today, think on your feet and yes or no. He couldn't hang around while your people set up a committee to talk about it. The way he told it, Costello might go for him any time. You knew how important

Costello was so you said "yes", but you told him he had to let you bring in a freelance as the gun, and he would have to act as beater. You couldn't do it yourself, first you don't have enough field experience and second, if you suddenly went AWOL from Berlin to do the job, all hell would break loose. He said OK and you said you needed a few days to set things up. He should go home and sit on Costello and when things were ready he'd be told to drive Costello onto the gun. Not Denmark but somewhere …'

'Yeah, yeah. Somewhere to muddy the water. And when Bronski gets Costello to where we want him, Bronski also gets a bullet in the head?' He shrugged as if to say, *what do you think*? 'No loose ends and like you say nobody to contradict me when I claim the glory. As far as my people are concerned it will be a brilliant piece of individual initiative in the field. So who will be the gun?'

'One of ours, someone good.'

'So we finally get Costello. What about the gun?'

'I told you, it will be one of ours. There'll be no problem, not during, not after. No loose end there either.'

'No, I guess not.'

'And you go on up the ladder more than a few rungs.'

'If it goes right. If it goes wrong, I go down the shit hole, and more than a few feet - in fact, well over my head.'

'Look, if you don't think it'll work, say so and we'll end it. But if you're in, I need to know now, because I've got to get things lined up. Well, in or out? It's crunch time.'

She didn't like it, but she couldn't fault it.

Costello dead was better than no Costello at all and they might not get a better chance.

'What about my end?'

'Just the way you got the call to sort. I told you, you'll have to find a way so that you got Bronski's call and you've got to invent the contact that brought him to you. He'll be dead so he isn't going to argue and there's got to be enough guys like him from your past who'd fit the bill as a contact.' She was hesitating. Was it a weak spot? 'Look, you already said setting up a fake contact would be OK, that there'd be no problem.'

'That was when you were telling me what this was all about. When I said that, I was only seeing where you were going. Now it's different. I might actually have to figure something out and it would have to be watertight.'

'For God's sake, Candice. When we last met you were a control, you ran people and you had balls. Have you had surgery or have you been flying an office desk since then? Make a fucking decision, will you?'

He waited.

'OK, I'm in.'

At last. He knew Candice. She still had balls all right, but this time she would be lying to her own people. It hadn't been easy for her to agree, even though she was getting something for them that they obviously wanted very badly. He had known it would be hard work, and it had been, harder than he had expected. But he was home now. She had decided and, having decided, she would give it one hundred and ten per cent. He knew it.

'OK, Candice, now I need something from you so that I get up the ladder as well. You know what it is, so why don't you let me have it?'

And Candice began to pay the price they had agreed for her to climb the ladder.

SIXTEEN

At five she was back by the beach, standing on the path between the bungalows and the bathing piers, making a call. Charlie picked up his mobile from beside him on the settee.

'Yes? Hello, Henry, very prompt, dead on five ... I'm at home ... of course. You said I should be alone. There's just me. Elspeth's gone, like you wanted. She left for the UK from Copenhagen at one this morning to stay with her father ... What do you mean, go and open the back door? You're here! What the hell are you here for?'

The call ended. He got up, threw the mobile on the settee and went to the back door, opened it slightly then went back into the living room and stood looking out of the window. He saw her walk up through the garden, heard the back door close and then she came into the living room.

'Nice set-up you've got here. Nice house, nice views. I can see how you wouldn't want to lose it.' She pulled the chair out from the desk and sat down facing him. 'And you won't lose it, not if you do as you're told.'

'You didn't say anything about coming here.'

'I didn't say anything about anything except you'd get your wish, which you will, if you do as you're told.'

Charlie looked at her sullenly. He knew what was coming. They were going to use him, to drag him into this as a field operative.

'What do you want me to do? Remember I've been out of it for a long time so don't expect too much.'

'You'll be OK, Yuri, or do you prefer Charlie now?'

'Let's stick to Charlie, I've got used to it.'

'You want Costello dead, so do we. A perfect communion of interests. We'll kill him for you, but you'll have to help.'

'If you kill him it won't be for me. I'm not stupid, I saw in Hamburg you had your own reasons for this and they're nothing to do with Costello trying to kill me.'

'Does it matter? You want him off your back and we'll see that it happens.'

She's right, thought Charlie, *why Costello dies doesn't matter so long as he dies*.

'So, what do I do?'

'Beater and gun, you'll be the beater. You drive him onto my gun.'

'Where?'

'Not Denmark. Make him run. The Balkans would be ideal for us.'

Charlie gave a sharp laugh. 'The Balkans? Why not Manhattan or Paris, for God's sake? What do you think I am – a sheepdog who doubles as a hypnotist?'

She didn't mind the outburst. He was just letting off a little steam before he settled down to work.

'I said the Balkans would be good for us, I didn't mean you had to get him there. Just get him where a killing like this won't raise too many eyebrows.'

'Like where?'

'Anywhere that used to be in the East would do, although the Balkans ...'

'I know, you already said; they'd be good for you.'

She could see that he was settling, getting used to the idea of going back to work. He went to the settee and sat down. Now she could get the details fixed.

'How long will you need to get him on the move?'

Charlie gave a half-shrug and spread his hands.

'That depends on him. If he scares easy, maybe a week. If

134

not, then how long is a piece of string?'

'Come on, Yuri, I've …' He looked at her. 'Sorry. Charlie. I'll try and remember. You've done this, or had it done, plenty of times.'

'Sure, I've done it, but this time it will be just me on my own, so it won't be easy. And remember, he's supposed to be the one after me, not the other way round, and if he's trained he won't be made to run easily and he won't run straight.'

'Do they ever?'

'It's not a solo job. Even with a team it wouldn't be easy; he's not an agent operating in enemy territory. How do you expect me to get him to run? Do I creep up behind him and say "boo"?'

'Don't worry, he'll run. Just make him think some friends of his have turned up. Friends he's not keen to talk to.'

'Are these friends likely to?'

'No.'

'Would it be a problem if they did?'

'Oh, yes.'

He wasn't interested in why the Brits wanted Costello dead. But he *was* interested in how dangerous this operation could get.

'Is there anything I should know, about Costello, or about anything else? It's bad enough working on my own, I don't want there to be any nasty surprises along the way, like these friends turning up.'

'There'll be no problems. Trust me.'

His face showed nothing but inside he laughed. *Trust her*! Or maybe it was British irony, maybe she was laughing at him.

'How long have I got?'

'I can give you a week at the outside.'

'A week! What am I supposed to do in a week, working on my own? I'll need more time than that, I'll need more information. I need to know what sort of target he will be.'

'He's flagged, he's a target, he's already on the run. Juice him and he'll run all right.' But Charlie didn't look convinced. 'We know of two agencies that are after him. We think he's a freelance, no permanent hook-up to anyone. Last job we know of was in Rome. If he *is* a freelance, maybe someone's paid him to come here and get you. Do this right and you could be doing both of us a favour.' She wanted Yuri fully committed to the job. Costello as a hit man and him as the target would be a great incentive. 'Just make him think the people who are looking for him know where he is, and he'll run.'

It was enough.

'OK, I'll try to get him moving.'

'Keep an eye on him, he may surprise you.'

'Surprise me, how?'

'He may run faster than you think. Sit on him tight – don't, whatever you do, let him get past you and get running before you're ready.'

Charlie didn't like it. What was she trying to say?

'Look, I'll say it again, if we're together in this I need to know what you know.'

'No you don't, Yuri, you need to do what you've been told and that's *all* you need.'

He didn't bother to correct her this time. 'So how do I contact you?'

She took a mobile out of her handbag and threw it to him.

'If there's a call it will be me. It's set for only one number, so when you call that will also be me. It's got a special battery, so it will last about twice as long as a normal one but for God's sake don't let it run down to where it might cause a problem. It needs a special charger. I'll need two reports daily, midday and around ten. Always call in. Never miss a call. An hour each way will be OK.' She stood up. 'Are they watching you?'

'I assume so. Since I did my little flit to Hamburg I have to assume I'm watched.'

'If anyone asks, I'm a freelance reporter from the UK. I got a whisper that the gas bottle explosion was really a car bomb. I came, you said it was a gas cylinder. Sorry, no story. I left.' She pulled a business card out of her handbag and flicked it to him. Sonia Krasko, journalist. He liked the name, it was a nice touch. English reporters with names like that sounded genuine. 'OK?'

'Sure, Henry. I still call you Henry?'

'You still call me whatever you like but Henry will do.

Phone me at ten.'

'Where will you be?'

'On the other end of that mobile. Call in tonight.'

'What do you expect me to have to say by ten tonight?'

'You'll think of something, Charlie. I'm sure you'll think of something.'

And she left. He went back to the window and watched her walk down the garden and turn right along the path.

About ten minutes after she left, there was a ring at the doorbell. It was the Comedian but he wasn't trying to be funny. He didn't ask to come in, he just walked past Charlie and went into the living room. When Charlie joined him he was standing waiting.

'You had a visitor. Who was she?'

The delivery was curt. It looked like the games were over, at least for the time being.

'A reporter from the UK, a freelance she said. It looks like there might have been a leak and not from any gas cylinder.'

'A leak?'

'She said she'd had a tip that it wasn't a gas bottle, that it was a bomb.' The Comedian went and sat on the chair at the desk, Charlie sat down on the settee. 'As me and Elspeth haven't told anyone I think we must assume that your side of things is where the information came from.'

'Did she give you anything?'

'A business card. It's on the desk.'

The Comedian turned, picked it up and looked at it. 'May I?'

'Feel free, I don't need it.'

And the Comedian pocketed the card. 'So you told her what?'

'That her information was wrong. It was a leaking gas cylinder and it went bang.'

'And she was satisfied?'

'Apparently. She asked me a few more questions, nothing in particular. What had the police said, how did I feel, was my wife OK? The interview sort of petered out and, when she accepted there was no story, she left.'

'In and out through the back door? Do your unexpected

visitors usually come to your back door?'

'No, but she wasn't unexpected. She phoned from the path by the beach and asked if she could talk to me about the explosion. I said there was nothing to tell but come in anyway. I would leave the back door open. She said I was lucky to live in such a nice place. She'd walked up to the house along the beach. She liked it here.'

The Comedian got up.

'I don't envy you, Mr Bronski.'

'Sorry?'

'I said I don't envy you. You are playing a game where the rules will change and change until someone gets hurt, perhaps even killed. At the moment, my money's on you. But I'll wait and see. As I said, things change.'

'I'm sorry, I don't know what you're talking about. What game?'

'A game people play, people who tell themselves that ends justify means. I will give you a piece of free advice to use in your game, perhaps you could pass it on.'

'Pass it on to whom, exactly?'

'The reporter, the friend you met in Hamburg, whoever put the bomb in your car. Perhaps even Fr Mundt and Mr Costello. Whoever else is involved.'

'And the advice is?'

'We don't play those sort of games in Denmark and we don't allow others to play them here. Take your playmates elsewhere, Mr Bronski, or you will all regret it.'

'I don't have the vaguest idea what you are talking about but I get the impression that you have just threatened me.'

'Yes indeed, Mr Bronski, a clear and very direct threat. As your reporter pointed out, you live very nicely here in Nyborg. Unless you and your friends move to another location to get your business done you will not live here for very much longer, nicely or otherwise. Please see that my advice is circulated amongst all interested parties. Good day.'

And he left.

Charlie sat for a moment and thought about his last visitor and the advice he had given. He didn't like it. The Comedian could make things difficult. He went and made himself a drink, straight whisky, and sat down again. He would get Costello on the move. The Comedian's advice was sound and timely, especially about what might happen to him. He was under no delusions about what happened to the last man standing when the music stopped. He had tied up too many loose ends himself to have any doubts about what was waiting for him. But he would be ready for it. He took a long drink. If it was going to be done, get it out of Denmark and get it done quickly, not because she told him to, but to keep the Comedian out of things. He had the Comedian tagged as someone who delivered on his promises, and his threats.

Charlie began to plan how Mr James Costello, supposed apprentice priest, probable freelance hit man, could be persuaded to walk into a bullet somewhere other than Denmark, preferably the Balkans, because they were 'good for us'.

SEVENTEEN

'You have everything?'

Jimmy looked down at the black holdall.

'I seem to have bugger all, but I suppose I've got all I really need.'

'You have euros for when you're out of Denmark?'

'Don't worry, I have everything.'

Udo gave him an encouraging grin. He liked Jimmy, he would miss him. They were alike in many ways, both lost souls trying to find their way to a God neither of them was sure existed. They both understood wickedness more than goodness, both were lonely and exiled. Had the circumstances been other than they were, they might have become friends. As it was, if Jimmy was going to run it was time for him to start.

'You remember what to do when you get to Lübeck and you have the number to call when you get close?'

'I remember and I've got the number.'

'You have the address as well? You have everything I gave you?'

'Udo, I'm not a kid. I remember what you told me. I know what to do.'

'Of course. I'm just nervous, that's all. It's been a few years since I was involved in anything like this. What time's your train?'

'The same time it was last time you asked.' Udo fell silent. It was questions for the sake of questions. He knew Jimmy was as ready as he'd ever be. 'What will you do when they come and ask about me?'

'Tell them the truth. You went out in the morning, you didn't come back. I have no idea what's going on.'

'That's the truth.'

'It's true enough. Do you really know what's going on? Do either of us?'

Jimmy smiled. He liked it.

'Very Jesuitical, not a lie but not quite the truth either. A sort of grey area of honest dishonesty.'

'All areas of life are grey, except to saints or fanatics. You're not a fanatic, are you, Jimmy?'

'Only if you're a saint.'

They both laughed and then shook hands.

'Take care, Udo. I'd have liked to stay. I'm really sorry it didn't work out.'

'So am I. I think we could have got on together. Is there anything else I can do?'

'Yes, one thing. Let Professor McBride know.'

'Know?'

'Everything. Maybe she won't be interested but I think she ought to be told. Can you do that?'

'Sure. I'll pass on the message through her tame Monsignor. Well goodbye, my friend, and remember, *Gott mit uns*.'

'Whose mittens?'

Udo laughed loudly and spontaneously then slapped Jimmy on the back.

'They're God's mittens, and it means we can't lose because we've got God's mittens on our side.'

Jimmy shook his head. Udo could be a strange bloke. 'Whatever. See you. Take care.'

Jimmy left and Udo spoke to the empty air.

'God with us, Jimmy. If he exists, which I sometimes doubt. But I hope you do exist, God, because I think we're going to need you.'

Her mobile rang. It was Charlie.

'Yes?' She checked her watch, it was just before ten thirty in the morning.

'Things have started.'

'Explain.'

'He's on the train and it's just pulled out of Nyborg.'

'What! You can't have got him on the move since yesterday.'

'It's nothing to do with me. I came to Copenhagen to watch him, get some idea of his movements. It was pure chance I was watching when he left the house.'

'What the hell's he doing on a train?'

'Travelling west towards Jutland, I don't know where to. I bought a ticket to Aarhus. The train finishes there.'

'Why do you think he's moving?'

'He's running, that would be my guess. If he thinks I'm on to him and that the police and Danish Intelligence have connected him to the car bomb, he would reckon it's only a matter of time before he gets picked up. He might even think that the friends you mentioned could get wind of where he is and turn up. Whatever the reason, he's on the move and moving fast.'

'Any guess where he's heading?'

'He could be making for an airport. There's one at Aarhus, another at Esbjerg. Or he could be making for Billund. Billund would be my bet.'

'Why Billund?'

'Because it's a tourist airport. It's near Legoland. One more Brit wouldn't be noticed.'

Henry Clarke-Phillips ran over it again. 'You sound very sure. Why do you think he's running?'

'Because before he got on this train he bought a ticket to Hamburg and he did it in a way that would get remembered. Fussed with his money, asked questions, made himself memorable. But he didn't get on the Hamburg train. Like I said, he headed west. I waited till Nyborg, there was an outside chance he had business there. He didn't, so I've called in. I thought you'd want to know.'

'Too damn right I wanted to know. Go on.'

'He's carrying a small holdall, travelling light and fast. He's running all right and I'd say he's good at it. He must have had practice.'

'Damn.'

Charlie waited but after a couple of seconds he pressed on. She was the one who warned him to be careful of the battery.

'What do you want me to do?'

'Give me a minute.'

He gave her another few seconds then he carried on again.

'If he picks up a plane to the UK I can hardly follow and do him there. I need instructions if we're going to do anything before he gets anywhere near an airport.'

Somebody had to make a decision and it was a big one. 'Keep an eye on him. I'll get back to you.'

She ended the call. Charlie put away his phone, pressed the flush and went back from the toilet into his carriage.

Henry Clarke-Phillips dialled a number. The direct line in London rang and the man answered it.

'Yes?'

'Costello is on the move.'

'Good. That was quick work. Where are you driving him?'

'We're not. He's running. He's on a train heading west towards Jutland. Once he's on Jutland he's got a choice of three airports.'

'You blew it! For God's sake, you bloody well –'

'Shut up.'

The sudden sharpness of the words silenced him. People who worked for him didn't tell him to shut up. But she went on before he could respond.

'It's not us. I don't know why he's running but it's not us. He's heading west, we think to an airport. Aarhus, Esjberg or Billund. And before you ask, Billund is near Legoland. Lots of Brit tourists in and out.'

He decided to forget the 'shut up'.

'Do you think the police have spooked him?'

'How should I know? If it was the police, that makes it worse for us. If they spooked him they may be watching him. If they are, they'll know he's on the move and can have airports watched. Do we want him picked up by the police?'

'Very funny.'

'All right, not picked up by the police. So someone has to make a decision.' There was a moment's silence. She had said the forbidden words. *He* must make a decision. He couldn't delegate it and he couldn't take it upstairs.

The silence went on.

'Hello, anybody there?'

'Don't try and be funny. I'm thinking. This is tricky.'

And she knew exactly what he was thinking. How to shift the blame? At the first little hint of trouble, his self-preservation instincts kicked in and took over. He finally spoke.

'If he gets on a plane for the UK we're in the shit. Either he'll get picked up at the airport, or get through and then go to ground. Both ways we lose him. What do you suggest?'

Oh great, she thought, *if I give him a way out and it works it will become his idea and if it doesn't he gets ready to make me the whipping boy.* But if they lost Costello or let him get taken by the wrong people, there would be enough shit coming from the fan to bury both of them and have plenty left over. Her best hope was to come up with something. Either that, or maybe find herself cast as a rogue agent acting alone, someone who set up a private party and organised it so she would get all the glory – except there turned out to be no glory.

'Can we do it in Denmark? Before he reaches the airport.'

'No, definitely not. Not Denmark.'

'OK, how about Bronski shows himself and tries to drive him away from where he can catch a plane?'

'That's no good. If he sees Bronski he might do anything, he might even call the police himself. Then where would we be? I wanted him to feel threatened, frightened. I wanted him to behave like a blown agent and run while we were in control. I didn't want him to just pack a bag and set off to God knows where.'

'So what do you want me to do? We need a decision. Can we call it off? Can we still salvage something by giving him to Mossad or the CIA?'

Silence. She could almost feel his nasty little mind turning, finding a way to get something for himself out of this instead of trying to come up with some sort of field decision.

'Make sure Bronski sits on him, stays out of sight and calls in hourly or at once if anything happens. I'll get back to you.'

He ended the call, then dialled.

'Candice, there's been a development. How far have you got at your end?'

Her answer was not good news. He forced enthusiasm into his voice.

'Good, that's great, everything's in place?'

Damn, she's all set, no changing anything now.

'The development? Oh, Costello is on the move, we've begun driving him. It's going like clockwork. We arranged it so he thought your people or Mossad had him located him and he ran, just like I told you he would.'

Christ, she's congratulating me.

'Yes, thanks, I know it was quick but why wait? The way I look at it, if we're going to get it done, let's get it done, especially as I knew you'd have everything ready at your end. I was sure you'd be efficient, as always.'

God damn and blast the bloody woman.

'You're sure you're ready?'

He tried a casual laugh but it petered out.

'Well, it looks like we're off. Thanks, I'll be in touch.' He put the phone down. 'Shit, shit, shit.'

She had set up her end, so they couldn't cancel now. Somehow it had to go through. *But how?* He tried to think of something, but field operations weren't anything he had much experience of, just enough to get him his desk, and all long ago now. How the hell to get Costello where he wanted him? No, not wanted him any more – needed him. What the hell to do? The irony of the thing was, there were half a dozen people in the building he could have asked who would have come up with any number of good ways to get it done. And he couldn't talk to any of them. He had to be Control on this one all by himself. Why in God's name had he started the whole thing?

He pressed a button. The door opened and his secretary

came in.

'Yes, sir?'

'Get me a couple of aspirin will you, Gloria. I feel a headache coming on.'

'Certainly, I have some in my desk.'

The secretary left.

He got up, went to a cabinet, opened it and poured himself a stiff Jack Daniels, then went back to his desk and sat down. Gloria returned and handed him the two tablets.

'No calls, no interruptions. If anything comes from upstairs, I'm out.'

'Very good, sir.'

She left, closing the door quietly behind her. She went back to her desk and checked how many aspirins she had left. He didn't often have headaches; usually they started when he thought he'd ballsed something up. Four left. If this was going to turn into a big balls-up she would probably need another packet. She'd get one when she went to lunch.

He took the aspirin and washed them down with a big pull at the whisky then got back to the problem in hand. He felt the incipient pain in his head begin to come alive. It was going to be a bad one, he could feel it building already. *Thank God for Gloria's aspirin*. But he would have to be careful.

He mustn't let her see that he was worried. He mustn't let anyone see.

And he returned to the problem of keeping Costello away from any of the airports.

Jimmy looked out of the window. He was still vaguely surprised at Denmark. When he had received the letter saying his placement was in Copenhagen his first thoughts had been of snow and fjords, a land of semi-permanent winter. He had lumped Denmark with all the things his ignorance associated with Scandinavian countries. Looking out of the train at the countryside he could have been in any rural English county. He watched as fields, hedges and small patches of woodland passed by.

Copenhagen hadn't been a surprise to him. It was European,

different, foreign, full of places for the tourists. He didn't like or dislike it. He felt about Copenhagen much as he felt about Southwark: different from Kilburn where he'd been born and brought up, but not that different.

But Copenhagen wasn't Denmark. The real Denmark was more like Nyborg, clean and well-looked after but with history and character. It would have been nice to have travelled, seen more places like Nyborg. He decided he liked Denmark and was sorry to be leaving. And that brought his thoughts back to what was happening.

How long would it take for anyone to notice he had left? Maybe a couple of days, maybe longer. He wasn't important to anyone in Copenhagen and as for that bloke Bronski, he'd somehow got his wires crossed. God knows how. But once he was gone, and stayed gone, Bronski would probably forget about him, especially if whoever fitted up his car had another go. He was pretty sure he'd seen the last of Bronski. And the police wouldn't think he was worth following, unless the Danish police had a damn sight more money to waste than the Met ever had.

Now he was leaving it all behind him he could put it into perspective. He had been in the wrong place at the wrong time and on the edge of something that was nothing to do with him. These things happened. Not often. But they happened. The important thing was not to let them get out of all proportion. If you're in the wrong place, go to some other place. He didn't think all that Hamburg ticket nonsense was needed but he'd done it like Udo had suggested. Enough fuss so he'd be remembered if anyone asked the ticket seller. But no one was going to come looking for him, no one that mattered anyway.

They passed a field. A fox was crossing it without a care in the world, heading for a small copse at the far end.

So this was cloak and dagger, was it? This was what Special Branch and the secret boys got up to, how to play hide-and-seek from the bad guys. It had sounded all very professional when Udo had told him, but now it didn't seem so very much. You just got on a train and headed off in the opposite direction from the one they expected you to take. No tail, no last-minute dash

148

from the shadows, no car chases. Not like the films or TV at all, really. Just get on a train and off you go. Still, he wasn't complaining. Keep it simple, keep it safe. *Who knows*, he thought, *maybe I'll get where I'm going, maybe I'll even make it all the way to somewhere*. Not that he cared. But he wasn't making it easy for them. He was just a bit surprised at how bloody easy it was to make it hard.

Jimmy looked out of the window again then at his watch. About an hour to Fredericia and the change of trains. Then south to Germany. Once he was out of Denmark he would be safe, for the time being anyway. Jimmy settled down to empty his mind and think of nothing. To forget Bronski, Udo, the police and everything else. And, as Denmark's clean and efficient rail service hurried Jimmy west, every half hour, in another carriage, a call got made.

'No change.'

Until the train pulled into Fredericia and Jimmy got off and bought a ticket to Hamburg. Then the call was made and the message was – all change.

In an office in London another whisky was poured and this time no more aspirins were needed. Costello was headed south, not to any airport. The man holding the glass smiled to himself. He'd toughed it out, kept his nerve. He'd been a true professional and he'd made it. Take your chance when it comes and see it through. Bold, incisive and clever. What was it they said? Cream and bastards always rise. The glass was held up in a salute and the man almost shouted, 'To cream and bastards.'

The door opened.

'Did you call, sir? Do you want another aspirin?'

'No, Gloria. My headache's gone. I'm fine.'

Gloria closed the door and went back to her desk. She was glad he felt better; he was an even bigger pain in the tits than usual when he had one of his headaches. Somebody must have sorted it out for him, whatever it was, and things were back to normal. She was pleased. She liked it when things were going well and everything was normal.

EIGHTEEN

'How should *I* know? I didn't even know he was going to run.'

What did the silly bugger think she was, a clairvoyant or a field agent? Maybe he expected her to be both, seeing as how he already expected 'one hundred and ten per cent'. Henry Clarke-Phillips sat on her bed beside her open suitcase and waited until London had worked out his next duff question.

'The ticket he bought at Fredericia was for Hamburg, yes?'

It was Bronski who answered. The three were on a conference call. She listened as Bronski explained.

Yes, Costello had bought a ticket to Hamburg, but he had also bought a ticket to Hamburg at *Copenhagen*. Buying a ticket to Hamburg didn't mean he was going to Hamburg. It only meant that he was, at the moment, headed in that direction. He might get off before then and head somewhere else.

There was silence. London was thinking. For Clarke-Phillips that was a bad sign. Once she let him start thinking, they could be on this bloody call all day. Decision-making wasn't his strong point, except in committees. Then he could make the decision fast enough. As soon as he spotted who was going to be the winner, he'd make the decision to be on that side. And this was a field decision, people's lives could depend on it. That was why she had to be careful. If he knew lives were on the line she could be on this conference call long enough for Costello to die of old age. She moved things on.

'What if he gets into Germany and heads west? What do you want me to do if he goes west? Do we do anything?' It got the response she expected. Not yet. More delay, never make a decision now if you can put it off till later.

'OK, what if he goes east?' This time he surprised her. He made a decision.

'Is that a definite yes? Once he's in the old East Germany we pick a spot and it gets done?'

He confirmed. So, she had her decision. But only if Costello went east into what had been the old German Democratic Republic. *Please God, make Costello go east so we can finish this and I can go home.* 'Did you get that, Bronski? Good. Well, pray he goes east. Until we know which way he's going, sit tight. Once you know which direction let me know. I'll head for Hamburg. No, by train; I want us to stay in contact. Keep phoning in every half hour.'

She ended the call, put away the mobile and picked up the hotel phone on the bedside table.

'Reception? Make up my bill, please. I will be leaving almost at once. And get me a taxi for the station.'

Then she began packing. Maybe this would work out after all.

Jimmy had never been an enthusiastic traveller and never developed any interest in foreign parts. Eastbourne on the south coast for a week with the wife and kids had been the limit, literally and metaphorically, of his horizon. He had expected to live and die in North London. And die he very nearly did, with the result that he had become an exile, forced to travel by circumstances then, just as he was being forced to now.

He left the train at Padborg station, as Udo had told him to. It didn't look much of a place. On one side there was nothing except big, squat, industrial sheds and on the other side what he could see of a small town. The train had passed a fair amount of tracks coming into the station where lines of containers loaded onto rolling stock were waiting to be hooked up to engines. It was obviously more a transit yard for freight than a busy passenger station.

Another train was already in and waiting. Jimmy got a sinking feeling that it was the train he wanted and if he didn't find out quick, he'd miss it. He looked around for directions to the ticket office.

Behind him the Hamburg train pulled out. He hurried down the platform to where a man in uniform stood watching the Hamburg train depart.

Jimmy held out a piece of paper Udo had given him. It asked for a single, second-class ticket for Bad Oldesloe.

The official looked at it then said something in Danish that Jimmy didn't understand. Jimmy looked at him blankly. The man tried again in German. It went over Jimmy's head again. The man took Jimmy's arm.

'*Kom, schnell.*'

He led Jimmy across to the other platform where the train was waiting.

Jimmy looked at it. 'This one?'

The man pointed to his piece of paper. 'Bad Oldesloe. *Ja.*' Then indicated by a sort of pushing gesture for Jimmy to get on. '*Schnell.*'

'Thanks.'

'*Bitte.*'

Jimmy got on the train, moved down into a carriage and found a seat. The train wasn't busy. He looked out of the window at the official who smiled at him.

Jimmy smiled back and gave a small wave. Then the train began to move.

Bloody hell, thought Jimmy, *that was close*. Obviously it was a connection, one waiting for the other to arrive. Thank God it was like Udo had said, nice and friendly. But not so slow; quick enough for him to have made it. He sat back as the train gathered speed. Almost at once, a sign by the trackside told him that he was no longer in Denmark. He had just crossed into Germany. Change at Neumünster, Udo had said. *Please God there's somebody just as helpful there. I'll spend the rest of my life on trains trying to get to bloody Lübeck if I have to do it on my own*. Then he sat back and watched the flat north German

153

farmland go past.

Two carriages behind, Charlie also sat by a window looking at the countryside go past. It was good and bad. Bad that Costello had jumped train at Padborg because there was nowhere on that station to give him cover. Good because Costello had got straight onto this train so he hadn't needed cover. Bad because Costello might decide to take a walk and stretch his legs and there was nowhere to go to avoid him if he came through the carriage. Good because it meant Costello was heading east. It was good and bad and might go either way. If Costello sat tight until he got to where he was going, it was good. If he got restless, it was bad and might get worse.

He took out his mobile.

'He's changed trains at Padborg on the German-Danish border and it's looking good, he's heading east. I just follow him, yes? OK. Where are you now? I see – if we're lucky, by the time you're in Hamburg we'll know where he's heading. One more thing, we're stuck on this train together. If Costello sees me, what do you want me to do?'

He put the mobile back in his pocket and thought about what Clarke-Phillips had said.

Don't let him bloody well see you.

What sort of fucking answer was that? Shit, he hated working with people who couldn't, or wouldn't, make a quick field decision, people who always needed to check. What was he supposed to say to Costello if he walked into the carriage – 'go back and wait, I haven't been told what to do yet if we bump into each other'? So Charlie sat back, trying to decide what to do if Costello came. But he had the same problem as Clarke-Phillips; what the hell *could* he do? In the end, he decided that, as there were four carriages between him and where Costello had boarded, and nothing to bring him this far back, maybe no decision was needed after all.

Jimmy watched the flat, uninteresting fields go by. The weather had turned steadily greyer and a thin mist had settled over the landscape. He looked at his watch. *How long to Neumünster*, he wondered? As if in answer to his question, the ticket collector came into the carriage. Jimmy waited until she reached him then showed her his piece of paper. She took it and, after a brief glance, handed it back.

'A single to Bad Oldesloe, yes?'

'You speak English?'

'Yes.'

'Thank God.'

'You wish a single, second-class ticket to Bad Oldesloe, yes? That is what your piece of paper says.'

'No, I've changed my mind.' He knew he was on the right train now, so the Bad Oldesloe thing didn't matter any more. 'Lübeck, I want to go to Lübeck.'

'You must change at Neumünster and Bad Oldesloe.'

'I know.'

She fiddled with her machine, produced a ticket and handed it to him, then told him the fare. He paid it and put away the ticket.

'What platform at Neumünster?'

'We arrive on platform five and you go to platform one.'

Do it all, he thought, *while you've got the chance.* 'What time does my train leave platform one?'

She went back to her machine.

'We arrive at thirteen twenty-one and your train leaves at thirteen thirty-seven.'

'Thanks.'

The ticket collector moved on.

So far, so good. In fact, so far, so bloody good.

Jimmy sat back and closed his eyes. He wouldn't sleep, he knew that, his mind wouldn't let him, but at least he could rest. He'd been travelling since around half past seven and it was now noon. There had been nearly an hour's wait for the right Hamburg train when he had arrived at Fredericia at nine fifteen so he'd had time to pick up a good breakfast.

What had the ticket collector said? We arrive just after twenty past and the Bad Oldesloe train goes just before twenty to.

Jimmy let his mind wander. He'd get something at the next stop, maybe a coffee or a beer. Maybe even a sandwich to keep

155

him going. A beer, he'd get a beer. If he was in Germany he might as well try their beer. Everybody reckoned the Germans knew their beer. Jimmy let his mind wander through pubs he'd known, beers he'd drunk and villains he'd drunk with. All very long ago.

The train pulled into Neumünster two minutes early. Jimmy got off and looked around for signs to the other platforms. Then looked again. Up the platform he thought he had seen a face, but it wasn't there now. It must have been his imagination. He was imagining things. He walked towards the sign which showed a figure descending stairs and left the platform in search of a bar and platform one.

Up the platform, Charlie Bronski slowly emerged and followed where Jimmy had gone.

I'm too old and too out of practice, he thought. *I'm careless, and even on a job like this that could be dangerous*. Still, now he was sure Costello was heading east he felt better. Once Clarke-Phillips arrived in Hamburg and Costello settled down somewhere, the thing could be done and he could go back to Nyborg. Elspeth would come home, he would get back to his writing and things would be normal again. A thought popped into his head: *East Germany in an English Kitchen*. Would it work? There was plenty of nostalgia for the old Cold War. He'd think about it. He got to the top of the stairs and looked down. It was clear. He went down to road level and looked both ways. There was no sign of Costello but he could see a sign for the bar down to his right under the elevated platforms. He walked towards it to check. Yes. Costello was in there buying a drink. Bronski walked away a little distance and waited just around a corner. Jimmy came out carrying his holdall in one hand and a bottle with a plastic cup resting over it in the other. He walked away from the bar to the first stairway and went up. Charlie waited, then followed.

The train was in and the platform was clear. Bronski went onto the adjacent platform and walked past a building which screened him from the waiting train. He then crossed back, walked up to the first carriage and got on.

Jimmy stepped out from behind the wall of the staircase and

looked to where Bronski had boarded. *So, not imagination, after all.* Bronski had come for him like Udo thought he would. He crossed the platform and got on the train. He threw his holdall onto a seat, sat down next to it and put his bottle of beer onto the table in front of him.

How the hell had Bronski managed to follow him? He shook his head. It didn't matter, what mattered was that he *had* followed him.

He had told Udo that he wouldn't fight the others if they came. What he hadn't told him was that he wouldn't get the chance to fight, because even if he saw them coming they were out of his league, and he knew it. If they found him he was dead. But Bronski was different, and he had seen Bronski coming. He would fight this one. Yes indeed. He wouldn't sit still for that bastard, whoever he was.

The train began to move. Jimmy lifted the plastic cup off the bottle, from which the top had been removed, poured some beer and took a drink. It was fine, it had a taste and it wasn't too cold. He sat back, took another drink and watched the town slip by. He gave his mind up to Bronski. He'd need a gun. Maybe Udo's friends could get one for him. Jimmy's eyes were looking out of the window but his mind was elsewhere. In his mind he was working out the best way to kill Charlie Bronski.

The train began to slow. Neumünster hadn't looked much of a place, not around the station anyway, but Bad Oldesloe looked quite attractive with plenty of trees and open spaces. Not that it mattered, as he would only be there for fifteen minutes and go from one platform to another. Unless there was a bar where he could get another beer.

A few minutes later the train pulled into the station and stopped. There wasn't much of a crowd waiting to get on and not many people got off but he didn't bother to look for Bronski. Bronski was there, somewhere. Jimmy walked over to a uniformed official and showed him his ticket to Lübeck.

'Which platform?'

The official looked at the ticket and held up his hand showing all five fingers.

'Five?'

The official nodded. '*Fünf*.' Then pointed.

Jimmy followed his direction to the staircase that led down from the platforms to street level. He walked along under the platforms and went up the stairs to where a sign told him platform five was located. He hadn't seen a bar anywhere, so he stood and waited.

The train finally pulled in and Jimmy got on, found himself a seat and waited until the last leg of his journey began. He smiled to himself. Somewhere on the train Bronski was sitting, still not knowing where he was going to finish up. If he hadn't been able to get something to eat or drink he must be feeling like shit. At least on the trains he should have been able to get to the toilet, or maybe he hadn't dared risk even that. Jimmy's smile turned into a grin. Udo said the blokes who would be looking after him could get whatever he wanted. Now he knew what he wanted. He would need a new set of papers, but the first thing he would ask them for was a gun.

NINETEEN

After an hour and a quarter the train arrived on the outskirts of
Lübeck and Jimmy made a call to the number Udo had given
him.

'Costello. I'm on my way in.'

No one at the other end had spoken. The phone had just gone
dead.

Lübeck station was a big place and busy. Jimmy left the
train. He knew Bronski was behind him somewhere but there
was nothing he could do about that yet, so he followed the signs
that took him out to the taxi rank. He showed the driver of the
first taxi a slip of paper with an address Udo had written on it.
The driver nodded. Jimmy got in and the taxi pulled away.

The address wasn't that far from the station, a side street of
run-down terraced houses among several side streets of run-
down terraces. The taxi stopped, the driver turned and said
something, then pointed. This was it.

Jimmy got out of the taxi, paid and watched it go, then
looked up and down the street. He wasn't looking for anyone,
he was just looking. He hadn't thought about what to expect but
he wished Udo's friend had had a better address. He went to the
door and rang the bell. It was opened by a dumpy old woman
who wheezed and looked at him without interest.

'I was told to come here. You are expecting me. I phoned.'

Nothing.

'Udo Mundt sent me.'

The woman wheezed on and still looked at him but now with a mixture of curiosity and fear. Obviously she had no idea what he was talking about and Jimmy had no idea what to do next. Then she said something in rapid German. Jimmy didn't speak any German but he didn't need to, he got the gist. Who are you? What do you want?

He didn't think it would do any good but he tried again anyway.

'Udo Mundt sent me.'

He held out the piece of paper. She took it, read it and then looked at him. Now she was confused and frightened; it must be the right address. She shoved the paper back at him and the rapid German began again, this time with gestures. Once more Jimmy didn't need an interpreter. I know nothing of this, go away, this is a respectable house. Go away or I will call the police.

Jimmy turned away and the door banged shut behind him. He walked up the street a short way then he stopped. He was alone in a city he didn't know with somebody following him who probably wanted him dead and he had no idea what to do or where to go. What the hell had Udo been playing at?

A black Mercedes pulled up beside him with the window down. The driver leaned across.

'Please get in, Mr Costello.' Jimmy didn't move. 'Udo Mundt sent me to meet you. He told me you were coming. That I should meet you at this address. I got the call you made, so I knew you were arriving.' Jimmy got in and the car pulled away. 'A little precaution, you understand. Udo was sure you would not give anyone the address but, well, things happen that one cannot foresee. If anyone got that address from you, it wouldn't take them anywhere. We have to be careful. You come from Udo, so of course we trust you, but still it is wise to be careful, yes?'

Jimmy nodded. Yes, it was wise to be careful.

The car pulled out of the side street and made a left turn. 'Where are we going?'

'If I told you, would it mean anything?'

'No. I was only making conversation.'

The driver laughed, he seemed a happy sort of bloke. 'We are going across the river to Hansestadt. You'll like it there, a lively place, lots going on, plenty of bars. You like beer?'

'Yes, I like beer.'

'Good, we'll go to a bar and talk. We have to talk. There is much to arrange.'

'Yes, and first on that list is the how much?'

The driver didn't laugh. He thought about it. Then he laughed because he'd worked it out.

'The how much? That is good, very good. An English joke. We will have a few beers and arrange the how much?' The voice became serious. 'Udo told you it would cost, that it would not be cheap.'

'He told me you were his friends.'

'Of course. We are very much Udo's friends. But even for friends …' He took a hand off the wheel and rubbed the tips of his fingers together. 'Nothing is free. There will be expenses, we all have to make a living. Not everyone can walk away from life and become a priest like Udo.' The laughter came back. 'The world needs its sinners. After all, if there were no sinners then the likes of Udo would go out of business, yes?'

They came to a junction where they made another left on to a busy main road. The run-down terraces were gone now and shops and offices lined the road.

'Udo isn't worrying, the supply of sinners was holding up pretty well last time he looked.'

The driver laughed again.

'Yes, plenty of sinners, always plenty of sinners making a living, keeping the Udos and the police in work. So the world goes, my friend, as you well know, I can see.'

Yes, thought Jimmy, *as I well know*. He looked at the driver, not big-built but tall, over six feet. Then he looked at the Merc. It was expensive and well-turned out just like the driver. Jimmy didn't know much about fashion but he could tell an expensive suit when he saw one, and the one the driver was wearing was very expensive. This bloke made a living from his sins all right, a good living. But it didn't matter. If you paid, you got the service; the more you paid, the better the service.

The main road went round a big traffic island and over a bridge across a river. Facing them was a long, formal park – at the far end was some sort of fortress made up of two massive, round towers. Between the towers and connecting them was an archway with two elaborate storeys above it. Each tower was topped off by a huge black cone. It was very impressive but to Jimmy it looked like something from Disneyland.

'The Holstentor, the Holsten Gate, very famous, very wonderful.'

'Sure, wonderful. I'll need a gun.'

It didn't even get a glance. It was as if he'd asked for a cigarette.

'Do you have any preference?'

'Preference?'

'Automatic, revolver, calibre? Will you need a silencer, special ammunition?'

'Just a gun. Something to stop somebody with.'

That got a glance.

'You are good with a gun?'

'I've never used one in my life. When you get it you'll have to show me how it works.' Jimmy looked at him. They both accepted that a number of lies would get told by each of them. But only small lies, ones that didn't really matter. 'I'll pay for the lesson, of course.'

That got a genuine laugh – Jimmy could tell the difference. The car crossed another bridge over another river or the same river that had found a different way round. Once over the bridge, the Mercedes turned right and drove along the riverside. The buildings facing the river were of a style Jimmy liked but didn't know, several storeys high with big windows and stepped gables at the top, some gables curly-wurly and decorated, some severely plain. The curly-wurly-topped frontages were painted, mostly white, the plain ones had been left red brick, but all had been built when there was plenty of old money and were well kept up now because there was plenty of new money. Somehow, he thought of them as Dutch, not German, but then,

162

what the hell did he know about architecture? *Lübeck seems a nice place*, thought Jimmy, *just like Udo said*.

'I like you, Jimmy. I may call you Jimmy?' Jimmy nodded. 'I like you. You make me laugh. When we get to the bar I will tell you how much to look after you. How much for the gun,' he laughed again, 'and of course how much for the lesson.' Jimmy looked past the driver at the riverside, all expensive and well turned out like him. He liked it and he decided he liked the driver. They would get along. 'And for you, we'll make it all a special price.'

Jimmy laughed, he felt it was expected. 'I don't mind paying the going rate.'

'Of course you don't. Udo said you could pay. But if I didn't make a special rate how could I ever look Udo in the eye again? You will get a special rate and tip-top service. I promise.'

'And the gun?'

'The best, German, no foreign rubbish. An East German gun. Ex-Stasi issue.'

'Will it stop somebody with one bullet? I told you, I'm a novice with guns. I may get one shot but I doubt I'll get a second.'

'You will stop him, whoever he is, but only if you hit him. I can answer for the weapon but not for the one who pulls the trigger.'

The car turned left, drove a short way, then made a right. It was a nice enough street. The same sort of frontages but not so big or grand as the riverside ones. Everything since they crossed the river looked like an old part of the city, the sort of place tourists would like, classy and historic, and he was sure the prices would be classy too. The car pulled up outside a bar. Jimmy looked at the name above the door: El Sombrero. Above street level, from the first floor up, the old Lübeck frontage seemed to try and distance itself from the large Mexican hat and the bright yellows and reds of the paintwork.

Bloody hell, thought Jimmy, *we're in the middle of a place that has decent-looking beer houses everywhere and he brings me to a Mexican bar*. Well, it was his town, let him get on with it. It was the middle of the afternoon at the tail end of the tourist season so the place wasn't busy, only a few of the tables had people talking and drinking. The driver was obviously known and, by the welcome he got, was a good customer. He introduced Jimmy, in German, to a man behind the bar, who didn't look Mexican but did look like he owned the place. The owner looked at Jimmy then reached across the bar and offered his hand. Jimmy shook it then followed the driver to a table. The waiter brought two beers. The driver raised his glass.

'Cheers, Jimmy.'

Jimmy raised his glass and took a drink. The beer was good, very good, so he decided to forget the Mexican decor that surrounded them and took another drink. So long as the beer was good, the look of the place didn't matter.

'So, I'm Jimmy. Who are you?'

'Otto. Long Otto, because even as a child I was tall.'

'Hello, Otto.'

There was something vaguely familiar about him but he had never seen him before. Why did he look familiar?

'Why do I get the feeling I know you from somewhere?'

'Because already we are such good friends. We laugh together, talk, drink beer. It is like we have known each other for years.' Whatever it was it wasn't that.

'Or maybe I remind you a little of Udo.'

That's what it was. A slightly younger, taller Udo, with money and style.

'Yeah, you remind me a bit of Udo.'

'Why not? I *should* remind you of Udo. He's my older brother.'

'Your brother? He never mentioned a brother to me.'

Otto shrugged. 'These things happen. Udo and I used to be close but when he decided to become a priest, well, I could see how my line of work would not have suited him. Now he goes his way and I go mine but we keep in touch.'

'Did Udo tell you what this is about?'

'No, and I don't want to know. You don't want to be found for a while. That's all I need to know. The rest is none of my business.'

'What if it's dangerous?'

164

'It will only get dangerous if anyone finds you, and no one will find you. We're good at what we do. Excuse me, I see friends.'

Otto got up and went to talk to a man and woman who had come in and gone to the bar. Jimmy thought about it. *It will only get dangerous if somebody finds you.* But it didn't really take any thinking about. If Otto was looking after him, he had to know. Otto came back and sat down.

'Somebody already has found me.' That got Otto's attention. 'I was followed here. There's a guy called Charlie Bronski who lives in Denmark. He's got the crazy idea I want to kill him.'

'And what gave him that crazy idea?'

'His car got blown up.'

'He survived a car bomb?' Surprise and disbelief were nicely blended.

'No, there must have been a warning of some sort. He got out.'

'Who plays games like that?'

'I don't know, but not me. Anyway, he's got it into his head the bomb was down to me so when I ran he followed. He got careless at Neumünster station and I spotted him. He's why I need a gun.'

Otto smiled.

'Then you don't need a gun.'

'No?'

'No. When we look after someone we supply the whole package. If this Bronski character becomes a problem he will be our problem, not yours.'

'OK, Otto, this is your turf, we'll do it any way you say.'

'Is there anybody else I should know about besides Bronski?'

Jimmy shook his head. It wasn't one of the small lies, but that didn't count because in a way it wasn't really a lie at all. Otto shouldn't know about Mossad and the CIA because they weren't Charlie Bronski on his own. If Otto knew about them he might change his mind about whether this hiding thing was worth the money. So ...'

'No, there's nobody else you should know about.'

'Good.'

'You were going to tell me how much this is going to cost.'

'Udo told you it wouldn't be cheap?'

Jimmy nodded. 'He told me.'

It turned out Udo was dead right. It wasn't cheap. Jimmy just hoped the standard of service Otto was going to give was as high as the price. They shook hands, it was a deal.

'I'll get us schnapps to drink to it.' And he waved to the waiter.

'I'll stick to beer if that's OK. It's good beer and I don't drink spirits as a rule.'

'Sure, just as you like.'

The waiter came and took the order.

'Now, tell me all about yourself. We will become friends, just like old friends.'

'Born in London, raised there, became a copper, retired, went to stay with Udo. From there on, you already know.'

'That's it?'

'Do you need any more?' Otto laughed.

'No, I do not need any more. The more I listen to you, the more I like you. You talk but you don't talk too much. You don't ask any questions that you don't have to and you answer the ones that need an answer. The only thing I don't like is that bit about being a policeman.'

'It was a long time ago, ancient history, like your Holsten Gate.'

The drinks came. Otto held up his schnapps. 'Here's to you, my friend, and a quiet life.'

Jimmy picked up his beer.

'God's mittens.'

'What?'

'God's mittens. It was something Udo said. We can't lose because we've got God's mittens. I don't know what he was on about. I thought it must be something German, like "mud in your eye". You know, a toast when you drink.'

Otto thought about it, then he laughed out loud. A genuine laugh.

'Of course, God's mittens!'

And he laughed again. Jimmy smiled. He didn't think it was that funny, but it had tickled Otto.

'Yes, Jimmy. How can we lose when we have God's mittens?' He looked across at the waiter and shouted to him in German. Jimmy couldn't follow him but he thought he caught God's mittens in there somewhere. When Otto finished the waiter burst out laughing and the few other customers joined in. Otto turned back to Jimmy and raised his glass. 'God's mittens, Jimmy.' And he finished the rest of the schnapps off at one go. Jimmy gave a shrug. He still didn't see the joke.

'God's mittens to you, Otto.' And he took a drink of his beer.

TWENTY

Udo had indeed been right about Lübeck. The whole town was full of history and interest, if you were interested in history. Jimmy wasn't. Just now Jimmy was interested in what Charlie Bronski was up to and whether he was still the only one watching him.

After they left the Mexican bar, Long Otto had taken him to an apartment above an office in another part of the old town away from the tourist frontline, saw him settle in, then left. There was food in the fridge and beer. Jimmy had showered, eaten, and then sat and thought for a while, or rather, let his mind run down. Then he had gone to bed and slept.

Otto phoned at ten a.m. and arranged to come round. They spent the rest of the morning looking at the immediate neighbourhood. It was quiet and gently anonymous, with plenty of narrow picturesque streets between terraces of old houses that were red brick or painted like their bigger, more splendid cousins that overlooked the river. Picture-postcard stuff. Beyond the roofs Jimmy saw several spires. The district didn't seem short of churches.

There was a place where some of the streets opened onto a cobbled square with an ancient-looking wooden structure in the middle, a roof held up by six dark, timber posts. Lying on the stone floor with his back up against one of the posts was a grey-

169

bearded, scruffy derelict. The empty bottle of whatever he had been drinking that morning or the night before still stood at his side. Jimmy liked that, it reassured him. The place had charm and old-world appeal. But if it needed or wanted tourists, they wouldn't have left a derelict who passed out in their square to sleep it off where you couldn't miss him. Around the square were shops, a restaurant and two bars that all looked as if they were laid out strictly for the locals. No special show or fuss to attract visitors, just street frontages that had been there for a couple of hundred years.

Long Otto told him to stay in the immediate neighbourhood, not to stray. He was safe so long as he stayed close to home. Then he took him into one of the bars in the square and told him to use it if he went out on his own. He would be safe in that bar. Jimmy looked at the barman and one of the waiters. He agreed with Otto. He'd be safe in that bar so long as Bronski didn't come at him with a grenade launcher, and if the barman got in the way he might still be safe. The one who was acting the waiter wasn't as big but instead he had a small bulge at his waist under his calf-length white apron. The white shirt and tight black waistcoat ruled out a shoulder holster. Otto noticed Jimmy looking.

'While you're with us they'll be on the staff here. Eat all your meals here, breakfast, lunch and dinner. Drink here when you feel like it. Everything is paid for. When you drink, do you get drunk?'

He asked like he was asking, do you prefer tea or coffee? 'No, I drink but I don't get drunk, not often.'

'Good, drunks get stupid. Get drunk if you need to, but do it here and someone will see that you get back to the apartment OK. That's your table.'

He nodded to an empty table which was out of a direct line of sight from either the big front windows or the door.

'Nobody else will be using it and nobody will try to join you.'

'Are your blokes on all day?'

'No, two shifts, but don't use the bar after ten. The other pair go off at ten. We all need a life, Jimmy. It can't be all work can it?' And he laughed. 'So. Girls?'

'Girls?'

'Will you want a girl? If you do, tell them in the office below your apartment. They'll see to it.'

'No, thanks anyway, no girls.'

Otto sounded doubtful but he still asked. 'Boys?'

'Good God. Nobody. No girls, no boys, no anybody.' Otto laughed again.

'I thought not but I had to ask, you understand? We need you settled, not going looking for anything.'

'I won't go looking, I promise.'

'Good. Everything will go well. I also promise.'

Jimmy liked Otto but he didn't trust him. He had known men like him in London, big blokes who laughed a lot. Nat had been like that. And Nat had wanted a hundred grand off him or he would send him out of London in five directions at once. But nobody had given Nat any warning so the bomb in his car had turned the laughter off, prematurely and permanently. Laughter didn't mean anything, laughter could go with violence just as easily as anything else. But he still liked Otto and believed he would keep to his side of the deal. Unless someone offered him more to hand Jimmy over or turn him into a permanent resident in one of their cemeteries. Otto was in business to make money, not to do favours for his big brother or make new friends.

'What about a church?'

'A church?'

'Yes, a Catholic church.'

'What would you want a church for?'

'Mass. I go to Mass when I can.'

'Maybe. I'll think about it. But not confession, I can't have a man in the confessional like I do here at the bar.'

Jimmy knew it was a joke so he smiled. 'Mass will do, Otto.'

Otto sat thinking for a moment.

'No, sorry, Jimmy, settle for being a sinner among sinners for a while. Let Udo do the praying for you. I can cover you here but not if you go wandering off into a church. I couldn't cover you in a church.'

171

'OK.'

They lunched together in the bar and drank beer. Then Otto left. Jimmy went back to the apartment and slept some more. He had time to kill so he killed it. He'd done it often enough before.

The next day Jimmy was on his own. He left the apartment and looked through the door of the ground floor office. Two girls and a middle-aged woman were doing something at desks with papers. They took no notice of him. Whatever it was, it didn't look like any whorehouse he'd ever seen. He went out and looked around the streets again. Everything was the same except the derelict had gone, but his empty bottle still stood by the wooden pillar.

Jimmy had his meals in the bar like Otto had told him and had a few beers, more than a few, to help the day pass. He found he was tired, tired of running, tired of looking over his shoulder, tired of trying to be the kind of man Bernie would think of as a good man. He had never been a good man. He had tried to change, he had tried hard. First in London, then in Rome, but he had failed both times, just as he had been failing in Denmark and was now failing in Lübeck. His were small talents: a talent for causing pain and a talent for working things out. Small things but they were all he had. He had no talent for big things: for goodness, for sacrifice. Maybe you had to be born with those. He was what he was, and he always would be.

George had been right when they had met at the Liffey Lad last time he was in London, about a hundred years ago. George had told him, 'If people change, Jimmy, it's just their underwear they change. You're the same.' And George was right. It was right then and it was right now. He hadn't changed and if, from some Heaven, Bernie was watching him, he would be causing her the same pain now as he had in their life together. Except there wasn't supposed to be any pain or sadness in Heaven, so either she was dead and gone and Heaven was just a fairy story or she didn't watch him or think about him. Either way he was alone, and would be for ever and ever. Amen.

Jimmy sat at his table. The day was over, it was just after ten and he was having a final beer before going back to the apartment. Otto came in and sat down. The waiter on the afternoon shift with the same bulge under his apron came over and stood by Otto.

'Beer.'

The waiter nodded and left.

'Come to say goodnight, Otto?'

'Come to ask you a question, Jimmy.'

'Ask away.'

'How long?'

It was a question Jimmy had been asking himself on and off all day. How long would he stay and where would he go next?

The waiter came and put the beer on the table and Otto took a drink.

'I don't know. Maybe it all depends on Bronski. You still not worried about Bronski?'

Otto shook his head.

'If I worry, I worry about you. Sitting around with nothing to do but wait and think isn't good for you. It isn't good for anyone. You can't stay here indefinitely. You should make plans.'

'What? Escape plans? Dig a tunnel maybe?' Otto didn't laugh this time.

'Seriously, you should decide what needs to be done. Udo said you wanted to disappear. I should look after you until it could be arranged. Do you want papers, a passport, a new identity? If you can pay you can have them, good ones, almost the real thing. Just say the word and you'll have them in a couple of days. Then you can get on your way, a new man, a man no one will be looking for.'

As Jimmy listened, he could feel his anger rising. Why? Why get angry? Otto was making sense. What had he bloody well come for if not to get away and start a new life with a new identity?

'And go where?'

'Anywhere. Forget Bronski. Just slip away, he'll never find you.'

The anger kept coming. Jimmy couldn't stop it.

'I've had enough of running. I've been running one way or another for too many years and I'm fucking tired of it. I'm tired of trying, I'm tired of people, I'm tired of pretending to be something I'm not. You know what I'd really like to do, what would really cheer me up right now?'

Otto slowly shook his head. He could see that Jimmy was getting angry. But who was he getting angry with? If he was getting angry at himself it might mean trouble.

'What would cheer you up, Jimmy?'

'What I'd really like to do is beat the living shit out of somebody, preferably Charlie fucking Bronski, but at the moment it could be anybody, anybody who comes to hand.'

'Me?'

'If that's an offer? Because if it is, don't be sure I won't take you up on it even with Godzilla and Billy the Kid to look after you.'

Otto reached out and put a hand on Jimmy's arm. Jimmy looked down at it and noticed his own hands on the table. His fists were clenched and his knuckles were white.

Then he relaxed. The anger was suddenly gone. Otto saw it, took away his hand and sat back. Jimmy sat in silence for a moment. Otto was right, he couldn't sit about doing nothing waiting for something to happen, so he made a decision.

'OK, I'll tell you what I'll do. Find out where Bronski is and I'll kill him. I don't need you to do it. I want to do it. I want to see his eyes when he closes them for the last time. I want him to see it was me putting the bullet into the bastard.'

'Are you sure? Is that what you really want?'

Jimmy nodded.

'OK. We know where Bronski is.'

'Where?'

'In a hotel. I can take you there.'

'Right, get that gun, tell me which hotel he's in and then stand back and let me finish this my way.'

'Sure. I'm glad you've come to a decision. Just one thing, I said half up front and half when you leave. I'll want the second half tomorrow. I'm glad you made a decision but I don't want to bet what you owe us on the outcome of your hotel visit. Not if you insist on going on your own.'

'I'll have your money for you by lunchtime tomorrow. Just see you have the gun.' He tried to get laughter into his voice. 'A German gun, no foreign rubbish.'

Otto smiled, but it was a sad sort of smile.

'No rubbish, good ex-Stasi issue. Soft-nosed bullets?'

'Just as they come, Otto, just as they come.'

Otto called the waiter over and ordered two more beers. They would sit for a while like two old friends, a drink and a talk at the end of another day. And tomorrow Jimmy would kill Charlie Bronski.

TWENTY-ONE

She had come to Bronski's hotel room from the station. It was late, but she seemed to want to talk and she was in charge.

'Why Lübeck?'

Bronski couldn't see that it mattered.

'Why anywhere? Running has to stop sometime. In his case, it stopped here. I thought East Germany was good for you. From Lübeck you could spit into the old GDR. Why are you complaining?'

'I'm not complaining, Yuri, just asking the question. If you stop running you have to have a reason. One reason is you've given up, another is you've run out of breath, the best reason is because you think you're safe. Does he think he's safe here?'

Charlie shrugged. He didn't care. The target was static and that made him vulnerable. Was this how the British did things? Sit, wait, endlessly talk about it but do nothing. No wonder the country was a basket case.

'Maybe he does, how should I know? He's here, we're here. Why not get on with it?'

'Does he know you followed him?'

'No.'

'Are you sure?'

'Sure I'm sure. If he thought he was being followed he'd have shown it. He'd still be running or he'd be looking and he isn't doing either. He's being looked after by a local called Long Otto. He just sticks close to home and uses one bar where he's looked after by two of Otto's boys. We don't have a problem unless Otto gets wind of us and even if he knew we were here he wouldn't be too much of a problem. He's just local muscle, a real provincial.' *No, that was going too far, don't overdo it.* 'But it's his town, so while it's just you and me he could be a problem.'

He waited but she just sat there. Was she thinking or waiting for divine inspiration? Why wouldn't she give the go-ahead? And why *was* it just the two of them?

'Why is it just you and me? Is it a cost thing? Why are you Brits always so strapped for cash?'

'Because we're not flashy or stupid,' was what she said. What she wanted to say was, 'Because we're too mean to pay for what we want or what we need. Because our political masters don't get votes from things nobody is allowed to talk about. Because these days we're a chicken-shit outpost for our American cousins.'

But nobody ever said those things, at least not out loud.

Her mobile rang. She took it out, listened for a moment then put it away.

'We go tomorrow. It's arranged.'

'Arranged? Arranged how? Who with?'

'With me. It's arranged and all you need to know is we go tomorrow. The place is to the north of the city, Herrenwyk; there's an old industrial site there, derelict, waiting for redevelopment. Come on, we'll need to give it a look-over so we can get the thing worked out.'

They went downstairs to the hotel car park where her rented Audi was parked.

Damn, thought Bronski. *Now she decides to be dynamic, at this time of night.*

About half an hour later a pretty young woman knocked at Bronski's hotel room door but there was no answer. After a couple more tries she gave up. Why wasn't he there? He had seemed to enjoy himself the previous night and seemed keen for a re-run. *Oh, well. Tricks. Who could figure how their minds worked*? At least she would get a good night's sleep. She certainly wouldn't miss him, he was a grunter with about as much finesse as a claw-hammer. She walked away down the corridor swinging her handbag, happy to have an unexpected night off.

The Audi was travelling fast, headed along the dual carriageway. Bronski had a road map open but wasn't looking at it. On leaving the city they had followed the signs for the Herren Tunnel and this motorway led them straight to it. They arrived at the tunnel, paid the toll, moved on and finally emerged on the far side of the river. As soon as they had left the bright artificial lights Bronski indicated a right turn. Clarke-Phillips moved the car over onto the slip road and followed it round until they were heading back towards the river. They came to a T-junction.

'Left here.'

The Audi turned onto a road that ran parallel with the river on their right. This was a world away from the old-world charm of central Lübeck. They drove past floodlit lorry parks, industrial buildings with the names of the company lit up and fenced yards piled high with building materials. Bronski studied the road map by the light of a torch and gave instructions.

After a while the lights gave way to darkness and, from what they could see in their headlights and the occasional street lamps, the places looked older, less prosperous, then run-down and finally broken-down and boarded-up.

'It should be here on your right somewhere.'

They pulled off the road and slowly drove through a wide area of missing mesh fencing onto an old concrete car park with tufts of weeds growing strongly from the cracks and pot-holes. The headlights showed them a squat, one-storey building, one of several that had once been some sort of industrial complex. From what Charlie had managed to see of the last part of their journey, they were in a really scummy area, dirty and with anything that hadn't already been knocked down slowly crumbling away. He would say one thing for it, though – it wouldn't be a busy part of town.

Clarke-Phillips switched off the engine and held her hand

out for the torch. Charlie gave it to her and threw the road map over onto the back seat. They got out and she led the way to a pair of wide, rusty steel doors. Inset into one of them was a smaller door, which was slightly ajar. She pulled it open and they went in. She shone her torch around so they could both get a look at the place.

It was perfect. An empty, concrete box with small windows and steel doors at each end. There was rubbish scattered all over. Broken boxes, paper, cardboard, worn tyres. It was just one big space and, apart from the square pillars which held up the ceiling, there was nowhere to run to and nowhere to hide. Once Costello was inside, it was all over. Bronski was impressed.

'How did you find it?'

'I found it, never mind how. It'll do the job. Just be sure and bring Costello here.'

'And how do I do that? Either he's in his apartment, near the apartment or in that bar. How do I pick him up? And if I pick him up, how do I persuade him to come here so you can put a bullet in him?'

'How about asking nicely?'

'And how about you come up with an idea? I told you we needed more people on this. I can't strong-arm him into the car off the street, cover him with a gun – if I had a gun – and drive him here in a car.'

'No, I can see how that might be a trifle difficult.'

'So how do we get Costello here?'

'We send a car for him and like I said, you ask him nicely.' And when she had explained he understood. The way she explained it, asking him nicely would work. It would work fine. He should have had more faith. Maybe these Brits weren't all idiots after all.

He wondered what the time was. Maybe if they hurried back he could still arrange things with his call girl.

'OK, back to your hotel and we can sort out our exits and tie everything up.'

'What's to sort out? We do what we have to, we leave.'

'We do what we have to and we leave the way I *say* we

180

leave. I want us both clean away and no slip-ups.'

Damn, thought Charlie, *there goes my sex*.

They went back to the car and retraced their journey back to the Herren Tunnel then headed towards the city, making good time on the big, straight road. Neither spoke during the journey, both were thinking. Both thought things had gone very well, better than expected. And both were right and both were wrong.

In his apartment Jimmy slept soundly. He had made his decision and tomorrow it would all be over, one way or another.

TWENTY-TWO

It was barely one when Otto arrived and sat down at the table. Jimmy was having a couple of sandwiches and a beer.

'Hello, Otto. Been busy?'

'The usual, this and that.'

'You're early, I've only had one sandwich.'

'Last night you seemed ready to go so I didn't want to keep you hanging about.'

'You've got it?'

'Not on me, Jimmy, not even in here can I pull out a gun and hand it over. It's in the glove compartment of the car. When you've finished your beer, we'll go and get it.'

'Ammunition?'

'Just what's in the clip. You said one shot, remember, no second. But I made them soft-nosed. Hit him and you'll blow some of him off wherever the bullet goes. That should hold him long enough for you get another shot, even if you only get him in the arm.' Jimmy finished his coffee. 'And you? You have something for me?'

Jimmy put his hand into his inside jacket pocket and pulled out an unsealed envelope. He handed it over to Otto who took it and put it into his inside pocket.

'You don't want to look?'

Otto shook his head.

'I trust you, it'll all be there, you wouldn't welch on a friend. Besides, I know where you live.'

And he laughed, but Jimmy knew from the laugh he wasn't kidding.

'How did you know I'd have it? I don't even know where the nearest bank is.'

'You paid the first time by banker's draft and you didn't know when you'd need the second payment. If you needed it in a hurry or on a day the banks would be closed you wouldn't risk not being able to get it. I guessed you'd have it where you could get it at short notice.'

'Or maybe you had someone look at the apartment while I was here. If I left here before your man was finished they'd have got a call. I think looking was a better way of making sure you'd got your money than guessing. Somehow I don't think you base much of your business on guesses. I think you prefer to know for sure.'

Otto gave a loud laugh and slapped the table hard with an open hand.

'By God, Jimmy, you're a smart one, I'm glad we're on the same side. I see you could be a handful if you needed to be. Was yours a guess or did you know?'

'I knew, I had the drawer set up. When I went back after lunch I saw it had been gone over. The envelope wasn't hard to find, I left it where anyone would look.'

'I hope you understand. I had to know, it's a lot of money. I liked you from the first but one has to be careful. You came from Udo but maybe these days Udo isn't as sharp as he was. I had to check.'

'Of course you did, I expected you to. You don't know me and like you say, it's a lot of money. Don't worry about it, it's nothing. Anyway you've got it now so we can forget about it. How much will the gun cost?'

Otto waved a hand. 'Nothing, it's a gift, from one friend to another.'

'I said I'd pay. I don't mind paying.'

'No, I couldn't let you pay. Guns are cheap, they almost give them away.'

'So it's a cheap gift then?'

It took Otto a fraction of a second to react but when he did the frown that had appeared dissolved in laughter.

'A joke, yes? A British joke. A cheap gift for a cheap friend, is that it? No, no, you are not a cheap friend, you are a very valuable friend.'

And he laughed again.

Jimmy decided that Otto's laughing could be bloody wearing. He overdid it. He wouldn't be sorry to sort the Bronski thing out and be on his way. He'd had enough of Lübeck and Otto. He was ready to go to the station or the cemetery, whichever way it turned out.

He got up and so did Otto. They left the bar and crossed the pavement to the Mercedes. Jimmy got into the passenger seat and opened the glove compartment. There was an automatic there. He took it out as Otto got into the driver's seat.

'You like it?'

'Should I?'

It was heavy and Jimmy was holding it in his right hand with his arm across his stomach. The muzzle was pointing towards Otto.

'It's a good gun, like I told you. But don't point it at me like that, it might go off.'

And Jimmy pulled the trigger, then pulled it again. All that happened was that it gave two clicks.

Otto wasn't laughing now. Jimmy held up the gun and examined it.

'It doesn't seem much of a gun to me, it just makes a clicking sound.' He turned to Otto. 'If it was any good as a gun shouldn't you have a couple of bullets in you?' Otto said something. It was in German but Jimmy guessed he was swearing.

'Is he coming out now or do we have to wait some more?'

From behind Jimmy a head rose and Charlie Bronski got up and sat on the back seat.

'Put the gun away, Jimmy. No, not in your pocket, back in the glove compartment. It may be empty but I still think it's safer in the glove compartment.'

Jimmy put it back. When he sat back he saw Otto was now holding a similar automatic and it was pointed at him.

'So what happens now? You drive the car from the back seat and Otto covers me, or do we play musical chairs and all change seats?'

'Put the gun away, Otto, you can see Mr Costello understands how things are. It looks like he understood before he got into the car. Get going.' Otto put away his gun, started the car and it moved off. 'You won't be silly will you, Mr Costello? Otto isn't the only one with a gun and mine's not like yours, it has bullets in it.'

Jimmy didn't answer. He had seen it coming but he hadn't seen how he could stop it. He was on his own in a place he didn't know. They were organised and it was their town. So, would it all end in Lübeck? Well, why not? It had to end somewhere. Soon it would all be over. He didn't mind. It would be painless, just a bullet in the head and then ... then what? Heaven, Hell or just black oblivion? But he'd asked himself that question many times. Long ago he had decided that whatever had waited beyond life for Bernie would be OK for him. If she was in Heaven then it might be a long wait, but Bernie would get him in if anyone could. If anyone ever deserved Heaven it was Bernie. If there was a Heaven. If there still was a Bernie. If there was nothing, fine. If she was nothing now, he would soon be nothing, not even a memory.

The car was moving out of the narrow streets into the traffic of a main road. Charlie spoke from the back seat.

'I hope you're not trying to work anything out, there's nothing you can do.'

'Then I'll do nothing, won't I?'

'How did you know? What tipped you off?'

'Otto told me.' The car swerved as Otto turned and looked at him before quickly getting his eyes back on the road. 'Careful, Otto, I'm the only one supposed to die today, don't bugger it all up and kill all three of us.'

Otto didn't look at him or say anything but Jimmy could see he was truly pissed. It was Charlie who wanted to talk.

'Otto told you?'

186

'As good as, last night. All that crap about papers and moving, about how hanging about wasn't good for me. Why the big hurry? I'd only just arrived. I could see he wanted some sort of opening so I gave him one to see where he'd go. He went straight for the money. I knew he'd had the apartment checked to make sure the money was there but he still played the innocent. Can you get it, Jimmy? I can't bet what you owe me on any shoot-out.' Jimmy looked at Otto who was staring straight ahead. 'Your acting was good, Otto, but the script was crap.' He looked back at the road. They'd crossed a bridge, not either of the ones he'd been over before. They were heading out of the city. 'Why the act unless he was planning something for me? It wasn't hard to guess what that something was. He'd sold me out. If he'd put a "sold subject to contract" sign round my neck he couldn't have made it more obvious.'

'Is that it?'

It didn't matter but it was something to do. Make Otto look like an arsehole. *Why not*?

'His two goons stayed. I didn't leave the bar until about quarter to eleven. Otto was with me, so they could have gone, but they stayed. That meant I was being watched, not protected. Otto wasn't taking any chances. There was nothing I could do, so I did nothing. I just went to bed, got up and had breakfast and walked about until lunchtime. Friend Otto turns up, thinks everything's just as he wants it and goes into his laughing routine. The gun thing gets me into the car. He has it parked so the passenger door is at the curb. I get in and look for the gun, that way I'm not supposed to notice you down behind the seat.'

'You saw me?'

'I didn't look. Why should I look? If Otto was driving there had to be someone behind me. Either you were behind the seat or somewhere very close so you could get in once I was in. It didn't matter one way or the other.'

'So you just walked into it? Why not at least try to run?'

'I wanted to see if I could make Otto wet his pants. I think I nearly did. At least I stopped that bloody laugh – it was getting on my nerves.'

Charlie sat back, he didn't want to talk or listen any more so they drove on in silence. Once out of the Herren Tunnel, Charlie gave directions and they followed the same route he'd made the previous night with Clarke-Phillips until Otto pulled the car off the road onto the car park in front of the crumbling industrial complex. They drove up to the set of double steel doors. The small door set into them was open. Otto stopped the Mercedes by the open door, got out and moved round the car towards the door, watching Jimmy, the automatic back in his hand. Jimmy and Charlie got out. Charlie had his gun out as well. He gestured with it.

'In you go, Mr Costello, and remember, nothing silly.'

'My, my, so many guns and so few brains. Am I supposed to be worried that if I try anything you might have to shoot me? It's hardly a threat, is it?'

Otto moved to just inside the door where he could still cover Jimmy with his gun.

'Just go inside, keep the jokes for later.'

Jimmy walked into the building. Charlie followed. Once they were all inside, Charlie turned to Otto.

'Wait in the car.'

'You don't need me here?'

Charlie shook his head. 'No.'

Otto turned towards the door and began to put his gun away. Charlie took one step towards him and shot him once in the back of the head. Jimmy blinked at the noise which the emptiness of the place magnified. Otto pitched forwards into the door and then fell to the floor. Jimmy looked at him. He was very dead.

'Goodbye, Otto. It wasn't a pleasure knowing you.'

Jimmy looked away from the body. Charlie's gun was pointing back at him now.

'No loose ends. The people I work for don't like loose ends.' He gestured with the gun. 'On your way, there's somebody waiting for you by that window over there.'

Jimmy looked. She was standing to his right, by one of the windows. It wasn't bright inside but enough of the glass in the grimy windows was smashed, so it was clear enough to see her. He walked towards her. She wore a smart suit, had longish brown hair. Jimmy had never seen her before in his life. Her arms were by her sides and in one hand, pointing at the floor, was a gun. He walked up and stood in front of her. He wasn't far away, she couldn't miss. Neither spoke, there was nothing to say. They both knew what was going to happen. The gun started to come up and the sound of the shot filled the warehouse with noise, echoing and bouncing around the stained concrete walls. Then there was a silence. Jimmy looked at her. She lay crumpled against the wall under the window. Charlie went to her side, made sure she was dead, picked up her gun and then looked at Jimmy. Now he had a gun in each hand. One was pointing at Jimmy, the other he was holding out.

'Take it.' Jimmy looked at him in a dazed way but didn't move. Why wasn't he dead? And who the hell was *she*? 'Take the bloody gun, will you?' Jimmy moved forward and took the gun by the barrel. Charlie stood up and moved away. 'Now, moving very slowly, put a bullet in her head.'

Jimmy looked at her. She was dead. 'What?'

'Mr Costello, you're alive. If you want to stay that way don't ask questions, just do as you're told. Put a bullet in her head.' Jimmy bent down, held the muzzle of the gun against her head and pulled the trigger. Once again the place filled with noise and the dead woman pitched violently sideways onto the floor. Charlie pulled out a plastic bag from a pocket, dropped it on the floor and stood back. Jimmy stood up and turned to face him, he still had the gun he had been given. It was pointing straight at Bronski's stomach, he couldn't miss, but Bronski didn't look worried. Jimmy pulled the trigger. There was a click. He wasn't surprised. It wasn't his day for guns. 'That's right, Mr Costello, I had just three bullets in mine, enough to get the job done. This is hers and it's fully loaded. Put the gun in the bag and put it back on the floor.' Jimmy picked up the bag, put the gun in it, put it back on the floor and stood up. 'Stand back.'

Jimmy took a couple of paces back and Charlie picked up the bag and stuffed it in a side pocket.

'What now? Is now when you shoot me?'

'Now you have a choice. You can get in the car with me or you can stay here. If you stay here I'll make sure the police find this gun.' He tapped his side pocket. 'It's got you all over it and it's killed two people. Think fast, Mr Costello, this place is derelict but three shots might bring somebody and I don't want to kill anyone else today.'

There was nothing to think about, so he didn't think about it. He was alive.

'OK, let's go.'

And they walked back to the steel doors, stepped over Otto, and left.

TWENTY-THREE

When Jimmy got to the Mercedes, there was someone sitting in the driver's seat and the engine was running. The driver turned and looked at him. It was Udo. Charlie opened the back door.

'In front, where I can see you.'

Jimmy did as he was told and Charlie got in the back. Udo had the engine running but he didn't seem ready to go anywhere. He nodded towards Otto's feet, which were visible by the open door.

'Haven't you forgotten something, Jimmy?'

'No.'

'Don't you want your banker's draft back? If I know Otto, it should be a lot of money.'

'It's a piece of blank paper in a unsealed envelope. Why would I have given him a lot of money? I switched it once I was sure he'd had my room searched.'

Udo looked at him for a moment then laughed and the Mercedes moved off.

'I should have guessed. If this had turned out the way Otto expected you'd still have had the last laugh. My God, would he have been pissed at you.'

Bronski's voice came from the back seat.

'Nice one, Jimmy.' Jimmy looked round at Charlie. 'Come on, I can call you Jimmy now. I just saved your life.'

'Do I get to know what this is all about? If you didn't follow me to kill me what sort of game are you playing?'

'Ask Udo. It's his game now. It has been ever since I got to Lübeck.'

Jimmy turned back.

'Well, Udo, do I get to know what this is all about or do I have to guess?'

'Now that would be interesting. If you had to guess, what would you say this was all about?'

Charlie joined with Udo.

'Yeah, come on, Jimmy. We've got time until we get to the station. What do you think it's all about? You used to be a detective. Make a guess.'

So Jimmy thought out loud as the car headed back to the city. 'Well, it's not about what happened in Nyborg, about you thinking I was responsible for some nutty car bomb.'

Charlie was happy to talk.

'No, it was never really about Nyborg. And it stopped being about me as soon as your name got mentioned.'

'I think you're ex-Intelligence, Stasi or KGB. Somebody the British thought worth paying money for. They set you up with a new identity and you fetched up in Nyborg because it's a quiet, out-of-the-way spot, a nice place to live and a nice place to hide. But somehow your past caught up with you. The bomb was a warning – I've found you and I'm going to kill you. You shouted for help and got a hurry-up call to Hamburg. For reasons I still don't understand you had me down for the bomb. When you met your contact you gave them my name and that's when it stopped being about you. From then on it was about my past catching up with me. It looks like Nyborg let us both down.'

'Very good, I'm impressed. And it was KGB originally but then it was Russian Intelligence. I still don't know who you are or what you did but your name certainly carries some punch. You should have seen that bird rocket when she heard it. Come on, why not even things up, what's your story? You seem to know mine, let's hear yours.'

Jimmy could hear the false, friendly smile in Charlie's voice.

He was sure it would be on his face if he turned and looked, but he kept his eyes on the road.

'Why don't you go and fuck yourself, Bronski? I'm not going to tell you shit.'

Udo glanced in the rear mirror and saw the smile get wiped off Charlie's face.

'Enough, both of you. Enough.'

It was an order from someone who was used to giving orders. It was a voice you didn't ignore. Udo drove on and Charlie sulked. Jimmy stared ahead and tried to look on the bright side, but it wasn't easy. They went through the tunnel and along the dual-carriageway in an uncomfortable silence. Back in Lübeck, Udo pulled the car over in a side road near the railway station.

'We're here. Get out, Jimmy. Charlie, you take the car and lose it. Then get home any way you want.' Charlie began to open the door. 'The gun, Charlie, don't forget the gun.' Charlie pulled out his gun and held it out. 'Very funny, the other one, the one in the plastic bag.' Charlie put his gun away and took out the plastic bag and handed it over. Udo handed it to Jimmy. 'Get rid of it in bits. Throw it into the sea when we get to Nyborg.'

They all got out and Charlie got into the driver's seat. Udo stood by the window. 'I wouldn't hang about if I were you. This car is a bit conspicuous and Otto's people will be looking for him. If you make it I'll see you back in Nyborg.'

The Mercedes pulled away. Jimmy watched it go, then turned to Udo.

'Will he make it?'

'I wish I could tell you they'll get him, that we'd seen the last of Yuri Kemedov. But no, he'll make it all right. Charlie's still good and he's a survivor. And this is Lübeck, it's not Hamburg or Berlin or anywhere like that. Charlie will get past Otto's boys. They're just violent amateurs. Charlie is and always was a professional.'

'Like you?'

Udo looked at him. He didn't look surprised. They began to walk.

'How long have you known?'

'I was sure when you gave me the route to Lübeck. It came out pat, too pat for someone who was a minor official in a small government department. You were never a clerk who did a "bit of smuggling on the side with a few friends". It was your business. If you were East German that made you the police. The ones who caught the ones who did it.'

'Or?'

'Or something else. You didn't strike me as any kind of ex-copper I've ever come across, so I guessed Stasi.'

'You're not exactly a typical ex-copper either but that didn't make me put you down as someone from the British Security Services.'

'No, but you went into the act so smoothly. You'd done it before so many times it still fitted without any effort. Getting people in, getting them out. Getting them where they could be dealt with. Picked up, shot, whatever was wanted. You made it look like riding a bike, something you never forgot.'

'You said that was what made you certain. When did you first suspect?'

They walked arrived at a pedestrian crossing, pressed the button and when the lights changed crossed over.

'I don't know but I think it started at the hospital on the day of the car bomb and went on from there.'

'And what was it?'

'Same as Charlie, you were too calm, too in control. You were good, you played your part well, but it showed. You kept your eye on all the moving parts. You pretended to swallow Bronski's story about a publisher because it gave you a chance to visit Mrs Bronski and see where she fitted in. You found out she didn't. After that you lost interest and kept your eye on me and Bronski. How did you know for sure he'd come back from Hamburg? He could have run.'

'There were too many loose ends and he wasn't of any real value to them any more. They wouldn't invest in a new life for him again, whatever bind he was in. They'd tell him to clear off and sort it out for himself. Or maybe kill him. But once Bronski put your name in the frame it all changed. When Professor

McBride told me to take you on as a placement, she made it clear in her own way that I should look after you, so I knew you were something special.'

'That was really what put me on to you. McBride knew what I might be up against and I don't think she'd put me alongside anybody who couldn't look after themselves if anything happened. You had to have the right sort of background, not the sort that you get in the more learned professions.'

Jimmy saw the sign for the railway station ahead. 'Are we going home?'

Udo nodded. 'It's over so we go home.'

'Straight home or the roundabout route?'

'Straight home.' Udo took a package from his pocket. 'Here, take these.'

Jimmy took the package and opened it. It was a pair of glasses, a small false moustache and a British passport.

'You're joking, a bloody disguise?'

'Look at the passport.'

Jimmy looked at the passport photo. It was him in glasses with a small moustache. It was amazing what they could do with computers these days. He looked at the name. John Christopher Crippler.

'What sort of name is Crippler for God's sake?'

'Until we get home it's your sort of name. Now put them on.'

Jimmy put them on. The glass in the lenses was plain. 'How do I look?'

'You'll do. We probably won't need them but it's just possible they'll have your name and description from Otto's people while we're on the train. It's a long journey.'

They went into the station and Udo bought the tickets.

Then they went to the station bar and Udo bought beers.

'How long?'

'Not long. We leave at two-ten from platform seven. Drink your beer.'

Jimmy drank.

'Are we OK here? What about Otto's friends? Aren't we a bit exposed?'

'Trust me. This sort of thing is what I used to do. Nobody is going to be looking for you. I told you, Otto was small-time; they're all small-time in Lübeck. Don't worry about them. I doubt his friends will do anything even when they know he's dead. He wasn't the big man he pretended to be and he wasn't as good as he thought he was. He would have got it one day, probably from one of his friends when he got that bit too greedy or made one double-cross too many. The day just came sooner than he expected. Forget him, nobody will miss Otto. He was a nobody who got to think he was somebody for a while. But it's over now.'

Jimmy took another drink of his beer. It wasn't as good as at the bar Otto had made him use but it was OK.

'You make it sound as if you didn't think much of your brother. He said you used to be close.'

Udo put his glass down.

'My brother? What the hell makes you think Long Otto was my brother?'

'He said he was.'

Udo laughed.

'My God, what a liar. He was a sort of cousin, wrong side of the family, wrong side of the blanket, wrong side of the law but the right side of the border, so I made use of him, but we were never close. He was in the black market in a small way. I used him as an informant, not that he ever brought me anything worth having. But sometimes I planted information we wanted on the street through him. I'd meet him here in Lübeck and let him think we were playing cousins. I'd drink and then tell him things he thought he'd wormed out of me or that I'd told him in confidence, things he could sell on.'

'So they'd come from a source that would be believed in a way that would be believed?'

Udo nodded.

'It was really just like I told you. I was a small cog in the government machine, I wasn't anyone important, just an enforcer, a frightener or muscle for field agents, an odd-job man. I got run-of-the mill stuff to do.'

'Like arranging train journeys?'

'Things like that. The details of getting people in, getting them out. I didn't do much thinking or planning. I just did what I was told to do. I really was what I said, a sort of clerk. Then reunification came along and suddenly no one wanted the Stasi any more. The higher-ups edited their files and became solid citizens and set about making money the capitalist way instead of the communist way.'

'They took business graft instead of government graft?'

'Of course. You didn't think they'd change the habits of a lifetime just because the political system changed?'

'And you?'

'Me and the rest were left to do the best we could. I had no skills, at least none that had any really legitimate application. I was used to a decent standard of living so I rounded up Otto and a few others and went to work. I did OK, we all did OK for a while. There were still shortages and now stuff didn't have to be smuggled in. All you needed was a safe, cheap supply of what people wanted. So I got one.'

'Bent goods?'

'Sure. People asked me for things, fancy cars mostly, and I arranged for them to be stolen, fixed the paperwork to make it look legitimate and sold it on. Not that my customers were that bothered about where anything came from.' Udo looked at his watch and finished his beer. 'And now you have the story of my life, just like you got Charlie's. You know all about me and I know nothing about you.'

He got up. Jimmy finished his beer and got up as well. 'I told you all about me in Copenhagen, remember.' They left the bar and headed for their platform.

'But you didn't tell me what this is all about.'

'Because you don't want to know. Unless you like running and looking over your shoulder while you do it. Or maybe being dead isn't a problem for you either.'

'Oh, I'm not ready to meet my maker yet. I doubt I'll ever be, and I'm certainly not in any hurry to find out.'

'Then hang on to ignorance.'

'If you say so, Jimmy, if you say so. It doesn't really matter because the truth is, I don't care any more.'

'No, I know what you mean.'

And they followed the signs to platform seven where the two ten Hamburg train would be waiting.

TWENTY-FOUR

There was no going back, was there? It was that urgent, bloody secure meeting site she'd asked him for. He'd had to go and get one in a hurry from Simpson and that made it undeniable. He forced his brain to work harder. Maybe if he said … perhaps he could …

He pressed the button, the door opened and Gloria came in.

'Yes, sir.'

'Have you any aspirin, Gloria?'

'Of course. I'll get you one.'

'Make it two. In fact bring the box, will you.'

Gloria left and went to her desk. *It must be some bloody balls-up*. He looked like death warmed up and there was already an empty glass on his desk. It must be something to do with what was going on. The whole place was buzzing. She hadn't seen anything like it for years. It was like the old days again, when they'd lost someone in Soviet territory. She got the aspirins out of a drawer and went back into the office. He was at the drinks cabinet pouring himself what looked like a stiff one.

'Do we know what's going on yet, sir?'

He turned. 'Going on? What do you mean, going on?'

'The flap, sir. Do we know what the flap is all about? Is someone in the field in trouble?'

He put the bottle back and closed the cabinet. 'What flap? What do you mean, flap?'

He came back to his desk and sat down, took a small sip of his drink then picked up a folder and held it open as if he was reading it. It was upside down, but he had been looking at it for about ten seconds before he noticed, blinked a couple of times and put it down. It was the yellow three-star folder. Costello's folder. She held out the box of aspirin.

'Not too many, sir. Not with alcohol.' He took the box.

'Of course ... I, er ... of course.'

She turned and left. She wasn't inclined to stay and chat. He wasn't a pretty sight. She closed the door after her, went back to her desk and picked up the phone.

'Hello. He's got a box of aspirins and he's drinking ... yes, it's a full box ... whisky, it looked neat and a big one ... well, you told me this morning to keep an eye on him, sir, and if there was anything that I thought you should know ...' She listened. 'Very well, sir.'

She put the phone down and went back to work. A few minutes later a man came into her office. He took a chair, put it by the door, sat down and folded his arms. She didn't recognise him. They ignored each other. After about ten minutes the office door opened and Gloria looked round.

'Yes, sir? Do you want something?'

He stopped dead in the doorway when he saw the man sitting by the door, a look almost of horror on his face. He had his overcoat on.

'Er, I was going out. I was ... I was going to go out. I had something that needed ... but it will keep. I'll do it later.'

The office door closed. The man continued to sit and Gloria resumed work.

Sod it, this meant a new boss. She hated it when she had to break in a new boss. They were all desk pilots these days, men or women who could arm-wrestle the software and the paperwork, were Olympic-class ladder-climbers who had no field experience. She wondered how long her present master had; there were things that needed a signature. She glanced at the man sitting by the door. By the look of things, no time at all.

It must have been the mother and father of all balls-ups.

In another part of London a BBC news presenter was preparing to go on air. The producer waited while the presenter settled again. In a way, and for the first time, she was almost impressed. She never thought he had it in him.

'Just read the words, Nigel, just read the bloody autocue.'

Nigel read the autocue.

'News is coming in of the murder today in Lübeck, Germany, of an English tourist.'

Nigel stopped looking at the autocue.

'For God's sake, Linda, an English tourist? Why not say it's an English secret agent. Why piss about with this tourist rubbish? Why should we be lying for them?'

'Because, Nigel darling, we are not reporters, this is the BBC news, we read what we're told to read. Somewhere, a reporter who knows all about real news will, as we speak, be trying to get the full story. When that happens, it will be filed and the gods upstairs will get what clearances they can and, in the fullness of time, you will read to a public who don't give a shit what it has been deemed fit for them to know. Which, if previous form is anything to go by, will be precious little because it's Intelligence-related. For the moment, she is an English tourist brutally murdered by Johnny Foreigners – better still, Germans. And as the clock is ticking its inexorable way to air-time can you just read the words, darling, and stop wasting everyone's fucking time?'

Nigel began reading the words. 'News is coming in ...'

The man by the door stood up when the Director came in. The Director ignored him, walked past Gloria into the office and closed the door behind him. The man at the door sat down again and Gloria made a small note to buy a replacement box of aspirin.

The Director sat down and motioned for the man at the desk, who had risen on his entry, to sit down. The man tried to smile but it died at birth. The Director got straight into it.

'We're not barbarians. Nor do we go in for extraordinary

rendition. But our American cousins are and do. And today I feel I can see the advantages of their approach. They're screaming for you and I don't see how we can avoid letting them have you. If we don't, they may come and get you and that must not happen at any cost.' The man felt his bladder control slipping. 'They say the CIA woman you used, the one from their Berlin office, was injured in a car crash yesterday. In many ways I hope for her sake she was but I think the likelihood is that she's already been shipped to one of their foreign holding and interrogation units, after which she will stay without trial in some other place of irregular confinement until they decide what to do with her. There is of course no question of a trial in your case either. I will try and get the best deal I can, not, I hasten to add, for *your* sake but to salvage anything I can for the reputation of this department. Personally I would like you to be taken to some nice, soundproofed cell and have the man sitting by the door outside beat you to death with his bare hands. That would give me some small satisfaction, give him some useful practice, and help erase you from sight and memory. You have, after all, betrayed the Service and your country, which is treason.'

The man lost the battle with his bladder and felt a warmness spreading inside his shorts.

'Thanks to your insane delusions we have lost Costello. The Americans and Israelis rightly blame us for it.' The Director gave a wintry smile. 'Just as a matter of academic interest, psychological not professional, what on earth did you think you were doing?' The Director waited for a moment but the man in the damp trousers was asking himself the same question. He had been asking it ever since she had stopped calling in, hadn't answered her phone and he hadn't been able to contact Bronski. 'You misused department funds and personnel to mount an unauthorised field action which involved subverting a US agent, eliciting top-secret material from her, and involved handing over to her a man you had specifically been ordered to terminate. What on earth did you stand to gain by it?'

Yes, it was a good question he only wished he had a good answer. His pants were turning cold and he had the distinct impression he was going to be sick or faint, or both. On balance probably both.

The Director stood up.

'I did not enjoy breaking this to the Prime Minister. He took it badly. I take a small comfort that after a rare example of his masterful decision-making which initiated this ill-starred cock-up, at least he will now go back to dithering where Service matters are concerned and not make any more decisions. If I can take only that much from the mess, it will be something. I will also gain what comfort I can over the coming months from the knowledge that, after what I'm sure will be a rigorous interrogation by the CIA, you will begin a number of years rotting in some American secure facility. If I am asked, I will suggest somewhere for the criminally insane would be appropriate. It won't be much, but time and the thought of it may yet heal the wound I bear from ever having agreed to your getting this desk in the first place. A desk, which it has become obvious during your tenure, was well beyond your competence. You will wait here until arrangements can be made to escort you out of the building and pass you on to our American friends.'

The Director stood up, turned and left the office, walked past Gloria and the man standing at the doorway and left. He didn't close any doors behind him. Once he was gone the man at the door closed it quietly, sat down and folded his arms. Gloria carried on with her work. She was submitting her master's expenses chits, as she knew now, for the last time. God, he was a cheeky bugger, he scrounged almost as much in expenses as she earned. From the office there was the sound of someone vomiting, followed by a moan, then of a heavy body falling to the floor. The man sitting at the door stared sightlessly ahead of him and Gloria continued work on submitting the chits. Life had to go on, expenses chits had to be submitted through the proper channels even 'midst shot, shell and almighty cock-ups'. The only true survivor, she had learned in her many years in the Service, was the admin, which never died, faded away or got the bullet. She tapped the keys on her keyboard and the man by the door sat and stared into space. It was nothing to do with either of them. Whatever had fallen to the floor of the inner office would be taken away and disposed of and life would go on. As the BBC used to say in the old days when things went wrong – normal service would soon be resumed as soon as possible.

TWENTY-FIVE

'It was simple. I followed you when you left Copenhagen. I was ready to go when you left. I knew you would need back-up but I also knew that you would never agree to me coming. At the station I saw Charlie pick you up. I followed him. He had no reason to suppose anyone would follow him, so he never looked.'

They hadn't been able to talk on the train about what had happened and why. It was too busy. At Hamburg station they had found a quiet bar and sat with drinks at a table where, with lowered voices, they could talk.

'Who was she?'

'British Intelligence. It seems they wanted you dead.'

'For Christ's sake, why? I never did anything to them. Looked at properly, I never did anything to anyone. I just got caught up in the machinery.'

'Well, I only know what Bronski told me. She was British Intelligence, with orders to terminate you.'

'Did you believe him?'

'Yes.'

Jimmy took a drink and thought about it. How did bloody British Intelligence fit into things? The Americans and the Israelis wanted to find out what he knew about Rome and, if necessary, make sure he got permanently silenced. He didn't like it, but he understood it. He asked Udo.

'It was your line of work. Have you any idea?'

'Maybe they were doing it as a favour for the Americans or Israelis. You're the one who knows what this is really all about, not me, remember?'

Jimmy turned it over in his mind and decided Udo could be right. If British Intelligence found him, maybe killing him as a favour made sense. What the hell? The why didn't matter any more. The woman was dead and he was alive.

'So how did you turn Bronski round?'

'It wasn't difficult. If he joined me I'd take the bomber off his back.'

'Just like that?'

'No, not just like that. I explained and he listened. In the end he decided I was a better bet than London if he wanted to come out of the whole thing alive. To London he would be a loose end. To me, him living or dying didn't matter. All he had to do was take Otto out of the equation, shoot her before she shot you, and there he was, home and dry. It wasn't much to ask, seeing as how he was going to shoot her anyway.'

'What!'

'There was some sort of double-cross going on out of London. The woman's control had phoned Bronski and told him to hit her, then parcel you up until he could arrange for your collection.'

'And who was doing the collecting?'

'Well, it had to be Mossad or the CIA. A dead Jimmy Costello is a small favour, a live Jimmy Costello could obviously command a much higher price. My guess is they'd both want you to be thoroughly interrogated before they put a bullet in the back of your head.'

Jimmy picked up his beer and then put it down again. He suddenly found he wasn't enjoying it any more.

'What a world. I scratch your back, you poke my eye out. I'm glad I was only ever a bent copper, all this makes me feel like it was almost honest. Your world is too rich for me.'

'My ex-world, Jimmy. I'm a priest now.'

'Will you do it?'

'Do what?'

'Take the bomber off his back?'

'I've been too busy saving your English hide to think about it. Let's make sure we get you sorted first.'

Suddenly Jimmy remembered something.

'Thanks, Udo. I should have said it before but, somehow ...'

'That's OK, you've said it now, so forget it.'

'Will you do it, when we get back? He kept his side of the deal.'

Udo thought but not for long. 'We've got what we wanted. Maybe it would be best to let Yuri sort out his own problems.'

'God, you're a devious bastard, for a priest.'

'With the Yuris of this life, you have to be devious or dangerous, and preferably both. The one thing you can't afford is not to be a bastard.' He looked at his watch. It was three fifteen. 'Come on, we should get moving if we're going to catch that train.'

They got up, Udo paid. They left the bar and headed off together.

'You know, I thought the time had really come on this one. When Otto got me in the car and Bronski popped up. And in the warehouse, standing opposite that woman, I realised something.'

'What was that?'

'I was scared. Scared of dying.'

'That's natural, anyone would have been scared in that situation.'

'I've told you, I thought dying wasn't something that bothered me. But when it was about to happen I found I was wrong. It scared the shit out of me.'

They walked on in silence until they arrived back at the station and went to the platform where the Copenhagen Express was waiting. They boarded and sat down together. The carriage only had a few passengers and they sat at a table at one end away from those already in their seats. At three twenty-five, dead on time, the train slowly began to move. As it did a couple came through the door and sat at the table on the opposite side of the aisle. Jimmy looked at Udo who shrugged. It was going to be a long, quiet journey.

The sleek express slid out of the vaulted engine shed into the daylight and Hamburg began to pass by. Jimmy watched it while his brain tried to run back over what had happened and what Udo had told him. A question, as unexpected as it was unbidden, popped into his head. One he could talk about.

'Do you believe, Udo?'

'Believe what?'

'Religion, the Catholic Church. What we're supposed to believe.'

Put like that, Udo had to think. Straight out with no frills, it was a hard question. And Jimmy wasn't a lecturer in the seminary. It wasn't an academic question where you put certain words together for the right answer, the acceptable answer. Jimmy waited.

'No, I don't think so. I want to believe and I try to go through the motions with sincerity so that maybe, one day, belief will come. But now, at this minute, no.'

Udo waited. This was Jimmy's conversation; Udo the priest let him do it his own way. He could guess how hard it was.

'If there's nothing, then Bernie wasted her life, wasted it on me and for me. And if there's a God and a Heaven, well, I'm not the sort who goes there. If it's there at all, it has to be fair. The Bernies get to go there, the ones who've done some good in their lives. It's not for the Jimmy Costellos of this world. If I could get into Heaven then it wouldn't be fair so it wouldn't be Heaven, which means it's all just wishful thinking. I want there to be a Heaven for Bernie's sake. But I also don't want there to be one for my sake.'

'Because it's not just about Heaven, is it? If you have Heaven, then you have to have Hell.'

Jimmy nodded.

'But I can't let myself believe in nothing or, like I said, it means Bernie's life was wasted. There's only one thing I can really believe in. Standing in that warehouse made me see it. Me. I believe in me, me being alive and me staying alive.'

Udo waited but nothing more came.

'You know what you are, Jimmy?'

208

'A bad Catholic?'

'No, just a half-Catholic.'

'A half-Catholic, what the hell is a half-Catholic?'

'It's what most Catholics are, at least most of the ones I've known.'

Udo paused to see if Jimmy wanted the talk to go on.

'Well, go on then, explain.'

'It's not easy. Maybe onion-Catholics is better. You're layers and layers of things, Catholic things, like going to Mass, saying prayers, the Pope, bishops, the whole set-up. But if you strip away those things, the layers, what is there at the heart of it for you?'

'What do you think?'

'What is there at the heart of an onion?'

Jimmy thought about it.

'Nothing, an onion is just an onion.'

'Like you, layers and layers of acquired Catholic stuff. Stuff you've been told to do so you do it. Stuff you've been told to believe, so you try to believe it. When you put aside all the layers and ask the question "what am I?", you're nothing, just another guy, just another life. If you allow yourself to think about it, to really think about it, there's nothing to think about.'

Jimmy looked out of the window and tried thinking about it. But what was there to think about? When you came right down to it there was life. And that's all there was, until death took even that away.

'So what can an onion-Catholic do about it?'

Udo shrugged.

'Live. What else is there? Find a way to live and then get on with it.'

'Is that what you've done?'

'Yes.'

'You became a priest.'

'It works all right for me. I wouldn't recommend it, though.'

'You don't have to, I tried it. I can see now that it wouldn't work for me. I couldn't change, I still can't.'

'Why change? What's changing got to do with it?'

Jimmy was puzzled. 'You have to change don't you? Isn't

that what it's all about?'

Udo smiled. 'Nobody changes. Once you're who you are, what you've chosen to be, or what life has made you, that's it. That's the one you stay.'

'And you think that's how it is for everybody?'

'Oh, there'll be exceptions. There'll always be saints and monsters. But for ordinary people in the middle, people like you and me, I think it's pretty much true. You won't change.'

Jimmy believed him. Udo wasn't the first to point it out, but this time Jimmy knew it was true. The conversation didn't pick up again so Udo left it. The train travelled on. After a minute he leaned his head back and closed his eyes.

Jimmy sat and looked at him. Udo was right. It was true and he would have to live with it. At least he had found out one thing. He didn't want to die. In fact, he was shit-scared of dying; he wanted to live. The problem was, *would* he live? Had all this Bronski thing put the word out on him? Somehow, talking with Udo, he felt he was finally getting close to something important, something about himself, about living. He was finally getting close to making a sort of sense of things. But it would be typical of God to let him lift the curtain a little on what his life was all about only to have someone turn up and bring down the curtain once and for all. In primary school, the teachers used to say God was a mystery, that we weren't meant to understand. He had grown up thinking that was just a cop-out. A way of avoiding the difficult questions with impossible answers. Maybe he had been wrong. But it wasn't God that was the mystery. It was his bloody sense of humour.

Udo had slept for over an hour and now woken up. The people sitting at the table across the aisle had just got up and were going through the door. *Probably going to the Bordbistro to get something to eat or drink.* Jimmy had been thinking while Udo slept and now he wanted to talk. Jimmy leant forward and put his elbows on the table to ask his question.

'You're going to leave the bomber in place, aren't you?'

Udo leant forward to answer it. 'What do you mean?'

'Come on, Udo, I haven't known you long but I know you

well enough. If you turned Bronski it was because he really believed you could take the bomber off his back. If you can do that it means you're on the inside of whatever it is. You could have stopped it at any time, but you didn't. I also know you well enough to know you take being a priest seriously. So how come you're letting someone kill Bronski?'

Udo gave a tired smile.

'There's no way round you, is there, Jimmy?'

'You don't have to tell me if you don't want to.'

'OK, why not? Yuri Kemedov, now Charlie Bronski, operated in East and West Germany and the Baltic States. He ran some agents and did counter-intelligence work but he also operated against internal anti-state elements. He arranged for the infiltration of any group or organisation the government thought might be trying to subvert the revolution or be sympathetic to the West. Religious groups, liberal-minded academics, artists and writers who didn't toe the Party line. The way things were, he was never short of work. But he wasn't happy just to operate against legitimate targets. He was busy getting a name for himself and moving up. He started to set up groups, groups that weren't anti-state but weren't officially approved, that were in a sort of grey area. He did everything from faith healing to reading groups. He'd sucker people into them, groom a few who looked like he could fit them up as the leaders, then rig it to look like they were involved in subversive activities. When he was ready he'd roll up the whole thing and take the credit.'

'How come he could do that? People must have known.'

'We all knew, but we were the ones doing the work for him and he was back at head office with the full confidence of the high-ups. What would you have done? Blown the whistle or kept your mouth shut and obeyed orders?'

'Yeah, I can see how shopping him wouldn't really be an option.'

'And it wasn't anything that was big-deal. It was lots of small-time stuff. The high-ups were glad he was doing it but they never really took a close look into any of it.'

'Did you actually work for him?'

211

'Yes, I was on quite a few of his operations, legitimate ones and set-ups. I acted as an enforcer, a sharp-end man. I saw him a few times and knew all about him but he never noticed me.'

Jimmy understood but he was still surprised. It was payback time, revenge. Seeing the bad guy get what he deserves. But he still couldn't see Udo as the bomber, not unless he'd been more wrong than he'd ever been before.

'What happened? You came to Copenhagen as a priest and there he was, a happily married Catholic writer living with his wife in Nyborg?'

'Yes. I recognised him straight away. It didn't take a great brain to see how he had got there. He had wormed his way up the ladder and then, when he was worth something, sold out to the Americans or the British. Someone had given him a new life, a nice one at that.'

'And you decided, what?'

'To end the bastard's cosy little retirement.' *Christ*, thought Jimmy. It wasn't the answer he had expected. Udo went on, as much to himself as to Jimmy. 'We once did a job for him in Tallinn. He had arranged for an unofficial reading group to be set up amongst some university students. He got them books from the West, titles you couldn't get in the East. At first it was nothing much, bestsellers the state wouldn't let people read, harmless. But slowly he began to get them stuff that wasn't so harmless. Things that had political implications. Subversive. When he was ready he sent us in to roll it up.'

'Why use the Stasi?'

'Because he couldn't trust the local police. They would spot what was going on and most of them weren't, how shall I put it, unconditionally committed to the Russian revolution. They might see to it that the job got bungled, let the leaders slip through their fingers. He didn't want that because this time it wasn't a small-change thing. He had a big fish in play. One of the students he'd groomed as a leader was the daughter of a prominent Estonian politician thought to be in favour of independence. To smear him through his daughter would be a big feather in Kemedov's cap and move him quite a few rungs up the ladder. We did the job, she and a few others got swept

212

up, there was a secret trial and she and two others got bullets in the back of their heads.'

'Christ, Udo, that was dirty work by any standards.'

'For Yuri it was routine. Kemedov was an *apparatchik*.' Jimmy's face asked the question. 'It was a term, a name for the bureaucrats who had no convictions, no loyalties except to the system. Kemedov didn't believe in any ideology, not communism, not anything, except succeeding. And that meant serving the system he found himself in. So long as it served him well, he'd be a good servant. Until he got far enough to get a better deal elsewhere.'

'So when you saw him at Mass in Nyborg you decided he deserved some more appropriate reward for his years of service to the State?'

'Yes. The girl's father had shot himself just ahead of being arrested but she had a big brother. He was in the army at the time, a captain, serving in Afghanistan. When the Soviet Union fell apart and Estonia got independence he joined their new army and got to be a colonel before he retired. I passed on the information I had about Kemedov through old contacts. I didn't hurry, there was no need. Kemedov wasn't going anywhere. I waited until there would be no way he would suspect me. Unfortunately you turned up at the wrong moment, he added two and two, got five, and the rest you know.'

Jimmy was relieved in one way. Udo wasn't the actual bomber. But it wasn't far off the mark. He'd brought the bomber in and set up the target. Bomber, fixer? If you were talking right and wrong there wasn't much to choose between them, was there?

'So, will your colonel kill him?'

'I suppose so. That's what he came for. He lost a sister and a father because of him. It's what Kemedov deserves.'

'What about forgiveness, mercy?'

'What about justice?'

'Oh well, it's your game not mine. I'm just an innocent bystander.'

It was still another hour and a half to Copenhagen. There was nothing to do but think and talk.

'Tell me, Udo, what are the chances that all this will get to the others who might be interested in me?'

'How should I know?'

'It was your world once, it was never mine. However poor your guess is it would be better than any I might make.'

'I think they'll probably know where you are, if not now, then soon. Too many people got involved and it was messy.'

'So you think they'll come?'

'If it's important to them. But only you know how important it is so the question is, do *you* think they'll come?' Udo stood up. 'Come on, I'm hungry.'

Jimmy realised that he was hungry too so they went down the train into the Bordbistro. They ordered beer and sandwiches and sat in one of the semi-circular booths. The Bordbistro was almost empty, passengers who'd wanted to eat had mostly already done so. The couple who had been opposite them were drinking coffee and talking at a table at the far end. The other two booths next to theirs were empty.

'If they come is there anything I can do?'

Udo slowly shook his head.

'Not that I can see. If it's the Americans they'll fit you up for something then put in for your extradition. If it's the Israelis it will be a snatch. They're both good at what they do, they've had plenty of practice. That's about all I can tell you, except that if they're coming they won't waste any time.'

'Should I run?'

'You tried running from Bronski and where did it get you? You got out OK because you had me as back-up. The people who come after you this time will be better than Bronski, better equipped and there won't be just two of them and I'll be no good to you. If you run, where will you go and what will you use for papers? If they've got a definite fix on you they'll get you. Sorry, that's how it is.'

Jimmy felt like a rabbit who had just escaped from a fox by running across the road only to see the headlights about to hit him. Now you're safe, now you're not.

'Have you anything to suggest?'

'Nothing that will help. Make a will. Say your goodbyes and

214

say some prayers. Get drunk and stay drunk.'

'Thanks. I'll try and remember.'

They both sat in silence. Jimmy turned to one side and looked out of the window. He had never liked travelling, these days it seemed he did nothing else. Not that he was actually going anywhere. Maybe soon it would be over and he would settle down somewhere. Permanently.

Strangely enough, all he felt was tired. Not weary, not frightened, just tired. He was close to knowing something important, something about himself. It was all building up to something. He couldn't change who he was and he wouldn't try any more. He had finally realised that he didn't truly believe in anything except himself and staying alive. He wasn't even a bad Catholic, only an onion-Catholic. None of it made any sense, not yet. But he was close.

'Please, God, let me get there before it all ends.'

Udo surfaced from his own thoughts. 'Sorry, I missed that. I wasn't listening.'

'It was nothing, just me talking to someone with a funny sense of humour who isn't there and wouldn't do anything even if he were.'

'I see, a prayer. Well, why not? I hope it gets answered.'

'So do I, Udo. So do I.'

TWENTY-SIX

Jimmy came into the living room in his dressing gown with a mug in his hand.

'What time is it?'

Udo looked at his watch.

'Just after nine. Did you sleep well?'

'I slept well enough, I just didn't sleep long enough. I think I'll need three days solid to get back to anything near normal. I don't even remember what the time was when we got back here yesterday.'

'I know. I was the same. The first time you sleep after an operation your body goes to sleep, but your brain is only beginning to wind down. Sheer tiredness can switch off the body but not the brain. It's been a long time, but I remember the feeling. You'll be back to normal after a few days - you've been through a grinder and you're new to this sort of thing. It takes some real rest to put things back together.'

Jimmy sat down.

'How long have you been up?'

'Since eight. We had a caller, the policeman with the funny sense of humour who came and asked us about Bronski's visit to Hamburg. I'm pretty sure he's Security Service.'

'Did he want to know where we'd been?'

'Strangely, no. It didn't even get mentioned. He wanted

217

some information from me.'

'Anything I should know about?'

'He wanted me to tell him who was after Bronski.'

Jimmy was taking a drink of his tea and he spilled some down his dressing gown.

'God, how did they make that connection?'

'No idea, but they did.'

'What did you do?'

'What could I do? I told him.'

'And when they pick your man up …'

'They won't. I was told to phone and tell my man, as you call him, that if he left Denmark today he would be allowed to go. If he was still here tomorrow, he would be arrested and charged with the bombing.'

'Did you agree?'

'Of course, what else could I do? He sat there while I phoned.'

'And?'

'He's leaving, going back to Estonia. He's doing as he's told.'

'Just like that?'

'He's got a wife and two kids back there. He wants Bronski dead but he doesn't want it to cost him twenty years or more in a Danish prison.'

'So was that it?'

'No. I was told to tell him that if Bronski died in any way that might be interpreted as a professional hit, there would be an extradition warrant out inside twenty-four hours.'

'So no ideas about paying for it to be done?'

'No. It looks like Bronski gets to stay alive. When I'd made the call the funny man left and that was that.'

They sat in silence for a moment.

'What does it all mean?'

Udo shrugged. 'No idea, but it looks like Bronski will get on with his retirement after all. He gets out free and clear.'

Somehow Jimmy wasn't surprised.

'Yeah. I found that most of the really clever ones always did. How do you think your clever bugger of a visitor got to know about your involvement?'

'How should I know? He did, that's enough.' Udo looked into his empty mug and got up. 'Well, I'd better get on. There's a lot to catch up with, phone calls mostly. If you're away for just a few days it all backs up.'

'Why don't you take it easy for a while. It was tough for you as well.'

'No, the world doesn't stop just because you're doing something else and it doesn't stop because you're tired. They get born, they die, they want to talk, they need you to visit. So you forget you're tired and you get on with it.'

Jimmy was impressed. It had been a struggle for him to make himself a hot drink of tea and here was Udo going back to work like nothing had happened. He must be tough as old boots or dedicated to the point of obsession. Jimmy stood up and followed Udo to the kitchen.

'How on earth did you get to be a priest anyway? Were your family Catholic or what?'

'No, and I never met any professionally. All the religious ones I interrogated were Protestants or sect people. I suppose I just started to get interested.'

'In religion?'

'No, religion itself never interested me. People did. I interrogated many people. Often I used a degree of coercion, you understand?'

'I understand, torture.'

'I obeyed orders, it didn't bother me. It had to be done so I did it. Some lasted longer than others and a few held out until they died. The ones who interested me were the religious ones.'

'They were the ones who held out?'

Udo finished drying his mug and put it away but he stayed to talk so Jimmy stayed to listen.

'No, not particularly, they were about the same as the rest, some weak, some strong, a few who died. No, it was something about quite a few of them. Even when you broke them you had the feeling you still hadn't quite got them. That somewhere inside you'd missed something. That a small part of them was still beyond your control. Free in some way. It was interesting, from a professional point of view.'

'And you followed it up?'

'Good God, no. To associate with that sort for any reason was suicide in my job. But I was interested. Then, when I was in business for myself I was in a bar in Munich and I got talking to this guy. It turned out he was a Catholic priest on holiday. We talked about things and I asked him about confession, about how could a man forgive the sins of others.'

'An odd choice of conversation.'

'Not really, I wanted to talk to him about what interested me and it was a way of turning the talk in that direction. He told me a story. There was a German priest, a theologian called Bernard Häring who got into trouble with the Vatican. Something about what he wrote in his books, I can't remember, I wasn't interested. Häring said that he had been seriously interrogated only twice. As a soldier in the war by the SS, and as a theologian by the Vatican. The SS were polite and efficient. It was the Vatican that had scared him to death. They were the ones he had found hard to forgive.'

'And that set you on the road to being a priest?'

'I suppose you could say it did.'

'How come?'

'It occurred to me that any Church that could accommodate men like Häring and the sort who interrogated him at the Vatican would be worth looking into. I was a systems man. I had been brought up and worked all my life in a system, one that I believed in. Then it had gone, just like that. The Catholic Church was a system and it had been around for a very long time. I figured it wasn't about to suddenly disappear, so I started looking into it and ended up here.'

'That's it?'

Jimmy rinsed out his mug and began drying it.

'Yes, that's it. And now I must get going. You take it easy; in six or seven hours you'll be ready to go back to bed. Don't fight it, go to bed and sleep. Let your brain readjust. We'll start getting back into some sort of routine tomorrow.'

'Will your visitor be a problem? Do you think he'll come back?'

'I don't see why he should. I think he got all he wanted.'

Udo left the kitchen and went to his study to make his phone calls. Jimmy put his mug away. Udo was right; already he was feeling the tiredness seeping back. Maybe it wouldn't take as long as Udo said. Maybe he could help it along. He went back into the living room, to some bookshelves. Most were in German but a few were in English. One was called *The Way to Nicea* by someone called Bernard Lonergan. It looked promising so he took it out and went and sat down. Normally he didn't read much, but at this moment he felt he had need of the right kind of book. He opened the book at the flyleaf. The subtitle was "A Dialectical Development of Trinitarian Theology". That sounded promising. He turned to the Introduction. The first sentence ran, "In a recent study of 'Biblical Hermeneutics' published in *Semeia*, Paul Ricoeur not only conceived live metaphor as creative expression but also attributed a similar power to parable, proverb and apocalyptic ..."

Jimmy yawned. It was perfect. A couple of hours with this and he would be ready to go back to bed, never mind any six or seven hours. And he settled down to read.

TWENTY-SEVEN

Two days after Jimmy and Udo returned, Elspeth Bronski came home to Nyborg. Charlie had phoned her as soon as he'd got back and told her everything was over. The problem was solved. He also told her to take as long as she liked, not to hurry if she was having a good visit. But she didn't want to stay. Hugh was becoming querulous and rambling. The house was a mess. She would stay long enough so that her departure didn't look too sudden, but she would leave as soon as she could.

Charlie was uncomfortable waiting for her at the airport. She hadn't hurried home because of Hugh. She was still worried. He met her as she came out of Arrivals, gave her a hug and a kiss, took her bag and began work.

Everything was fine, the FBI had found the man and now he was gone. It had all been a case of mistaken identity. He was some kind of nut who was convinced that Charlie had been responsible for the deaths of two of his family. God knows how he made any connection, but that's what had happened. The FBI said it was definitely all over. The man would get treatment, the help he needed. There would be no charges, no court case, nothing. It was all over. It was what Elspeth wanted and she seemed to accept it.

Everything was back on an even keel.

Charlie didn't make any fuss when they got home. He sat

223

Elspeth down on the settee, got her a glass of white wine, then went to the desk and switched on his laptop. With him at his desk and her sitting on the settee things were just like they used to be. Write, do something normal, something routine. Elspeth gave him a smile. It wasn't much of a smile but she was trying.

'Still the black bread thing?'

'No, that was too rich. I couldn't even redeem it with vodka. This is something else, cold stuffed goose neck.'

'My God, I think I preferred the black bread.'

Elspeth sat and watched Charlie as he began working, reading from the old cookery book and making notes on screen. She took the occasional sip. She didn't want it but she had to try.

'How can you just get back to writing as if nothing had happened?'

He turned and smiled at her. He was ready for that.

'Because nothing did happen. We had a bad dream, that's all. Now we're awake and we can forget it. Everything is back to normal. Like I said, remember?'

'I suppose so.'

'I know so.'

Charlie turned back to his writing and Elspeth stood up.

'I'll go and unpack then maybe we can go out somewhere for lunch.'

Charlie didn't stop writing. 'Yes, I'd like that. There's a couple of letters for you. I left them on the dressing table.'

Elspeth went to the bedroom. Her case was on the bed. She went to the dressing table, put down her glass and picked up the two letters. One from England, the other from Denmark.

She opened the one from England. It was about Hugh. Her sister Angela wanted her to support the idea of putting him in a home.

Now that you've seen it for yourself, I'm sure you'll agree that the best thing for everyone, but especially for Daddy, would be if Nigel and I found somewhere he could be looked after ...

The place was certainly a mess and he *had* become unbearable to live with. But that wasn't the real reason Angela had written. She had her eye on St. Anthony's. If she could get Hugh put in a home, she and her family would move in. Well, Daddy was a lot worse now in many ways but he certainly wasn't ready to go into a home, and, as far as Elspeth was concerned, the longer Angela was kept waiting to take possession of St Anthony's, the better. *Self-centred bloody cow. And as for that prick of a husband, Nigel …*

Suddenly she was shocked by her words, even if they were only spoken in her own head. She didn't use language like that.

She put Angela's letter down and picked up the other. The envelope was postmarked Odense and was handwritten, so was the letter. It was quite short, almost scrawled, as if written in a hurry.

Dear Mrs Bronski,

You do not know me but I have some information I think you should know. The man you think is your husband, and now goes by the name of Charles Bronski, is in fact Yuri Kemedov, formerly of Russian Intelligence and before that the KGB. He defected to the British and was given a new identity, the one he has now. I am the man who put the bomb in his car. He was responsible for the deaths of my sister and father and many more innocent people. For reasons you do not need to know, he is safe from me now but I pray to God that some relative of one of his other many victims will do my work for me. I will do my best to see his present location becomes known. Leave him, Mrs Bronski, or you may die with him. Whatever you do, do not try to warn him. If he became aware that you know his real identity, your life would be in danger. You will not believe what I have written but you can confirm its truth by talking to Fr Udo Mundt in Copenhagen.

There was no name. Elspeth re-read it, then quickly put it back into its envelope and put it in her handbag. She stood for a moment. Then she went to the bed and began to unpack. She needed to occupy herself while she thought.

At his desk in the living room, Charlie had stopped writing. His mind was circling a problem he had been working on ever since he had got back. If Costello was so important, how could he sell him, and who would the likely buyers be? The British wanted him dead but that didn't help. The British didn't count these days – they did as they were told, and the ones who told them were the Americans. He had to find a way of contacting the Americans and testing the water. One thing was certain, he could do nothing from Denmark. He needed to go to a European capital and make initial contact through an embassy. Paris seemed a good option. He got up and went to the bedroom door. Elspeth had her back to him, hanging things in the wardrobe.

'What about a break?'

Elspeth started and dropped a jacket on to the floor. She turned round and looked at Charlie. He walked to her, picked up the jacket and held it out.

'Are you OK? You look frightened.'

Elspeth gave him one of her weak smiles. She took the jacket from him.

'I try to tell myself it was all a bad dream, that it's over now and I can forget it. But I was always a hopeless liar, so I don't convince myself any more than I could convince anyone else.'

Charlie put his arms round her and held her to him. 'What you need is a break. We both do.' He stood back. 'Let's go to Paris. Autumn on the boulevards. We can relax and forget Denmark for a few days. What do you say?'

'Do you want to?'

'It's what you want that matters.'

Elspeth gently pushed his arms away and went past him and sat on the bed still holding the jacket.

'It doesn't seem to have affected you at all. Somebody put a bomb in your car, you had to go the FBI and then we had to run away and hide. Now it's all over and you just pick up where you left off. I can't do that, Charlie. I just can't do that.'

Charlie came and sat beside her.

'I was in base security for most of my Air Force time. You get used to alerts and then standing down. It's something I learned to do. As far as I'm concerned there was a short alert, I went to stay with an old friend and his wife. The specialists came and sorted out the problem and now we're stood down. Things are back to normal.'

Elspeth looked at him.

'Did you ever have to kill anyone, Charlie, in the line of duty, as part of your job?'

Charlie looked surprised.

'Good God, no. What made you ask that?'

'I don't know. I can't seem to make myself look at it the way you do. If you'd ever had to kill someone it would make you different, wouldn't it?'

'I bet it would, but base security was about being careful, not about being violent. Now, what about Paris? A change, a rest, a good time.'

'If you want to.'

'Do you want to?'

Suddenly Elspeth seemed to pull herself together. She stood up and smiled at him.

'Well, I'm not going to Paris looking like this. If we're going to Paris, I need a new outfit. We can go to Paris if I can go to Copenhagen and buy a proper suit.'

Charlie stood up.

'I thought the right idea was for a woman to do the shopping *in* Paris?'

'It is. But I couldn't go into a Paris shop looking like I do. I'll go to Copenhagen today and you can arrange everything. Please, Charlie, if we're going, let's go straight away.'

There was almost a pleading in her voice. Charlie stood up and took her hand.

'Of course. Go and get a suit that will knock a Paris shop girl's eye out and when you come back I'll have it all arranged.'

'Thank you.'

Elspeth stood up and pulled on the jacket. Then she went to the dressing table and picked up her handbag.

'Did you read your letters? Anything interesting?'

'No, nothing. Nothing important. Angela's still trying to get that awful family of hers into St Anthony's. She wants me to agree that Daddy should go into a home.'

'What a bunch. I'm glad I got the one who's the exception to the rule. What was the other one?'

Elspeth paused. Her mind was racing. Confront him? Tell him? Lie to him? *Do not warn him or your life will be in danger.*

'Er, that was a note from …' Charlie waited, suddenly alert. 'From Fr Nguyen. I wasn't going to tell you because, well, you know how you get when … he didn't want to bother me in person but he wanted me, us, to …' Charlie waited. 'He wanted us to donate some money for a centre they're trying to establish in Odense for immigrants. There's a big Vietnamese population and lots of them are Catholics. I suppose he must have got our name from someone.'

Charlie relaxed.

'My God, priests. It's always money, isn't it? Did he say how much?'

'No, just that he was contacting Catholics who lived anywhere near Odense.'

'Don't worry, we'll cough up. We always do. You get going to Copenhagen and I'll start sorting out the bookings.' He walked to the bedroom door. 'And make sure the suit will knock them dead in Paris. No expense spared. I'll claim it as a business expense. Who knows, I might even actually get a bit of business done.'

And he was gone.

Elspeth stood for a moment hardly daring to breath. Then she walked to the living room doorway.

'Bye, Charlie.'

He didn't look round from the desk. 'Bye.'

Elspeth left the bungalow and walked quickly towards the station. She pulled out her mobile and dialled.

'Father Mundt? Oh, Mr Costello, is Father Mundt in? May I speak with him? Yes, it's important.' She walked on as she waited for Fr Mundt to come to the phone. 'Hello, Father. I need to talk to you. Yes it's urgent. As soon as possible, this afternoon. I'm on my way to the station now. Yes, I can tell you. It's about someone called Yuri Kemedov.' There was a silence. Then Udo answered. 'Thank you, Father, I'll be there as soon as I can.'

Udo put the phone down and went back to the living room.

'That was Elspeth Bronski.'

'I thought I recognised the voice.'

'She's coming to see me.'

'When?'

'She's on her way to the station at Nyborg now. She should be here in a couple of hours.'

'What does she want.'

'She wants to talk to me about someone called Yuri Kemedov.'

Jimmy put down his book. 'Oh, Jesus. What will you do?'

'What can I do? If she asks I'll tell her.'

'And if Bronski finds out?'

'What do you think?'

'Oh, Christ. What a mess.'

'Yes, as you say, a mess.' And Udo went out.

Jimmy was sitting in a chair. He picked up the book he was reading and looked absently at the page.

"*Marcellus of Ancyra, however, according to the testimony of Eusebius, held that there was one tri-personal, thrice-named hypostasis in God ...*"

What did it all mean? Who had told her about Kemedov and why was she bringing it to Udo? Thank God I can walk away from this one. Whatever problems Bronski is going to have with his wife aren't anything to do with me. Jimmy stood up and went to the doorway of the study. It was open and Udo was working.

'I'll go and do some hospital visits when she comes.'

Udo didn't bother to look up. He kept on working.

'Sure, Jimmy. This is my affair, it's nothing to do with you. I'll get on with some work here until she arrives.'

Jimmy went back to the living room and picked up his book. "*... and Eusebius judged that this opinion was openly Sabellian.*"

He closed it. What a mess, but things were always a mess. Nothing changed. Nothing ever bloody well did.

TWENTY-EIGHT

Udo answered the door.

'Hello, Elspeth, please come in.' Udo led the way to the living room. 'Sit down.'

'Thank you, Father.'

They sat down and Udo waited. Elspeth half-smiled then looked round the room avoiding Udo's eyes. Udo waited. Elspeth looked at him, almost spoke, then looked down at her handbag. She was having trouble getting started, wanted to talk but didn't know how to begin. It didn't matter because Udo could start it for her.

'Ask me your question, Elspeth. It's why you've come, so ask it.'

She looked up, slightly startled. Then she understood.

'Is it true?'

'Yes.'

Elspeth held her handbag on her lap with both hands. She looked down at it for support but it remained stubbornly neutral, as handbags do. She looked at Udo looking at her, waiting. She couldn't bear his eyes on her. She looked at the window and studied the pattern on the net curtains. Small flowers with twiddly bits in between. Cheap and common. A priest should have better in his house. She looked back at her handbag. It still reserved judgement.

'Would you like a drink, tea or coffee?' She didn't answer. 'Perhaps something stronger?'

Elspeth looked up. She never drank spirits. Hugh had taught her that strong drink made women prone to sins of the flesh and that beer was a plebeian drink, coarse and common, a drink for the working classes, something to replace the sweat of hard physical labour. Ladies didn't sweat. If a woman wanted alcohol then it should be wine. But only in moderation and never port.

'Yes please, Father, I'd like something to drink.'

'Tea, coffee?'

'Something stronger. A large one.'

It was a phrase she had heard Charlie use.

'Sure. Vodka. Would that be all right?'

'Are you having a drink, Father?'

'Yes, and drop the Father, Elspeth. If you want to call me anything, make it Udo.'

'I'll have whatever you have.'

'Fine.'

Udo got up and left. Elspeth took a handkerchief out of her handbag. There were no tears yet, just fear. In the train, she had found a hundred ways to tell herself it wasn't true, that it was all just some horrible story. A malicious letter written to hurt Charlie through her. But she had known, deep inside, that she was only finding one of a hundred ways to avoid admitting it was the truth. What do you do when your whole world suddenly comes to an end, when you suddenly find you don't know your husband and you don't know yourself? Who was she now?

Udo returned, put a glass on the table in front of her and sat down. He took a drink and waited. Tentatively she picked up the chunky tumbler of clear liquid. It looked harmless, like water. She took a very small sip. It didn't taste of anything. Was she now a fallen woman? She found the words eventually.

'Can you tell me anything?'

'What do you want to know?'

'Who is Yuri Kemedov?'

'Yuri Kemedov worked for the Soviet Secret Service, the KGB. When the Soviet Union was disbanded, he worked for

232

Russian Intelligence. He wasn't so very high up or important but the British thought he was worth buying when he offered to defect. They gave him a new identity and a new life. He became Charles Bronski and went to live in England. After that you know more about him than I do.'

Elspeth put the glass down and opened her handbag. She took out the letter and handed it to Udo.

'Read it please, Father.' Udo didn't correct her. He took the envelope from her, took out the letter and read it. Then he put it back into the envelope and handed it back. Elspeth took it and sat for a moment looking at it. 'Is it true? Did he kill people?'

'He may have done. I know he had people killed.'

'Isn't that the same thing?'

'No. The hand that holds the gun does the killing. Yuri gave the orders.'

Suddenly words she had heard many times in her life slipped into her head, words that had never had any impact when they were part of the routine Gospel readings in Mass. They had never really meant anything, just words you listened to reverently. Holy but meaningless words that somehow saved you from Hell.

You would have no power over me at all if it had not been given to you from above. That is why the man who handed me over to you has the greater guilt. Those who handed Jesus over to Pilate for execution had the greater guilt.

She had been wrong about the words. They didn't save you from Hell. They put you there.

'Did he order the killing of the people in the letter? The sister and the father.'

'He had the sister killed. The father committed suicide.'

'And were there many others?'

'Enough.'

There was a silence. Udo took a drink and waited. She would have to do this in her own way, he couldn't help. He waited. Elspeth took a sip, then a big drink and immediately choked. She held her handkerchief to her mouth as she coughed and spluttered. She almost threw the glass on to the table. It fell over and what was left of the drink spilled as the glass rolled over and fell to the floor. Udo watched. Elspeth finally got control of herself. Her eyes were watering but it was not tears. She sat for a moment, breathing carefully. Then she noticed the table and the glass on the floor.

'Oh dear. I'm so sorry, Father.' She looked around in a vague way and then remembered the handkerchief she was still holding. She mopped up the vodka with it then bent down and picked up the glass, put it on the table and put the damp handkerchief in her handbag. Udo watched. He had seen it all before. People trying to deal with something that couldn't be dealt with. People trying to hang on to a normality that was utterly gone. Elspeth calmed down and looked at Udo. It was time.

'What shall I do?'

'What do you want to do?'

It was not the answer she expected, nor the one she wanted. She wanted to be told what to do. Priests did that. They told you what to do. You told them your sins and they forgave you in God's name and then named God's price. Always a small price, just a few words, meaningless holy words that saved you from Hell. 'Say three Hail Marys and make a good Act of Contrition' was what she wanted. You said your penance and everything was right again. They didn't ask you what you wanted to do.

'I don't know. Is there anything I *can* do?'

Udo though about it. It was a very sensible question. He was slightly surprised. Elspeth had always struck him as a woman who allowed herself to be ruled by others, someone who had never developed any real personality. A beautiful but essentially empty person. Now, as she sat there looking at him, waiting for his answer, she seemed to be changing. Unless he was mistaken, the emotion which she had finally allowed to emerge was not fear but anger.

'Stay or go.'

She thought about it.

'And that's all? Stay with him or leave him?'

'It's all I can think of.'

'Are you, as a priest, telling me I should stay with a man I'm not married to? A man it turns out I was never married to?'

'No, not as a priest. As a friend. As a priest I would have to say that now you know the truth about your supposed marriage, any continuance of your sexual union would be sinful. But, frankly, Elspeth, sinful or not sinful isn't the issue here.'

'The letter said I could be in danger if he found out I knew who he really was. Is that right?'

Udo nodded. 'Very much so.'

'Well, I don't believe you, either of you. I think whoever wrote that letter wants to get at Charlie through me. I think Charlie isn't the same man who did those horrible things, if anyone did them. I think he wanted to start a new life and did. He loves me and is trying to be a good man and a good husband. If any of it is true, I think he's trying to make up for what he did in the past. If he ever was as you say then he's changed. And as for sinful, well you can ...' she paused to summon up her courage, 'well you can fuck your sinful and you can fuck your Church.' There, it hadn't been so bad. Swearing out loud wasn't so difficult, nor even so terrible. All you needed to do was say the words. Then suddenly the fact that she had said them to this man, a priest, in his own home crashed in on her mind. 'Oh, Father, I'm sorry, so sorry. I didn't mean ...'

And a lifetime of oppression and Catholic guilt crushed the small flame of rebellion, snuffed it out. She lowered her eyes and awaited her punishment. It would be very terrible, she knew, but she would deserve it.

'Yes, I know how you feel. I sometimes feel the same myself. But I'm afraid you're wrong about Charlie. He hasn't changed. He can't change and I don't think he wants to try. If he thinks you know the truth about him, my guess is that he will kill you.'

Elspeth looked up at Udo. This wasn't any kind of priest she'd ever known. This was a glimpse of that shyest of animals in her limited world, the man behind the priest. And he was telling her the truth.

'How can you be sure?'

'Because a few days ago he went to Lübeck and killed two people. It was the price that British Intelligence wanted to keep him safe. *His* was the hand that held the gun this time; it was someone else who ordered the killings.

'Oh my God.' Then a thought occurred to her. 'How do you know so much about him, about what he was and what he did?'

'Because I worked for him, amongst others. We were both in the same line of business. God forgive me, mine was the hand that held the gun. I was the one who carried out the orders that the likes of Yuri gave.'

Elspeth tried to let it sink in. Then a small light dawned. 'But you, you've changed. Why couldn't Charlie, if he loves me? Do you think he loves me?'

'Possibly. I think you are a person someone could easily love. But even if he loves you, he won't let that stand in the way of what he thinks he has to do to protect himself. Lose one wife and you can always get another. Lose your life and it's permanent.'

'Then I can't stay. I can't live with him and pretend I know nothing. He'd find out just as if I told him.'

'You'll go?'

'Yes, I'll run away like some scared little girl.'

'Have you any experience of running?'

'Pardon?'

'Do you have money, can you get papers in another name or could you get them? Do you have somewhere to run where Yuri couldn't follow or find you? If he comes after you, could you be ready for him and kill him before he kills you? What if he pays someone to do it for him? You understand? It's not so easy to run in situations like this. You wouldn't know how and Yuri is a trained professional. People like me and him were trained to find people and do what had to be done.'

He wasn't helping, he was advising and then throwing difficulties in her path.

'But if I can't stay and I can't run, what can I do?'

'There's only one thing you can do ...'

Elspeth knew what was coming. The priest was back. The man had gone. Her anger returned. Anger was all that was left.

'I know. I've heard it a hundred times. Pray. Prayer is the answer. Put it all in God's hands. Prayer was the answer when Daddy wouldn't let me apply for university. The nuns at school listened and said I should pray about it. Well, I prayed, but I still didn't go to university. And when I asked priests what I should do about Daddy bullying me into staying at home to be his unpaid housekeeper instead of having a life of my own, the answer was always: pray about it. And I prayed. I prayed and I prayed until Charlie came along and just swept Daddy aside and married me. I thought God had finally heard me, that Charlie was the answer to my prayers. But he can't be, can he? Not if he's who you say he is. He was just someone else, like Daddy, who wanted to use me. So what's the good of praying? It will change nothing. Don't tell me to pray, I've tried it and it doesn't work.'

The anger was in full flow and Udo was glad, it was better than despair.

'I wasn't going to tell you to pray about it. Pray about it if you like. It would be good to pray about it. But like you said, it won't change Yuri. Nothing will change Yuri.'

Elspeth's anger disappeared. This man wasn't the one who had destroyed her world.

'So what were you going to say?'

'Choose bad.'

'Bad?'

'When your choice is between bad and worse, choose bad, not worse. Work out which is bad and which is worse, staying or running. Then do whichever is the bad option, not the worse. I'm sorry, it's all I can suggest.'

Elspeth thought about it. 'I could go to the police.'

She wasn't hopeful. She had thought about it a lot on the train. What did she actually know? Only what was in the letter and there wasn't even a name on the letter. True, she now had Fr Mundt's confirmation, but was that worth anything?

'Yes, you could go to the police.'

'Would it do any good?'

'No.'

'Would you tell them what you told me?'

'What have I told you?' Elspeth didn't understand. 'All I have told you is that a long time ago Charlie had another name and did another job. So what? Now he has a new name and is a

British citizen with a history which he can prove and which the British government, if asked, will back up. What could the police do? And once you'd told them, Yuri would know.'

'But he couldn't kill me then, could he?'

'If you mean would he put a gun to your head and blow your brains out, no, he wouldn't do that. But there are many ways to make someone die, more than you can imagine.' Elspeth looked down at her handbag. It offered no comfort. There was no comfort anywhere. 'What did you tell him?'

Elspeth looked up. 'About what?'

'About coming here.'

'Oh, he wants us to go to Paris, a break to help me get over what has happened. I said I'd come and buy something to wear and then we could go as soon as he wants. Straight away.'

'I see.'

There was a silence between them. Udo tried to offer what words he could.

'I'm sorry, Elspeth, truly sorry for what you have learned, for what I have had to tell you.'

She gave him a twisted smile.

'The trouble was I already knew something was wrong.'

'Well, a car bomb ...'

'No, after that. After he came back from Hamburg. A man came to the house. Charlie told me afterwards that he was police, but he didn't behave at all like a policeman. He asked Charlie about why he had gone to Hamburg so suddenly. Charlie told him a lie, or he had already told me a lie.'

'A lie?'

'He told me he had gone to get help, that there was an FBI agent in Hamburg who could help us. When he told me he said the man he met would help us. He said the agent was a man. But when he told the policeman who came, it had become a woman, a woman who worked in London. I suppose he had to say it was a woman because they could check. But it meant he'd lied to me. I couldn't understand why he'd lied but I just put it away. Tried to forget it. And the way he behaved when he met me at the airport and when we got home. It was as if nothing at all had happened. So when I got the letter, I knew.'

Udo waited. She was almost finished not least because she was running out of time if she was going to stick to her story.

'One last question, Father. Am I married?'

'I told you, Charlie is a British citizen, you married him legally so, yes, you're married.'

'In the eyes of the Church?'

'You know the answer to that, Elspeth. You don't need me to spell it out.'

She nodded. Yes, she knew the answer. She waited for a moment then looked at her watch. If she told Charlie she'd searched through all the shops but couldn't find anything then she still had a little more time.

'Can you hear my confession, Father?'

'Sure.'

Udo got up, went to a drawer and pulled out a stole, a scarf-like strip of embroidered cloth. He put it to his lips, draped it round his neck and sat down again. Elspeth made the Sign of the Cross and began. Udo sat and listened. Priest and penitent both with their own thoughts behind the words. She, coming to terms with what awaited her. He, wondering why Yuri would be on the move again so soon, and why Paris?

Jimmy came back about an hour after Elspeth had left.

Udo told him what had happened.

'He's on the move, Jimmy.'

'And?'

'For God's sake, he has to have a reason.'

'And?'

'He must be trying to sell you out. He's going to Paris to set it up. Can't you see it?'

'Yes, I suppose I can. But what can I do about it?'

Udo sat and thought. What could Jimmy do about it? It was a good question, unfortunately he didn't have a good answer. 'Can you get me a gun?'

'What?'

'Can you get me a gun? A nice, reliable gun. Like Long Otto said, German, efficient, ex-Stasi issue. It will only have to make one shot from close range. Can you do that?'

'And if I got you this gun, what would you do with it?'

'I'll put a bullet in his head.'

'He'll be in Paris, maybe by tomorrow, if not tomorrow then soon. If I'm right, by the time I could get you a gun he'd already have sold you. What good will it do to kill him when he comes back? It won't save you.'

'At least she'll be free of him and he'll have got what he deserves. Udo, they'll get me sometime, I'm running out of places to go. But before they get me I can at least remove one nasty bastard from this planet.'

'How?'

'It shouldn't be too difficult. Tell him you need to talk to him, ask them to dinner, just think of something. All I need is to be able to do is get close enough to hold the gun to his head when he's not expecting it.'

'It's not so easy. You make putting a bullet in someone's head sound easy but, believe me, it's not.'

'I know, Udo.'

'Do you? Do you really know?'

'Yes.'

'You've done it?'

'Long ago. It was something I thought I had to do, so I did it. And you're right, it wasn't easy.'

'What about the police? You can't blow someone's brains out at the dinner table and just walk away. What will you do afterwards?'

'Nothing. He'll be dead, she'll be free of him and I'll get what I should have got years ago. I'll spend the rest of my life in prison. God knows I deserve it.' Jimmy smiled. 'And it won't be so easy for them to get at me in prison, will it? Their kind of writ doesn't run so well on the inside. For that, you have to have been on the wrong side of the law.'

'Don't be so sure. They have long fingers.'

'So?'

'I'll get you your gun, as self-protection, not to assassinate Yuri. If they come after you, at least you'll be armed.'

'And dangerous?'

'No, you're not dangerous any more. I can see how you

might have been once. Very dangerous. But not any more. I'll tell you something. There are times when I think some people are chosen, that there are people who God has chosen. You may be one of them.'

'That's crap and you know it.'

'Do I? Then why aren't you dead? Or serving that long stretch you say you deserve in some British jail? Why are you still going, what keeps you going, and where is it you're going to?' Jimmy didn't answer. There was no answer. 'You see what I'm saying, I don't know and you don't know, but maybe God knows.'

'If there is a God, which I more and more doubt. And if he exists, he isn't a watchmaker and he doesn't play chess. If he does anything he just waits and watches. So let's leave him out of it, shall we? Just get me the gun, get Bronski where I can put him on the end of it and leave the rest to me.'

'OK, Jimmy. I'll get you your gun. Anything else is up to you.'

TWENTY-NINE

Jimmy's mobile rang. He took it out. It was Udo. 'That's handy. I was going to call you. Do we need eggs?'

'No, Jimmy, we don't need eggs. Finish shopping and come back, you've got a visitor. It's a Monsignor from Rome, the one who asked me to take you on. Very smooth, very ...'

'Bland?'

'That's it, that's the exact word, bland. Very smooth, very bland. He wants you here, so come running.'

Jimmy put his mobile away and headed for the checkout. It wasn't busy. He didn't like shopping so he always tried to do it during a quiet time. He finished paying and left the small supermarket with a carrier bag in each hand. Suddenly a young woman was at his side. She had a mac over her left arm which hid her hand. With her right hand she took Jimmy's arm. He stopped and looked at her. She was a stranger. She smiled a big smile and leant forward to kiss his cheek. With both hands holding carrier bags there was nothing he could do. But he would have done nothing anyway for two reasons. One was what she said, very quietly.

'Get in the car.'

The other was the feeling of something hard held in the hand under the mac poking him in the ribs. A car was waiting next to them. The girl kept the big smile going while she opened the door with her free hand. Jimmy got in and sat down with his two carrier bags on his lap. There was another young woman beside the driver. She was half-turned looking at him but she wasn't smiling. Her hands were out of sight. Jimmy didn't need to see the gun to know it was there. The woman with the mac went round the car and got in beside him. The driver pulled away into the traffic. Nobody said anything.

The car drove up to the top of the busy Vesterbrogade with its shops and restaurants. They passed the Central station on their right with the Tivoli Gardens opposite and turned into Hans Christian Andersen Boulevard. Jimmy looked out of the window. Despite what was happening he found it difficult not to feel more like a tourist than someone snatched at gunpoint. He didn't know why, but he felt strangely detached. Maybe it was because he was helpless. Maybe he had just accepted that one day this would happen. Now it had.

The car crossed the bridge over the channel between Copenhagen and Christianshavn. Ancient defensive bastions jutting out into the water kept them company on the left until the car veered away following the main road round to the right. They headed on until they joined the long, straight Amagerbrogade which ran through the comfortable suburbs all the way down to Tårnby. *If we keep going we're headed for the airport*, thought Jimmy. Whatever they wanted to happen to him, it looked like they didn't want it to happen in Denmark. Then his mobile went off.

He looked at the woman sitting beside him. She shook her head so he let it ring until it stopped and he looked out of the window again. The roads weren't busy and everything looked exactly as it should look. *Why is it*, he wondered, *that you only notice how normal things are for everyone else when things have gone completely arse-up for you?*

The car moved on quickly but not speeding. No one was taking any chances, everything was very under control.

'Can I put this shopping on the floor. It's heavy.'

The woman beside him nodded.

'Don't do anything foolish, Mr Costello. Just put it there.'

Both of her hands were visible and the mac lay across her

knees. She didn't have her gun out but he guessed she probably didn't need one. If he did anything except put the carrier bags on the floor she'd probably break his arm with one hand. She might even do it with nothing more than a look. He put the two carrier bags on the floor between his legs. They weren't really heavy, it was just something to do.

They reached Tårnby. The main road leading to the airport was a left turn but the driver crossed straight over the intersection into more suburbs. He drove on until they were clear of the houses and the flat expanse of runways became visible on their left. Planes rose steeply into the sky at regular intervals and others slowly descended. The car was on some sort of service road which ran round the outside of the airport perimeter fence. They drove on for a while and eventually stopped by a pair of big wire gates.

The driver got out and went to the side of the gates. Jimmy watched him speaking into a box. Then he went to the middle of the gates and pushed them open and came back to the car. They drove through and the car stopped. The driver got out and walked back to the gates. It was then they saw a car coming at speed along the service road. The driver turned and ran back to the car. He got in and the car shot forward only to brake hard after about twenty yards. Coming towards them fast were two more cars from inside the airport. They all looked round. The car behind them had stopped, blocking the open gateway. Someone was getting out. In front of them the two cars skidded to a halt, one to the left one to the right. There was nowhere to go. The driver turned round to the woman sitting beside Jimmy. She didn't say anything. She was watching the two cars in front. Nothing happened. No one got out, they just sat there at a distance from them. Then a voice from a loudhailer came from behind them.

'Please do nothing. I have Major General David Weiss on the phone for you. I repeat, please do nothing, I have Major General David Weiss on the phone. He wishes to speak to Hannah Levi. I repeat, I have Major General Weiss on the phone and he wishes to speak to Captain Hannah Levi.'

The woman said something in a language Jimmy didn't

recognise. The driver got out of the car, left the door open and headed towards the car behind them. Jimmy watched him go and when he turned back noticed that a gun had appeared in her hand again and it was pointing at him. He hoped that this Major General, whoever he was, said the right thing.

The woman beside him had half turned to look out of the back window. Jimmy very gently turned his head so that he just got a glimpse of what was going on. He was slow and careful, at this moment any sudden move on his part would be a silly move and probably his last. The driver was walking towards the other car. The man beside it had a loudhailer in one hand and held out something small in the other. Jimmy slowly turned back. The woman in the front seat had turned round and was looking at him. Now she had a gun as well. Suddenly everybody had a gun, everybody except him of course.

The driver returned, put his head into the car and said something to the woman beside Jimmy. Then he got back in but left the door open. The woman, who Jimmy now supposed was Captain Hannah Levi, got out and closed the door. The driver turned to look out of the back window. Jimmy risked slowly turning his head. When Captain Hannah got to the man with the loudhailer, she took what Jimmy realised was a mobile and listened. While she was listening somebody else got out of the back of the car. He was dressed in a smart black suit and had on a purple shirt topped off by a clerical collar. It was an old acquaintance, the Monsignor from Rome. Had the US cavalry arrived in the nick of time? Please God they had. The Monsignor waited until the woman handed back the mobile, said something, then they both started to walk back towards her car.

The Monsignor opened Jimmy's door.

'Please get out, Mr Costello, but do only that.' He nodded towards Loudhailer. 'The gentleman at that car over there wants to be able to see you.'

Jimmy looked at the woman in the front who was still pointing her gun at him.

'OK?'

She wagged the gun indicating for him to get out. They

246

weren't a chatty group. Jimmy got out and stood by the car. The Monsignor turned to the woman in charge, Captain Hannah Levi. He held out his hand and she gave him the mobile. She didn't look a happy bunny. Things were obviously not going to plan, at least not to the plan she had been given.

'Hello, General, I have a message for you from Professor McBride. She wants you to know that for the last two days Mr Costello has been officially in the employment of the Vatican and that he now travels on a diplomatic passport. Neither the Vatican nor the Danish authorities could allow a member of the Vatican Diplomatic Service to be kidnapped and taken by force out of Denmark. It could, indeed would, create a major diplomatic incident. I need hardly add that if anything even more dramatic were to happen to Mr Costello at the hands of members of the Israeli Secret Service, the damage could well prove irreparable and provoke consequences of the most severe nature.' The Monsignor listened for a moment then resumed. 'Professor McBride understands that and agrees with you. She too feels this has gone on long enough and needs to be resolved.' He smiled as he listened. 'No, General, I think not. I can see how that would suit you but it would suit you alone and all parties must be happy with the outcome.' He listened again. 'I think we all understand that, but Professor McBride asked me to point out that Mr Costello has not spoken to anyone at all about his time in Rome. He has not tried to use anything you think he might know against you in any way. Nor has he used it to try and protect himself against any actions he thought you might take, indeed now have taken. He has made no provision for any information to be used by any third party in the event of anything untoward happening to him. It is the Professor's opinion, and I agree with her, that Mr Costello has shown that he represents no material threat to Israel, nor anyone else. He is now in the employ of the Vatican and Professor McBride herself will vouch that for as long as he stays a Vatican employee neither she nor Mr Costello will communicate with any other party about any information you might think they possess.'

There was a silence. The General was obviously weighing

up his options. The Monsignor had been good. But had he been good enough? Then the Monsignor took the mobile from his ear and signalled to Loudhailer. The man holding the loudhailer handed it back into the car and walked towards them. When he arrived he took the mobile.

'Yes, General, what can I do for you? Yes, I can authorise that at once. They will be free to leave, no charges will be made against them. Please understand, this whole matter has been carried out in a way that nothing of it will become known to anyone except our two Services and, of course, Professor McBride. If you can answer for yours, I will answer for mine. If you accept that Professor McBride can answer for the Monsignor and Mr Costello it can all be concluded here and now.' He listened. 'Certainly.'

He handed over the mobile to Captain Levi. She listened for a moment then handed it back, got into the car and closed the door. The new arrival looked at Jimmy. It was the policeman with the funny sense of humour.

'Stand away from the car please, Mr Costello.'

Jimmy didn't need to be told twice. He pushed the car door shut and stood back. The driver pulled his door shut and the Israeli team pulled away. Their car went between the two blocking cars and headed towards the Terminal buildings far away in the distance. The three men watched it go. Then the policeman waved to the two cars. They turned and left.

'Aren't you going to stop them?'

'The Israelis? Stop them, Mr Costello? What on earth for? I've just gone to considerable efforts to send them on their way. Why should I stop them?'

'You said you were a policeman when you came to see me and Udo. I want to report them. They've stolen my shopping. It's in the back of their car.'

The policeman wasn't amused and it was the Monsignor who spoke.

'Shall we all go to the car?'

The policeman led the way, Jimmy and the Monsignor followed. They got into the car, reversed out of the gates and stopped. The driver got out, closed the gates and said something into the box. He got back into the car and headed off the way Jimmy had come. No one was inclined to talk. The journey was going to be about as chatty as the last one. *But at least there are no guns this time*. None that he would see anyway.

The car retraced his recent journey and when it reached Copenhagen it drove to Udo's church and pulled up outside his front door. The Monsignor turned to Jimmy.

'We travel to Rome tomorrow, Mr Costello. I will call for you at nine sharp. Please be ready.' He reached into his inside pocket and pulled out a passport. 'Take this, please.'

Jimmy looked at it. He had never seen a Vatican diplomatic passport before. He took it and put it casually in a side pocket. The Monsignor gave him a pained look.

'You don't change, do you, Mr Costello?'

'Does anybody?'

Jimmy got out of the car and it pulled away. He went into the house. Udo was in the living room having a beer. He waited until Jimmy sat down.

'What was that all about? The Monsignor got a call and then there was a car at the door and he was off like a rocket. I was worried about you, that something may have happened. I tried to call you but you didn't answer.'

'It was nothing much. Three Israeli Secret Service agents were parachuted in to steal our shopping. They got away with it; it will be in Mossad HQ in Tel Aviv by this evening. I'll have to go to the shops again. But first I'm going to have a couple of beers.'

He went into the kitchen and came back with a beer and glass and sat down. Udo let him pour his beer and take a long drink.

'Ready to tell me now?'

'I think it's finally over.'

'Really?'

'I think so. Yes, I think so. And I'll be leaving tomorrow morning, our Monsignor is taking me back to Rome. Apparently I work for the Vatican now, although what the work is, I have yet to be told.'

'Congratulations.' Udo raised his glass then drank. 'I'll miss you, Jimmy.' He paused. 'No, on second thoughts, perhaps I won't. I like you, but things seem to happen around you, people get hurt, killed. But I'm glad it's over for you, whatever it was.'

Jimmy took a drink.

'Thanks. My only regret is that I wasn't able to put a bullet into that bastard Bronski's head.'

'Forget it. We can't have Vatican employees blowing people's brains out, not even people like Bronski. It would tarnish the image. Anyway, I think Charlie's run of good luck is about to turn.'

'Oh yes?'

'Nothing I can tell you about but, yes, I think friend Bronski has finally run out of good luck. Let's just say yesterday's sins may have finally caught up with him. Cheers.'

He raised his glass. Jimmy raised his.

'If you're right it almost makes up for the shopping being snatched. Cheers.'

THIRTY

Jimmy felt distinctly foolish at the airport, being treated as if he was somebody. He had followed the Monsignor's lead and everything had gone like clockwork. No fuss on arrival, just out of the taxi, through to Departures and ushered into the VIP lounge. It was while they were waiting in the VIP lounge that the Comedian turned up. The Monsignor had switched on his best smile.

'Come to see us off, Commander?'

'To talk to Mr Costello for a moment.'

'By all means. Anything we can do to help.'

'Alone.'

The Monsignor left them, but Jimmy could see from his back as he walked away that he wasn't happy about it.

Jimmy and the Commander sat together out of earshot of the few other VIPs scattered around the lounge.

'You may now be travelling on a Vatican diplomatic passport, but it won't stop me having you arrested if you ever set foot on Danish soil again.'

'Arrested for what?'

'Illegal parking, possession of a dog without a licence, aggravated jaywalking, I'll think of something. Just don't come back, Mr Costello. I hoped when you left Denmark last time that we had seen the end of you, but you came back. Don't repeat that mistake. Next time the Israeli Secret Service will be the least of your worries.'

'How did you know about that?'

'Because it's my job to know things. A car bomb goes off, it becomes my business. It isn't terrorist-related, so I find out what it is related to. My enquiries turned up a certain ex-Soviet, ex-Russian Intelligence officer, Yuri Kemedov, who defected to the British and now lives with his wife in Nyborg and calls himself Charles Bronski. I checked everyone he made contact with and turn up Udo Mundt, ex-Stasi, now a parish priest in Copenhagen. Father Mundt has a house guest, you. So I check on you. For a man with so many years as a detective in the Metropolitan Police your file is remarkably slim. There must have been very little crime in London while you worked there. Almost none at all according to your file. So I arrange to have the three of you watched but, as it turned out, perhaps not well enough. Bronski skips off to Hamburg. Then he comes back.'

'Did you follow him?'

'No, as far as I was concerned Bronski can do what he likes so long as he does it somewhere that isn't on Danish soil. Next thing, all three of you leave for Germany and travel in a curiously circuitous route. Again we didn't follow, again on the same principal. Outside of Denmark I didn't much care what any of you got up to. When you all left, including Mrs Bronski who conveniently flew off to the UK, I hoped that might be that. Unfortunately it wasn't; you all came back.'

'Do you know anything about what happened?

'I know what everyone knows. A local businessman and a female British tourist were found murdered in a disused industrial building near Lübeck.'

'And you believe that's what it was?'

'I don't care, Mr Costello. What happens in Lübeck is not my concern. It is only while you are in Denmark you are my concern. You arrive, a car gets blown up. You go to Lübeck, two people die. I wait to see what will happen next. What actually happens is I get a call from a Monsignor who is based in Rome. He is concerned about you. He says you are the target

252

of an Israeli snatch team and, as you are a member of the Vatican Diplomatic Service, he requests our protection for you. If I don't protect you, I will have a Diplomatic Incident to deal with.' He smiled. 'Now that *did* surprise me. That, I had not anticipated. I increased surveillance on you so I was told immediately you were picked up by the team. The rest you know.' He stood up. 'I don't know who you are or what you're doing but I know you're trouble. So go to Rome, Mr Costello. Go to Rome and stay there. And whatever you do, don't ever come back to Denmark.'

'What will happen to Bronski and Father Mundt?'

'Nothing. They have done nothing, not on Danish soil anyway. If they continue to do nothing, they will both be left alone. Goodbye. Have a pleasant flight.'

He left. Neither felt a handshake was needed.

An hour later he was on a business-class-only jet with a diplomatic passport in his pocket, leaving Denmark for good. He turned to the Monsignor who was sitting next to him reading a book.

'How did you know about the Israeli snatch team?'

The Monsignor stopped reading and looked at Jimmy, annoyed.

'Has it occurred to you we are not alone on this plane?'

'There's no one in the seats in front and I promise to keep my voice down. How?'

'We were tipped off by the Americans. The man you call Bronski had contacted their embassy in Paris with an offer to sell you to them. They told us what they thought would happen, so we did what we did. We were already prepared. Father Mundt had alerted Professor McBride and she anticipated that there might be some such complication. She had the necessary contacts in place. Personally I think we were wrong. We should have let them have you. It would have been a neater end to the mess you've managed to create around you.'

He returned to his book.

Yes, thought Jimmy, *I can see how you might have wanted that, but you're still not the one who gets to make the decisions, thank God. McBride still does that.*

'Will Udo be all right?'

The Monsignor did nothing to hide his annoyance at having his reading interrupted again.

'Udo?'

'Fr Mundt.'

'Yes, I should think so. Why shouldn't he be all right? Has he done anything?'

No, thought Jimmy, *only saved my life and ordered a small-time gangster and a British agent executed. That's all.*

The Monsignor closed his book with a finger marking his page. He had decided on a little light conversation now that his reading had been interrupted.

'I liked Fr Mundt. I was with him only for a short time but I liked him. I'm glad to say I was able to help him with a small problem that had been worrying him.'

'Oh yes?'

'Yes. Someone, an English woman I think he said, had come to him and asked him to hear her confession.' He lowered his voice even further and leaned towards Jimmy. 'It seems she told him that she was going to poison her husband.'

He leaned back and waited for a response.

'If it was her confession, should Udo have told you, and should you be telling me?'

The Monsignor made a dismissive gesture with his free hand.

'No, the seal of the confession doesn't apply in this case.'

'Why, because you're a Monsignor?'

'Not at all. It doesn't apply because there was no confession. You cannot confess a sin you are *going* to commit. Only sins you have already committed, are genuinely sorry for, and have a firm purpose of amendment not to commit again. Fr Mundt explained that to her.'

'So what advice did he need from you?'

'He asked me whether, if she was sure her husband was going to kill her, killing him could be classed as self-defence?'

'And?'

'I told him not. Proportionality applies. If she was indeed certain her husband was going to kill her, the correct response would to go to the police, not to kill her husband.'

'What if she couldn't go to the police?'

'Strangely enough, Fr Mundt asked me the same thing, but I hardly see the question arises. Claiming you are going to kill your husband because he is going to kill you is hardly what you would expect from a fully balanced mind, is it? I told Fr Mundt not to let it bother him.'

'Not even go to the police?'

'Good heavens, no. If one did that every time a wife said she wanted her husband dead or the other way round, the police would never get anything else done. Oh, no. I told Fr Mundt he should leave it alone. If he wanted to do anything at all, he might recommend a good analyst.'

The Monsignor opened his book and returned to his reading. He had finished having a little conversation. Jimmy signalled to the stewardess. He felt like celebrating. He didn't like wine as a rule, but this was an occasion that called for something special.

'Have you any champagne? I've just had some very good news.'

'Certainly, sir. A full-sized bottle or just a half-sized?'

Jimmy turned to the Monsignor who determinedly continued his reading. Jimmy waited. Finally, with a bad grace, the Monsignor shook his head, never taking his eyes off the page.

'Just a half-bottle.'

'Thank you.'

And she left to get his champagne.

So, thought Jimmy, *that was what you meant, Udo*. Bronski's luck had finally run out and the bastard was going to die. *Well done, Elspeth, you little star*. Well bloody done.

A few moments later the champagne came.

Charlie Bronski was finding it difficult to get to sleep. His stomach was unsettled just like it had been recently, but worse tonight. He thought about it. Maybe it wasn't just Elspeth's awful cooking. It wasn't only his stomach, the purplish rash on the back of his left hand was spreading. Tomorrow he would make an urgent appointment with the doctor.

Next to him, facing away, lay Elspeth, her eyes looking into the dark of the bedroom. She was silently praying an Act of Contrition to herself even though she knew it would do no good. For an Act of Contrition to work there had to be sorrow for the sin and a firm purpose of amendment. She had a firm purpose, but not one of amendment.

When it was over she would be able to make a proper confession. She would probably have to make another sort of confession as well, and not to a priest. A sudden death would mean an autopsy and the rat poison would certainly be identified. But she didn't care. Fr Mundt had been quite clear. She couldn't go to the police and Charlie would certainly kill her if she tried to leave him or gave herself away. And she knew that somehow she would give herself away so it was self-defence, not really a sin at all. The only sin was enjoying it. She shouldn't be enjoying it, at least not so much. She might go to prison, or she might not, but at least Charlie would get what he deserved.

She had not found it as difficult to poison Charlie as she had expected. She had simply said she wanted to have a go at some of his recipes. He was proud of his writing, rightly so, and she had played on that pride.

'I know I can't help you with ideas, but at least I can have a go and you can tell me where I went wrong. That would help, wouldn't it? Let you see it from the reader's side a bit. I do want to help, Charlie. And I need to feel I'm doing something useful.'

Of course he had agreed. After that, all she had to do was choose meals with plenty of spice in them, get it wrong and add the rat poison to his meal before she brought the plates to the table. And it had worked. He had eaten and then pontificated about how she had got it wrong. She smiled to herself. And he never mentioned rat poison once.

Tomorrow would be her fourth attempt. It would be a spicy goulash out of *Hungary in an English Kitchen*. She wondered, not for the first time, surely there had to be some taste to rat poison? But if there was, Charlie hadn't noticed, and the goulash would hide it just like the curry, the chilli con carne and the sweet, spicy lamb had. Then a thought struck her, what if she ran out of suitable recipes before the poison worked? How long did it take to kill someone with rat poison? She didn't know and couldn't very well ask. Was it working? Charlie had complained of bleeding gums yesterday morning and she had told him she'd get him a softer toothbrush. Was that a symptom? She'd make it a stronger dose tomorrow, as strong as she dared. The trick would be to get the goulash hot enough but not so spoiled that Charlie couldn't eat it. *Difficult.*

Slowly, dreamily mulling over her problem, Elspeth drifted off into sleep. Next to her, the pain in Charlie's stomach suddenly grew alarmingly, he felt violently nauseous as if he was going to throw up. Then there was a sudden, blinding pain in his head. He tried to sit up but he couldn't. He felt himself losing consciousness as the pain in his head increased. He tried to reach out to Elspeth, to shout to her, to tell her he was ill, but he couldn't. He could open his mouth but no sound came. His whole body refused to respond to his will and a terrible agony engulfed him. Then a spasm shook his body, he gave a final, small shudder and quietly died. The poison had caused massive haemorrhaging in his stomach and in his brain. Elspeth slept on, peacefully unaware that the problem of the extra-hot goulash was now solved.

THIRTY-ONE

Jimmy came to the top of the narrow staircase and looked down the dingy corridor. Nothing had changed. This building, one of many behind St Peter's Basilica in Rome, looked magnificent from the outside but inside, at the top of the stone staircase, the rooms were small and shabby. He walked to the door he had come to many times during his stay in Rome, when he thought he was a mature student in training for the Catholic priesthood. In those days a small plaque hung on the door – Rector, Duns College. There was no plaque now. That elusive, Brigadoon-type institution was in dormant mode. Jimmy knocked. A woman's voice told him to come in. Inside it was still the same. The small, grimy window that wouldn't open. The big old desk with the antiquated phone. One chair facing the desk, and behind the desk an immaculately turned-out Professor Pauline McBride looking as if her dark suit and white blouse had just been returned from an upmarket dry cleaners.

'Welcome back, Mr Costello. Please take a seat.'

Jimmy sat down.

'Apparently I work for the Vatican now.'

'Good heavens, Mr Costello, what on earth makes you think that?'

'The passport for one thing.'

'No, Mr Costello, at the moment you are a free agent or, if

you prefer, unemployed.'

'So I never worked for the Pope? Pity. Just a fairy story to take the Israelis off my back and get me out of Denmark.'

'I would call it an engineered outcome using available resources. However, if you are looking for employment, there may be some work you can do for me.'

She hadn't changed. Still no straight answers.

'Tell me, how do I get the job? Do I fill in forms, or am I being asked? Or was that passport business your version of a snatch and I don't get any choice?'

'Would you rather I had left things in Denmark as they were?'

'Oh no. I'm very glad you saved my life. I'd be grateful even if I didn't know there must be something you wanted doing that needed me alive to get it done.'

'What a terrible cynic you have turned into in the short time since you left Rome.'

'You're wrong. I was a cynic when I left Rome. Maybe it was Rome that made me that way.'

'Just as you like. I hope you haven't changed too much since we last spoke. If we work together I want you to be the James Costello I knew, not some new variety.'

'I haven't changed, not much anyway. A bit wiser, maybe. A bit older certainly. And a bit less sure of what everything is all about. Udo was right when he told me people don't change.'

'You liked Fr Mundt?'

'Yes, I liked him a lot. He saved my life as well. It's been a big time recently for saving Jimmy Costello's life.'

'I'm glad you two got on. I chose him with some care.'

'Out of interest, why did you choose him? Apart from the fact that Denmark was almost a good place to hide.'

'I wanted someone who, how shall I put it? Someone whom I knew would cooperate and not feel like asking awkward questions.'

'In other words you knew about his past so you had him over a barrel.'

'He was asked and he agreed to have you as a placement. Fr Mundt was at no time put under any duress, I assure you.'

'Then I'm assured, aren't I?'

'I also wanted someone with the right kind of experience if certain circumstances arose.'

'You chose well, they arose all right and Udo did bloody marvellously.'

She ignored the comment.

'Mr Costello, please try to understand. Fr Mundt, once he was made aware of what was needed, a discreet place for a special candidate, was more than willing to cooperate. No pressure of any sort was necessary. I want you to feel the same way if you decide to accept the offer of being in the employ of the College I work for. I do not want you to feel you are in any way coerced.'

'So it's definitely not the Vatican?'

'No. Not the Vatican.'

'Pity. And if I worked for you, I'd really get a choice? It would be because I want to? Not because you have me over a barrel?'

'You can put it that way, although now the Israelis and the Americans have decided to be sensible I don't see how you can think I could bring any undue pressure. If you work with me there must be mutual trust.'

'With you, not for you? There's a difference.'

'I know the difference. We will be working together.'

'At what?'

'From time to time situations arise in the Church in various parts of the world that need to be looked into.'

'What sort of "situations"?'

'We'll get to that. You said Fr Mundt told you people don't change. In a way he's right and he's a good example. He is a man lost without a strong system to serve. In the Stasi, his job was to persuade people, to talk, to spy, to do all sorts of things, but essentially his job was to persuade. The methods he used were often immoral, criminal in any civilised society, and sometimes inhuman. Now he works for the Catholic Church and he still tries to persuade, but he only uses words, patient listening and good example. Alas, it doesn't get the same results but he sleeps at night and now he can live with himself.'

'And me?'

'You were a detective, a detective sergeant in the London CID. Maybe the best of your generation. Don't change that, use it. Use it to help the Church.'

'Be your own special private detective?'

For the first time ever, he saw her smile a genuine smile. It lit up her black face.

'It is not the way I would have put it, but, yes, it sums up what is required.'

'Rome's own Sam Spade.'

'I'm sorry?'

'Or Philip Marlowe if you prefer Raymond Chandler to Dashiell Hammett.'

Now she understood the reference.

'Ah, yes, a shamus, a private eye. It will not be that exciting or glamorous, Mr Costello, and it will not pay well. The Collegio Principe is more than adequately funded from the original bequests of its founder, but finance for the special work we are sometimes asked to do is always in short supply. All expenses need to be accounted for. Are you still comfortably situated for money?'

'Not as well as I was. Lübeck put a dent in my savings but I'll be OK.'

'You will receive a small monthly retainer.' She mentioned a sum. It wasn't small, it was almost invisible. 'But all expenses, if you are required to travel, will be reimbursed.' She paused. 'Well, Mr Costello, will you join me?'

Jimmy didn't need to think about it. What else was he going to do now that he wasn't busy running and hiding full-time, trying to stay alive?

'Sure. Why not?'

'Good, I think you've made the right decision. I'm glad we will be working together again. But before we begin could you give me the passport the Monsignor gave you. You have it with you, I hope?'

Jimmy had it with him. He wasn't about to let a Vatican diplomatic passport out of his possession, not even when walking around Rome. He took it out and handed it over. She put it into her desk drawer.

'Does that mean I'm not a Vatican diplomat any more?'

'You never were. The passport you used was a forgery, not even a very good forgery, but I needed it quickly and people don't look closely at Vatican diplomatic passports for some reason. I felt it would pass muster under the circumstances. It obviously did.'

Jimmy couldn't help smiling. She was a live one, no question, and would certainly bear some watching.

'So, now I'm working again, what have you in mind? Is there something on at the moment?'

'Actually, there is.'

And he sat and listened as Professor McBride told him what she wanted done. It sounded interesting.

Jimmy Costello, the detective, was going back to work.